THE REEL WEST

THE REEL WEST

EDITED BY BILL PRONZINI
AND MARTIN H. GREENBERG

DOUBLEDAY & COMPANY, INC.

GARDEN CITY, NEW YORK

1984

ACKNOWLEDGMENTS

"Massacre," by James Warner Bellah. Copyright © 1947 by The Curtis Publishing Company. First published in *The Saturday Evening Post.* Reprinted by permission of the estate of James Warner Bellah.

"The Tin Star," by John M. Cunningham. Copyright © 1947 by Crowell-Collier Publishing Co., Inc.; copyright renewed © 1975 by John M. Cunningham. First published in *Collier's* for December 6, 1947. Reprinted by permission of Knox Burger Associates.

"My Brother Down There," by Steve Frazee. Copyright © 1953 by Mercury Press, Inc. First published in *Ellery Queen's Mystery Magazine.* Reprinted by permission of Scott Meredith Literary Agency, Inc., 845 Third Avenue, New York, N.Y. 10022.

"Three-Ten to Yuma," by Elmore Leonard. Copyright © 1953 by Elmore Leonard. Reprinted by permission of the author and his agents, H. N. Swanson, Inc.

"The Man Who Shot Liberty Valance," by Dorothy M. Johnson. Copyright © 1949 by Dorothy M. Johnson; copyright renewed © 1977 by Dorothy M. Johnson. Reprinted by permission of McIntosh and Otis, Inc.

"Town Tamer," by Frank Gruber. Copyright © 1957 by Short Stories, Inc. First published in *Short Stories.* Reprinted by permission of Scott Meredith Literary Agency, Inc., 845 Third Avenue, New York, N.Y. 10022.

"Jeremy Rodock," by Jack Schaefer. From *The Collected Stories of Jack Schaefer.* Copyright © 1966 by Jack Schaefer. Reprinted by permission of Don Congdon Associates, Inc.

Library of Congress Cataloging in Publication Data

The Reel West.

1. Western stories. 2. Western stories—Film adaptations.
I. Pronzini, Bill. II. Greenberg, Martin Harry.
PS648.W4R44 1984   813'.0874'08
ISBN: 0-385-19319-X
Library of Congress Catalog Card Number 84-1688
Copyright © 1984 by Bill Pronzini
and Martin H. Greenberg
All Rights Reserved
Printed in the United States of America
First Edition

CONTENTS

INTRODUCTION

The Reel West is a collection of outstanding stories that formed the basis for notable Western films. Western fiction has long been a major source of material for film, and we were surprised to discover that no book consisting exclusively of this source material had been compiled prior to this one.

The transition from words to film is chancy under the best of conditions, so it should be noted that several of the stories contained in these pages have not been faithfully transferred to the screen. We should also mention that the short story, because it *is* short, has to be greatly expanded when made into a feature-length film; thus some of these tales contributed only the basic idea of the movies they became.

A brief look at the films, in chronological order:

The Texan (1930), directed by John Cromwell and written by Daniel N. Rubin and Oliver Garrett, is based on O. Henry's 1905 Llano Kid story "The Double-Dyed Deceiver." Gary Cooper, early in a career that would make him a Hollywood legend, portrayed the Kid whose rough ways are changed by the love of a woman. Fay Wray, of later *King Kong* fame, also appeared in this sentimental but satisfying film.

The great John Ford's *Fort Apache* (1948), starring Henry Fonda, John Wayne, and Shirley Temple, is one of the best cavalry films ever made and the first of Ford's famous "cavalry trilogy." Based on James Warner Bellah's 1947 story "Massacre," its message was the importance of myth in the lives of a country's people; but most moviegoers responded to the tension between Fonda and Wayne (the latter in a somewhat cynical and deeply drawn role) and to the fine photography by Archie J. Stout.

Written by the soon-to-be-blacklisted Carl Foreman from John M. Cunningham's 1947 story "The Tin Star," *High Noon* (1952) is perhaps the best (and certainly the most suspenseful) Western ever made.

Gary Cooper's performance as ex-Marshal Will Kane remains un-equaled. The excellent cast included Grace Kelly, Lloyd Bridges, Katy Jurado, Thomas Mitchell, and Lee Van Cleef. Considered by many to be a scathing commentary on McCarthyism, it is also a homage to the Western vision of what it means to be a man. Directed by Fred Zinneman and produced by Stanley Kramer, the film won four Academy Awards and was nominated for others. Its score by Dimitri Tiomkin and title song (sung by Tex Ritter) are almost as famous as the film itself.

Stephen Crane's justly acclaimed story "The Bride Comes to Yellow Sky" (1898) served as the basis for one half of the 1952 film *Face to Face*, which was directed by Bretaigne Windust and featured Robert Preston and Marjorie Steele. *Face to Face*, a neglected film, consists of two stories (the other one was based on Joseph Conrad's "The Secret Sharer") with separate casts and directors—an outstanding anthology effort that is well worth watching for on television and in revivals. The Crane segment has a hardness that would not become common in Western films until years later.

Tennessee's Partner (1955) was directed by Allan Dwan, a veteran Hollywood director whose career began in 1909. Written by a team of four scriptwriters including Milton Krims, it was adapted from the famous story of the same title written by Bret Harte in 1869. John Payne starred, along with Ronald Reagan, Rhonda Fleming, and such veteran character actors as Anthony Caruso and Morris Ankrum. Angie Dickinson had a bit part.

Running Target is an underrated contemporary Western, made in 1956 and based on "My Brother Down There" (1953) by the equally underrated Steve Frazee. Directed by Marvin Weinstein, who co-wrote the screenplay, it features veteran "B" actors Arthur Franz as the sheriff, Doris Dowling, and Myron Healey and is an excellent chase film that entertains despite a tiny budget. Watch for it on the Late Show.

James Cagney made only three Westerns, and 1956's *Tribute to a Bad Man* is easily the best of them. The film—directed by Robert Wise from a screenplay by Michael Blankfort based on Jack Schaefer's 1951 story "Jeremy Rodock"—features a virtuoso performance by Cagney, who portrays a horse rancher who, in the film version, is in constant pain from a bullet in his back. Others in the cast include Irene Papas, the forgettable Don Dubbins, and such professional celluloid tough guys as Stephen McNally and Vic Morrow. Cagney's role was originally designed for Spencer Tracy, who turned down the part.

The 1950s were a great decade for the Western film, and 1957's *3:10 to Yuma* certainly ranks with *High Noon* as one of the very best ever made. Its theme of a sturdy citizen (Van Heflin) charged with guarding an infamous outlaw (Glenn Ford in one of his best roles) was frequently imitated but never equaled. The film was directed by Delmer Daves, with a screenplay by Halsted Welles based on the 1953 short story of the same title by well-known suspense writer Elmore Leonard. As in *High Noon*, tension builds steadily throughout and its ending is unforgettable. Felicia Farr played Heflin's wife, while the sinister Richard Jaeckel portrayed one of Ford's henchmen. Part of the excellence of the movie lies in Heflin's struggle to maintain his dignity and honor, a struggle with which many viewers can identify.

John Ford's *The Man Who Shot Liberty Valance* (1962) was based on the 1949 story of the same title by Dorothy M. Johnson. Its theme is aptly summed up by the now famous line, "This is the West, sir. When the legend becomes fact, print the legend." The film stars James Stewart as an idealistic lawyer and John Wayne as a gritty rancher and features a memorable performance by Lee Marvin as the murderous outlaw Liberty Valance.

Although *Town Tamer* (1965) has familiar plot elements, it is notable for an impressive cast of old-timers: Barton MacLane, Bob Steele, Bruce Cabot, Sonny Tufts, Lon Chaney, Jr., Pat O'Brien, and Richard Arlen. Dana Andrews and Terry Moore had the lead roles. Directed by Lesley Selander and produced by A. C. Lyles, *Town Tamer* was adapted by Frank Gruber from his 1957 short story and subsequent novel of the same title.

And now—

Here are the stories which brought these films into being—stories we think you'll enjoy as much if not more than the Hollywood productions themselves. They're proof positive that heroes *do* still exist, if only in the pages of history and the imaginations of some of our best popular writers.

—Bill Pronzini and
Martin H. Greenberg
December 1983

THE REEL WEST

TENNESSEE'S PARTNER
BY BRET HARTE
(Tennessee's Partner)

Once the highest paid short-story writer in America, Bret Harte (1836–1902) wrote perhaps the finest fictional accounts of the lusty and sometimes violent life in the mining camps and boomtowns during the great California gold rush of the 1850s—stories such as "The Luck of Roaring Camp" (filmed as a "B" picture under that title in 1937); "The Outcasts of Poker Flat" (filmed three times, once in 1919 as a silent, once in 1937 with Preston Foster and Van Heflin, and once in 1952 with Dale Robertson); and "Tennessee's Partner" (brought to the screen in 1955, with John Payne and Ronald Reagan). Somewhat lesser known than the other two stories mentioned, "Tennessee's Partner" (1869) is nonetheless a Bret Harte—and an Old West—classic.

I do not think that we ever knew his real name. Our ignorance of it certainly never gave us any social inconvenience, for at Sandy Bar in 1854 most men were christened anew. Sometimes these appellatives were derived from some distinctiveness of dress, as in the case of "Dungaree Jack"; or from some peculiarity of habit, as shown in "Saleratus Bill," so called from an undue proportion of that chemical in his daily bread; or from some unlucky slip, as exhibited in "The Iron Pirate," a mild, inoffensive man, who earned that baleful title by his unfortunate mispronunciation of the term "iron pyrites." Perhaps this may have been the beginning of a rude heraldry; but I am constrained to think that it was because a man's real name in that day rested solely upon his own unsupported statement. "Call yourself Clifford, do you?" said Boston, addressing a timid newcomer with infinite scorn; "hell is full of such Cliffords!" He then introduced the unfortunate man, whose name happened to be really Clifford, as "Jaybird Charley"—an unhallowed inspiration of the moment that clung to him ever after.

But to return to Tennessee's Partner, whom we never knew by any other than this relative title. That he had ever existed as a separate and distinct individuality we only learned later. It seems that in 1853 he left Poker Flat to go to San Francisco, ostensibly to procure a wife. He never got any farther than Stockton. At that place he was attracted by a young person who waited upon the table at the hotel where he took his meals. One morning he said something to her which caused her to smile not unkindly, to somewhat coquettishly break a plate of toast over his upturned, serious, simple face, and to retreat to the kitchen. He followed her, and emerged a few moments later, covered with more toast and victory. That day week they were married by a justice of the peace, and returned to Poker Flat. I am aware that something more might be made of this episode, but I prefer to tell it as it was current at Sandy Bar—in the gulches and barrooms—where all sentiment was modified by a strong sense of humor.

Of their married felicity but little is known, perhaps for the reason that Tennessee, then living with his partner, one day took occasion to say something to the bride on his own account, at which, it is said, she smiled not unkindly and chastely retreated—this time as far as Marysville, where Tennessee followed her, and where they went to housekeeping without the aid of a justice of the peace. Tennessee's Partner took the loss of his wife simply and seriously, as was his fashion. But to everybody's surprise, when Tennessee one day returned from Marysville, without his partner's wife—she having smiled and retreated with somebody else—Tennessee's Partner was the first man to shake his hand and greet him with affection. The boys who had gathered in the canyon to see the shooting were naturally indignant. Their indignation might have found vent in sarcasm but for a certain look in Tennessee's Partner's eye that indicated a lack of humorous appreciation. In fact, he was a grave man, with a steady application to practical detail which was unpleasant in a difficulty.

Meanwhile a popular feeling against Tennessee had grown up on the Bar. He was known to be a gambler; he was suspected to be a thief. In these suspicions Tennessee's Partner was equally compromised; his continued intimacy with Tennessee after the affair above quoted could only be accounted for on the hypothesis of a copartnership of crime. At last Tennessee's guilt became flagrant. One day he overtook a stranger on his way to Red Dog. The stranger afterward related that Tennessee beguiled the time with interesting anecdote and reminiscence, but illogically concluded the interview in the following words: "And now, young man, I'll trouble you for your knife, your pistols, and your money. You see your weppings might get you into trouble at Red Dog, and your money's a temptation to the evilly disposed. I think you said your address was San Francisco. I shall endeavor to call." It may be stated here that Tennessee had a fine flow of humor, which no business preoccupation could wholly subdue.

This exploit was his last. Red Dog and Sandy Bar made common cause against the highwayman. Tennessee was hunted in very much the same fashion as his prototype, the grizzly. As the toils closed around him, he made a desperate dash through the Bar, emptying his revolver at the crowd before the Arcade Saloon, and so on up Grizzly Canyon; but at its farther extremity he was stopped by a small man on a gray horse. The men looked at each other a moment in silence. Both were fearless, both self-possessed and independent, and both types of a civilization that in the seventeenth century would have been called heroic, but in the nineteenth simply "reckless."

"What have you got there?—I call," said Tennessee quietly.

"Two bowers and an ace," said the stranger as quietly, showing two revolvers and a bowie knife.

"That takes me," returned Tennessee; and with this gambler's epigram, he threw away his useless pistol and rode back with his captor.

It was a warm night. The cool breeze which usually sprang up with the going down of the sun behind the chaparral-crested mountain was that evening withheld from Sandy Bar. The little canyon was stifling with heated resinous odors, and the decaying driftwood on the Bar sent forth faint sickening exhalations. The feverishness of day and its fierce passions still filled the camp. Lights moved restlessly along the bank of the river, striking no answering reflection from its tawny current. Against the blackness of the pines the windows of the old loft above the express office stood out staringly bright; and through their curtainless panes the loungers below could see the forms of those who were even then deciding the fate of Tennessee. And above all this, etched on the dark firmament, rose the Sierra, remote and passionless, crowned with remoter passionless stars.

The trial of Tennessee was conducted as fairly as was consistent with a judge and jury who felt themselves to some extent obliged to justify, in their verdict, the previous irregularities of arrest and indictment. The law of Sandy Bar was implacable, but not vengeful. The excitement and personal feeling of the chase were over; with Tennessee safe in their hands, they were ready to listen patiently to any defense, which they were already satisfied was insufficient. There being no doubt in their own minds, they were willing to give the prisoner the benefit of any that might exist. Secure in the hypothesis that he ought to be hanged on general principles, they indulged him with more latitude of defense than his reckless hardihood seemed to ask. The Judge appeared to be more anxious than the prisoner, who, otherwise unconcerned, evidently took a grim pleasure in the responsibility he had created. "I don't take any hand in this yer game," had been his invariable but good-humored reply to all questions. The Judge—who was also his captor—for a moment vaguely regretted that he had not shot him "on sight" that morning, but presently dismissed this human weakness as unworthy of the judicial mind. Nevertheless, when there was a tap at the door, and it was said that Tennessee's Partner was there on behalf of the prisoner, he was admitted at once without question. Perhaps the younger members of the jury, to whom the proceedings were becoming irksomely thoughtful, hailed him as a relief.

For he was not, certainly, an imposing figure. Short and stout, with a square face, sunburned into a preternatural redness, clad in a loose duck "jumper" and trousers streaked and splashed with red soil, his aspect under any circumstances would have been quaint, and was now even ridiculous. As he stooped to deposit at his feet a heavy carpetbag he was carrying, it became obvious, from partially developed legends and inscriptions, that the material with which his trousers had been patched had been originally intended for a less ambitious covering. Yet he advanced with great gravity, and after shaking the hand of each person in the room with labored cordiality, he wiped his serious perplexed face on a red bandana handkerchief, a shade lighter than his complexion, laid his powerful hand upon the table to steady himself, and thus addressed the Judge:

"I was passin' by," he began, by way of apology, "and I thought I'd just step in and see how things was gittin' on with Tennessee thar—my pardner. It's a hot night. I disremember any sich weather before on the Bar."

He paused a moment, but nobody volunteering any other meteorological recollection, he again had recourse to his pocket handkerchief, and for some moments mopped his face diligently.

"Have you anything to say on behalf of the prisoner?" said the Judge finally.

"Thet's it," said Tennessee's Partner, in a tone of relief. "I come yar as Tennessee's pardner—knowing him nigh on four year, off and on, wet and dry, in luck and out o' luck. His ways ain't aller my ways, but thar ain't any p'ints in that young man, thar ain't any liveliness as he's been up to, as I don't know. And you sez to me, sez you—confidential-like, and between man and man—sez you, 'Do you know anything in his behalf?' and I sez to you, sez I—confidential-like, as between man and man—'What should a man know of his pardner?' "

"Is this all you have to say?" asked the Judge impatiently, feeling, perhaps, that a dangerous sympathy of humor was beginning to humanize the court.

"Thet's so," continued Tennessee's Partner. "It ain't for me to say anything agin' him. And now, what's the case? Here's Tennessee wants money, wants it bad, and doesn't like to ask it of his old pardner. Well, what does Tennessee do? He lays for a stranger, and he fetches that stranger; and you lays for *him*, and you fetches *him*; and the honors is easy. And I put it to you, bein' a fa'r-minded man, and to you, gentlemen all, as fa'r-minded men, ef this isn't so."

"Prisoner," said the Judge, interrupting, "have you any questions to ask this man?"

"No! no!" continued Tennessee's Partner hastily. "I play this yer hand alone. To come down to the bedrock, it's just this: Tennessee thar has played it pretty rough and expensivelike on a stranger, and on this yer camp. And now, what's the fair thing? Some would say more, some would say less. Here's seventeen hundred dollars in coarse gold and a watch—it's about all my pile—and call it square!" And before a hand could be raised to prevent him, he had emptied the contents of the carpetbag upon the table.

For a moment his life was in jeopardy. One or two men sprang to their feet, several hands groped for hidden weapons, and a suggestion to "throw him from the window" was only overridden by a gesture from the Judge. Tennessee laughed. And apparently oblivious of the excitement, Tennessee's Partner improved the opportunity to mop his face again with his handkerchief.

When order was restored, and the man was made to understand by the use of forcible figures and rhetoric that Tennessee's offense could not be condoned by money, his face took a more serious and sanguinary hue, and those who were nearest to him noticed that his rough hand trembled slightly on the table. He hesitated a moment as he slowly returned the gold to the carpetbag, as if he had not yet entirely caught the elevated sense of justice which swayed the tribunal, and was perplexed with the belief that he had not offered enough. Then he turned to the Judge, and saying, "This yer is a lone hand, played alone, and without my pardner," he bowed to the jury and was about to withdraw, when the Judge called him back:

"If you have anything to say to Tennessee, you had better say it now."

For the first time that evening the eyes of the prisoner and his strange advocate met. Tennessee smiled, showed his white teeth, and saying, "Euchred, old man!" held out his hand. Tennessee's Partner took it in his own, and saying, "I just dropped in as I was passin' to see how things was gettin' on," let the hand passively fall, and adding that "it was a warm night," again mopped his face with his handkerchief, and without another word withdrew.

The two men never again met each other alive. For the unparalleled insult of a bribe offered to Judge Lynch—who, whether bigoted, weak, or narrow, was at least incorruptible—firmly fixed in the mind of that mythical personage any wavering determination of Tennessee's fate; and at the break of day he was marched, closely guarded, to meet it at the top of Marley's Hill.

How he met it, how cool he was, how he refused to say anything, how perfect were the arrangements of the committee, were all duly reported, with the addition of a warning moral and example to all future evildoers, in the *Red Dog Clarion* by its editor, who was present, and to whose vigorous English I cheerfully refer the reader. But the beauty of that midsummer morning, the blessed amity of earth and air and sky, the awakened life of the free woods and hills, the joyous renewal and promise of Nature, and above all, the infinite serenity that thrilled through each, was not reported, as not being a part of the social lesson. And yet, when the weak and foolish deed was done, and a life, with its possibilities and responsibilities, had passed out of the misshapen thing that dangled between earth and sky, the birds sang, the flowers bloomed, the sun shone, as cheerily as before; and possibly the *Red Dog Clarion* was right.

Tennessee's Partner was not in the group that surrounded the ominous tree. But as they turned to disperse, attention was drawn to the singular appearance of a motionless donkey cart halted at the side of the road. As they approached, they at once recognized the venerable Jenny and the two-wheeled cart as the property of Tennessee's Partner, used by him in carrying dirt from his claim; and a few paces distant the owner of the equipage himself, sitting under a buckeye tree, wiping the perspiration from his glowing face. In answer to an inquiry, he said he had come for the body of the "diseased," "if it was all the same to the committee." He didn't wish to "hurry anything;" he could "wait." He was not working that day; and when the gentlemen were done with the "diseased," he would take him. "Ef thar is any present," he added, in his simple, serious way, "as would care to jine in the fun'l, they kin come." Perhaps it was from a sense of humor, which I have already intimated was a feature of Sandy Bar—perhaps it was from something even better than that, but two thirds of the loungers accepted the invitation at once.

It was noon when the body of Tennessee was delivered into the hands of his partner. As the cart drew up to the fatal tree, we noticed that it contained a rough oblong box—apparently made from a section of sluicing—and half filled with bark and the tassels of pine. The cart was further decorated with slips of willow and made fragrant with buckeye blossoms. When the body was deposited in the box, Tennessee's Partner drew over it a piece of tarred canvas, and gravely mounting the narrow seat in front, with his feet upon the shafts, urged the little donkey forward. The equipage moved slowly on, at that decorous pace which was habitual with Jenny even under less solemn circumstances. The men—half curiously, half jestingly, but all good-humoredly—strolled along beside the cart, some in advance, some a little in the rear of the homely catafalque. But whether from the narrowing of the road or some present sense of decorum, as the cart passed on, the company fell to the rear in couples, keeping step, and otherwise assuming the external show of a formal procession. Jack Folinsbee, who had at the outset played a funeral march in dumb show upon an imaginary trombone, desisted from a lack of sympathy and appreciation—not having, perhaps, your true humorist's capacity to be content with the enjoyment of his own fun.

The way led through Grizzly Canyon, by this time clothed in funereal drapery and shadows. The redwoods, burying their moccasined feet in the red soil, stood in Indian file along the track, trailing an uncouth benediction from their bending boughs upon the passing bier. A hare, surprised into helpless inactivity, sat upright and pulsating in the ferns by the roadside as the cortège went by. Squirrels hastened to gain a secure outlook from higher boughs; and the blue jays, spreading their wings, fluttered before them like outriders, until the outskirts of Sandy Bar were reached, and the solitary cabin of Tennessee's Partner.

Viewed under more favorable circumstances, it would not have been a cheerful place. The unpicturesque site, the rude and unlovely outlines, the unsavory details, which distinguish the nest-building of the California miner, were all here with the dreariness of decay superadded. A few paces from the cabin there was a rough enclosure, which, in the brief days of Tennessee's Partner's matrimonial felicity, had been used as a garden, but was now overgrown with fern. As we approached it, we were surprised to find that what we had taken for a recent attempt at cultivation was the broken soil about an open grave.

The cart was halted before the enclosure, and rejecting the offers of assistance with the same air of simple self-reliance he had displayed throughout, Tennessee's Partner lifted the rough coffin on his back, and deposited it unaided within the shallow grave. He then nailed down the board which served as a lid, and mounting the little mound of earth beside it, took off his hat and slowly mopped his face with his handkerchief. This the crowd felt was a preliminary to speech, and they disposed themselves variously on stumps and boulders, and sat expectant.

"When a man," began Tennessee's Partner slowly, "has been running free all day, what's the natural thing for him to do? Why, to come home. And if he ain't in a condition to go home, what can his best friend do? Why, bring him home. And here's Tennessee has been running free, and we brings him home from his wandering." He paused and picked up a fragment of quartz, rubbed it thoughtfully on his sleeve, and went on: "It ain't the first time that I've packed him on my back, as you see'd me now. It ain't the first time that I brought him to this yer cabin when he couldn't help himself; it ain't the first time that I and Jinny have waited for him on yon hill, and picked him up and so fetched him home, when he couldn't speak and didn't know me. And now that it's the last time, why"—he paused and rubbed the quartz gently on his sleeve—"you see it's sort of rough on his pardner. And now, gentlemen," he added abruptly, picking up his long-handled shovel, "the fun'l's over; and my thanks, and Tennessee's thanks, to you for your trouble."

Resisting any proffers of assistance, he began to fill in the grave, turning his back upon the crowd, that after a few moments' hesitation gradually withdrew. As they crossed the little ridge that hid Sandy Bar from view, some, looking back, thought they could see Tennessee's Partner, his work done, sitting upon the grave, his shovel between his knees, and his face buried in his red bandana handkerchief. But it was argued by others that you couldn't tell his face from his handkerchief at that distance, and this point remained undecided.

In the reaction that followed the feverish excitement of that day, Tennessee's Partner was not forgotten. A secret investigation had cleared him of any complicity in Tennessee's guilt, and left only a suspicion of his general sanity. Sandy Bar made a point of calling on him, and proffering various uncouth but well-meant kindnesses. But from that day his rude health and great strength seemed visibly to decline; and when the rainy season fairly set in, and the tiny grass blades were beginning to peep from the rocky mound above Tennessee's grave, he took to his bed.

One night, when the pines beside the cabin were swaying in the storm and trailing their slender fingers over the roof, and the roar and rush of the swollen river were heard below, Tennessee's Partner lifted his head from the pillow, saying, "It is time to go for Tennessee; I must put Jinny in the cart;" and would have risen from his bed but for the restraint of his attendant. Struggling, he still pursued his singular fancy: "There, now, steady, Jinny, steady, old girl. How dark it is! Look out for the ruts, and look out for him, too, old gal. Sometimes, you know, when he's blind drunk, he drops down right in the trail. Keep on straight up to the pine on the top of the hill. Thar! I told you so!—thar he is—coming this way, too—all by himself, sober, and his face a-shining. Tennessee! Pardner!"

And so they met.

THE BRIDE COMES
TO YELLOW SKY

BY STEPHEN CRANE *(Face to Face)*

Although not noted for stories of life in the Old West, Stephen Crane (1871–1900), the author of the classic Civil War novel The Red Badge of Courage, *published two quintessential Western tales during his tragically short lifetime (he died of tuberculosis at the age of twenty-eight). One is "The Blue Hotel"; the other, which first appeared in 1898, is "The Bride Comes to Yellow Sky," a sensitive, realistic, and gently humorous study of a just-married Texas lawman named Jack Potter. Like the segment of the 1952 film* Face to Face *which is based on it, it is a story guaranteed to please.*

The great Pullman was whirling onward with such dignity of motion that a glance from the window seemed simply to prove that the plains of Texas were pouring eastward. Vast flats of green grass, dull-hued spaces of mesquit and cactus, little groups of frame houses, woods of light and tender trees, all were sweeping into the east, sweeping over the horizon, a precipice.

A newly married pair had boarded this coach at San Antonio. The man's face was reddened from many days in the winds and sun, and a direct result of his new black clothes was that his brick coloured hands were constantly performing in a most conscious fashion. From time to time he looked down respectfully at his attire. He sat with a hand on each knee, like a man waiting in a barber's shop. The glances he devoted to other passengers were furtive and shy.

The bride was not pretty, nor was she very young. She wore a dress of blue cashmere, with small reservations of velvet here and there, and

with steel buttons abounding. She continually twisted her head to re-
gard her puff sleeves, very stiff, straight, and high. They embarrassed
her. It was quite apparent that she had cooked, and that she expected
to cook, dutifully. The blushes caused by the careless scrutiny of some
passengers as she had entered the car were strange to see upon this
plain, under-class countenance, which was drawn in placid, almost
emotionless lines.

They were evidently very happy. "Ever been in a parlour-car before?" he asked, smiling with delight.

"No," she answered; "I never was. It's fine, ain't it?"

"Great! And then after a while we'll go forward to the diner, and get
a big lay-out. Finest meal in the world. Charge a dollar."

"Oh, do they?" cried the bride. "Charge a dollar? Why, that's too
much—for us—ain't it, Jack?"

"Not this trip, anyhow," he answered bravely. "We're going to go
the whole thing."

Later he explained to her about the trains. "You see, it's a thousand
miles from one end of Texas to the other; and this train runs right
across it, and never stops but four times." He had the pride of an
owner. He pointed out to her the dazzling fittings of the coach; and in
truth her eyes opened wider as she contemplated the sea-green figured
velvet, the shining brass, silver, and glass, the wood that gleamed as
darkly brilliant as the surface of a pool of oil. At one end a bronze figure
sturdily held a support for a separated chamber, and at convenient
places on the ceiling were frescos in olive and silver.

To the minds of the pair, their surroundings reflected the glory of
their marriage that morning in San Antonio; this was the environment
of their new estate; and the man's face in particular beamed with an
elation that made him appear ridiculous to the Negro porter. This
individual at times surveyed them from afar with an amused and supe-
rior grin. On other occasions he bullied them with skill in ways that did
not make it exactly plain to them that they were being bullied. He
subtly used all the manners of the most unconquerable kind of snob-
bery. He oppressed them; but of this oppression they had small knowledge, and they speedily forgot that infrequently a number of travellers
covered them with stares of derisive enjoyment. Historically there was
supposed to be something infinitely humorous in their situation.

"We are due in Yellow Sky at three forty-two," he said, looking tenderly into her eyes.

"Oh, are we?" she said, as if she had not been aware of it. To evince surprise at her husband's statement was part of her wifely amiability. She took from a pocket a little silver watch; and as she held it before her, and stared at it with a frown of attention, the new husband's face shone.

"I bought it in San Anton' from a friend of mine," he told her gleefully.

"It's seventeen minutes past twelve," she said, looking up at him with a kind of shy and clumsy coquetry. A passenger, noting this play, grew excessively sardonic, and winked at himself in one of the numerous mirrors.

At last they went to the dining-car. Two rows of Negro waiters, in glowing white suits, surveyed their entrance with the interest, and also the equanimity, of men who had been forewarned. The pair fell to the lot of a waiter who happened to feel pleasure in steering them through their meal. He viewed them with the manner of a fatherly pilot, his countenance radiant with benevolence. The patronage, entwined with the ordinary deference, was not plain to them. And yet, as they returned to their coach, they showed in their faces a sense of escape.

To the left, miles down a long purple slope, was a little ribbon of mist where moved the keening Rio Grande. The train was approaching it at an angle, and the apex was Yellow Sky. Presently it was apparent that, as the distance from Yellow Sky grew shorter, the husband became commensurately restless. His brick-red hands were more insistent in their prominence. Occasionally he was even rather absent-minded and far-away when the bride leaned forward and addressed him.

As a matter of truth, Jack Potter was beginning to find the shadow of a deed weigh upon him like a leaden slab. He, the town marshal of Yellow Sky, a man known, liked, and feared in his corner, a prominent person, had gone to San Antonio to meet a girl he believed he loved, and there, after the usual prayers, had actually induced her to marry him, without consulting Yellow Sky for any part of the transaction. He was now bringing his bride before an innocent and unsuspecting community.

Of course people in Yellow Sky married as it pleased them, in accordance with a general custom; but such was Potter's thought of his duty to his friends, or of their idea of his duty, or of an unspoken form which does not control men in these matters, that he felt he was heinous. He had committed an extraordinary crime. Face to face with this girl in San Antonio, and spurred by his sharp impulse, he had gone headlong over all the social hedges. At San Antonio he was like a man hidden in the dark. A knife to sever any friendly duty, any form, was easy to his hand in that remote city. But the hour of Yellow Sky—the hour of daylight—was approaching.

He knew full well that his marriage was an important thing to his town. It could only be exceeded by the burning of the new hotel. His friends could not forgive him. Frequently he had reflected on the advisability of telling them by telegraph, but a new cowardice had been upon him. He feared to do it. And now the train was hurrying him towards a scene of amazement, glee and reproach. He glanced out of the window at the line of haze swinging slowly in towards the train.

Yellow Sky had a kind of brass band, which played painfully, to the delight of the populace. He laughed without heart as he thought of it. If the citizens could dream of his prospective arrival with his bride, they would parade the band at the station and escort them, amid cheers and laughing congratulations, to his adobe home.

He resolved that he would use all the devices of speed and plainscraft in making the journey from the station to his house. Once within that safe citadel, he could issue some sort of vocal bulletin, and then not go among the citizens until they had time to wear off a little of their enthusiasm.

The bride looked anxiously at him. "What's worrying you, Jack?"

He laughed again. "I'm not worrying, girl; I'm only thinking of Yellow Sky."

She flushed in comprehension.

A sense of mutual guilt invaded their minds and developed a finer tenderness. They looked at each other with eyes softly aglow. But Potter often laughed the same nervous laugh; the flush upon the bride's face seemed quite permanent.

The traitor to the feelings of Yellow Sky narrowly watched the speeding landscape. "We're nearly there," he said.

Presently the porter came and announced the proximity of Potter's home. He held a brush in his hand, and, with all his airy superiority gone, he brushed Potter's new clothes as the latter slowly turned this way and that way. Potter fumbled out a coin and gave it to the porter, as he had seen others do. It was a heavy and musclebound business, as that of a man shoeing his first horse.

The porter took their bag, and as the train began to slow they moved forward to the hooded platform of the car. Presently the two engines and their long string of coaches rushed into the station of Yellow Sky.

"They have to take water here," said Potter, from a constricted throat and in mournful cadence, as one announcing death. Before the train stopped his eye had swept the length of the platform, and he was glad and astonished to see there was none upon it but the station-agent, who, with a slightly hurried and anxious air, was walking toward the water-tanks. When the train had halted, the porter alighted first, and placed in position a little temporary step.

"Come on, girl," said Potter, hoarsely. As he helped her down they each laughed on a false note. He took the bag from the Negro, and bade his wife cling to his arm. As they slunk rapidly away, his hang-dog glance perceived that they were unloading the two trunks, and also that the station-agent, far ahead near the baggage-car, had turned and was running toward him, making gestures. He laughed, and groaned as he laughed, when he noted the first effect of his marital bliss upon Yellow Sky. He gripped his wife's arm firmly to his side, and they fled. Behind them the porter stood, chuckling fatuously.

The California express on the Southern Railway was due at Yellow Sky in twenty-one minutes. There were six men at the bar of the Weary Gentleman saloon. One was a drummer who talked a great deal and rapidly; three were Texans who did not care to talk at that time; and two were Mexican sheep-herders, who did not talk as a general practice in the Weary Gentleman saloon. The barkeeper's dog lay on the board walk that crossed in front of the door. His head was on his paws, and he glanced drowsily here and there with the constant vigilance of a dog that is kicked on occasion. Across the sandy street were some vivid green grass-plots, so wonderful in appearance, amid the sands that burned near them in a blazing sun, that they caused a doubt in the mind. They exactly resembled the grass mats used to represent lawns on the stage. At the cooler end of the railway station, a man without a coat sat in a tilted chair and smoked his pipe. The fresh-cut bank of the

Rio Grande circled near the town, and there could be seen beyond it a great plum-coloured plain of mesquit.

Save for the busy drummer and his companions in the saloon, Yellow Sky was dozing. The new-comer leaned gracefully upon the bar, and recited tales with the confidence of a bard who has come upon a new field.

"—and at the moment that the old man fell downstairs with the bureau in his arms, the old woman was coming up with two scuttles of coal, and of course—"

The drummer's tale was interrupted by a young man who suddenly appeared in the open door. He cried: "Scratchy Wilson's drunk, and has turned loose with both hands." The two Mexicans at once set down their glasses and faded out of the rear entrance of the saloon.

The drummer, innocent and jocular, answered: "All right, old man. S'pose he has? Come in and have a drink, anyhow."

But the information had made such an obvious cleft in every skull in the room that the drummer was obliged to see its importance. All had become instantly solemn. "Say," said he, mystified, "what is this." His three companions made the introductory gesture of eloquent speech; but the young man at the door forestalled them.

"It means, my friend," he answered, as he came into the saloon, "that for the next two hours this town won't be a health resort."

The barkeeper went to the door, and locked and barred it; reaching out of the window, he pulled in heavy wooden shutters, and barred them. Immediately a solemn, chapel-like gloom was upon the place. The drummer was looking from one to another.

"But say," he cried, "what is this, anyhow? You don't mean there is going to be a gun-fight?"

"Don't know whether there'll be a fight or not," answered one man, grimly; "but there'll be some shootin'—some good shootin'."

The young man who had warned them waved his hand. "Oh, there'll be a fight fast enough, if any one wants it. Anybody can get a fight out there in the street. There's a fight just waiting."

The drummer seemed to be swayed between the interest of a foreigner and a perception of personal danger.

"What did you say his name was?" he asked.

"Scratchy Wilson," they answered in chorus.

"And will he kill anybody? What are you going to do? Does this happen often? Does he rampage around like this once a week or so? Can he break in that door?"

"No; he can't break down that door," replied the barkeeper. "He's tried it three times. But when he comes you'd better lay down on the floor, stranger. He's dead sure to shoot at it, and a bullet may come through."

Thereafter the drummer kept a strict eye upon the door. The time had not yet been called for him to hug the floor, but, as a minor precaution, he sidled near to the wall. "Will he kill anybody?" he asked again.

The men laughed low and scornfully at the question.

"He's out to shoot, and he's out for trouble. Don't see any good in experimentin' with him."

"But what do you do in a case like this? What do you do?"

A man responded: "Why, he and Jack Potter—"

"But," in chorus the other men interrupted, "Jack Potter's in San Anton'."

"Well, who is he? What's he got to do with it?"

"Oh, he's the town marshal. He goes out and fights Scratchy when he gets on one of these tears."

"Wow!" said the drummer, mopping his brow. "Nice job he's got."

The voices had toned away to mere whisperings. The drummer wished to ask further questions, which were born of an increasing anxiety and bewilderment; but when he attempted them, the men merely looked at him in irritation and motioned him to remain silent. A tense waiting hush was upon them. In the deep shadows of the room their eyes shone as they listened for sounds from the street. One man made three gestures at the barkeeper; and the latter, moving like a ghost, handed him a glass and a bottle. The man poured a full glass of whisky, and set down the bottle noiselessly. He gulped the whisky in a swallow, and turned again toward the door in immovable silence. The drummer saw that the barkeeper, without a sound, had taken a Winchester from beneath the bar. Later he saw this individual beckoning to him, so he tiptoed across the room.

"You better come with me back of the bar."

"No, thanks," said the drummer, perspiring; "I'd rather be where I can make a break for the back door."

Whereupon the man of bottles made a kindly but peremptory gesture. The drummer obeyed it, and, finding himself seated on a box with his head below the level of the bar, balm was laid upon his soul at sight of various zinc and copper fittings that bore a resemblance to armour-plate. The barkeeper took a seat comfortably upon an adjacent box.

"You see," he whispered, "this here Scratchy Wilson is a wonder with a gun—a perfect wonder; and when he goes on the war-trail, we hunt our holes—naturally. He's about the last of the old gang that used to hang out along the river here. He's a terror when he's drunk. When he's sober he's all right—kind of simple—wouldn't hurt a fly—nicest fellow in town. But when he's drunk—whoo!"

There were periods of stillness. "I wish Jack Potter was back from San Anton'," said the barkeeper. "He shot Wilson up once—in the leg —and he would sail in and pull out the kinks in this thing."

Presently they heard from a distance the sound of a shot, followed by three wild yowls. It instantly removed a bond from the men in the darkened saloon. There was a shuffling of feet. They looked at each other. "Here he comes," they said.

A man in a maroon-coloured flannel shirt, which had been purchased for purposes of decoration, and made principally by some Jewish women on the East Side of New York, rounded a corner and walked into the middle of the main street of Yellow Sky. In either hand the man held a long, heavy, blue-black revolver. Often he yelled, and these cries rang through a semblance of a deserted village, shrilly flying over the roofs in a volume that seemed to have no relation to the ordinary vocal strength of a man. It was as if the surrounding stillness formed the arch of a tomb over him. These cries of ferocious challenge rang against walls of silence. And his boots had red tops with gilded imprints, of the kind beloved in winter by little sledding boys on the hillsides of New England.

The man's face flamed in a rage begot of whisky. His eyes, rolling, and yet keen for ambush, hunted the still doorways and windows. He walked with the creeping movement of the midnight cat. As it occurred to him, he roared menacing information. The long revolvers in his hands were as easy as straws; they were moved with an electric swiftness. The little fingers of each hand played sometimes in a musician's way. Plain from the low collar of the shirt, the cords of his neck straightened and sank, straightened and sank, as passion moved him.

The only sounds were his terrible invitations. The calm adobes preserved their demeanour at the passing of this small thing in the middle of the street.

There was no offer of fight—no offer of fight. The man called to the sky. There were no attractions. He bellowed and fumed and swayed his revolvers here and everywhere.

The dog of the barkeeper of the Weary Gentleman saloon had not appreciated the advance of events. He yet lay dozing in front of his master's door. At sight of the dog, the man paused and raised his revolver humorously. At sight of the man, the dog sprang up and walked diagonally away, with a sullen head, and growling. The man yelled, and the dog broke into a gallop. As it was about to enter an alley, there was a loud noise, a whistling, and something spat the ground directly before it. The dog screamed, and, wheeling in terror, galloped headlong in a new direction. Again there was a noise, a whistling, and sand was kicked viciously before it. Fear-stricken, the dog turned and flurried like an animal in a pen. The man stood laughing, his weapons at his hips.

Ultimately the man was attracted by the closed door of the Weary Gentleman saloon. He went to it and, hammering with a revolver, demanded drink.

The door remaining imperturbable, he picked a bit of paper from the walk, and nailed it to the framework with a knife. He then turned his back contemptuously upon this popular resort and, walking to the opposite side of the street and spinning there on his heel quickly and lithely, fired at the bit of paper. He missed it by a half-inch. He swore at himself, and went away. Later he comfortably fusilladed the windows of his most intimate friend. The man was playing with this town; it was a toy for him.

But still there was no offer of fight. The name of Jack Potter, his ancient antagonist, entered his mind, and he concluded that it would be a glad thing if he should go to Potter's house, and by bombardment induce him to come out and fight. He moved in the direction of his desire, chanting Apache scalp-music.

When he arrived at it, Potter's house presented the same still front as had the other adobes. Taking up a strategic position, the man howled a challenge. But this house regarded him as might a great stone god. It gave no sign. After a decent wait, the man howled further challenges, mingling with them wonderful epithets.

Presently there came the spectacle of a man churning himself into deepest rage over the immobility of a house. He fumed at it as the winter wind attacks a prairie cabin in the North. To the distance there should have gone the sound of a tumult like the fighting of two hundred Mexicans. As necessity bade him, he paused for breath or to reload his revolvers.

Potter and his bride walked sheepishly and with speed. Sometimes they laughed together shamefacedly and low.

"Next corner, dear," he said finally.

They put forth the efforts of a pair walking bowed against a strong wind. Potter was about to raise a finger to point the first appearance of the new home when, as they circled the corner, they came face to face with a man in a maroon-coloured shirt, who was feverishly pushing cartridges into a large revolver. Upon the instant the man dropped his revolver to the ground and, like lightning, whipped another from its holster. The second weapon was aimed at the bridegroom's chest.

There was a silence. Potter's mouth seemed to be merely a grave for his tongue. He exhibited an instinct to at once loosen his arm from the woman's grip, and he dropped the bag to the sand. As for the bride, her face had gone as yellow as old cloth. She was a slave to hideous rites, gazing at the apparitional snake.

The two men faced each other at a distance of three paces. He of the revolver smiled with a new and quiet ferocity.

"Tried to sneak up on me," he said. "Tried to sneak up on me!" His eyes grew more baleful. As Potter made a slight movement, the man thrust his revolver venomously forward. "No; don't you do it, Jack Potter. Don't you move a finger towards a gun just yet. Don't you move an eyelash. The time has come for me to settle with you, and I'm goin' to do it in my own way, and loaf along with no interferin'. So if you don't want a gun bent on you, just mind what I tell you."

Potter looked at his enemy. "I ain't got a gun on me, Scratchy," he said. "Honest, I ain't." He was stiffening and steadying, but yet somewhere at the back of his mind a vision of the Pullman floated: the sea-green figured velvet, the shining brass, silver, and glass, the wood that gleamed as darkly brilliant as the surface of a pool of oil—all the glory of the marriage, the environment of the new estate. "You know I fight when it comes to fighting, Scratchy Wilson; but I ain't got a gun on me. You'll have to do all the shootin' yourself."

His enemy's face went livid. He stepped forward, and lashed his weapon to and fro before Potter's chest. "Don't you tell me you ain't got no gun on you, you whelp. Don't tell me no lie like that. There ain't a man in Texas ever seen you without no gun. Don't take me for no kid." His eyes blazed with light, and his throat worked like a pump.

"I ain't takin' you for no kid," answered Potter. His heels had not moved an inch backward. "I'm takin' you for a damn fool. I tell you I ain't got a gun, and I ain't. If you're goin' to shoot me, you better begin now; you'll never get a chance like this again."

So much enforced reasoning had told on Wilson's rage; he was calmer. "If you ain't got a gun, why ain't you got a gun?" he sneered. "Been to Sunday-school?"

"I ain't got a gun because I've just come from San Anton' with my wife. I'm married," said Potter. "And if I'd thought there was going to be any galoots like you prowling around when I brought my wife home, I'd had a gun, and don't you forget it."

"Married!" said Scratchy, not at all comprehending.

"Yes, married. I'm married," said Potter, distinctly.

"Married?" said Scratchy. Seemingly for the first time, he saw the drooping, drowning woman at the other man's side. "No!" he said. He was like a creature allowed a glimpse of another world. He moved a pace backward, and his arm, with the revolver, dropped to his side. "Is this the lady?" he asked.

"Yes; this is the lady," answered Potter.

There was another period of silence.

"Well," said Wilson at last, slowly, "I s'pose it's all off now."

"It's all off if you say so, Scratchy. You know I didn't make the trouble." Potter lifted his valise.

"Well, I 'low it's off, Jack," said Wilson. He was looking at the ground. "Married!" He was not a student of chivalry; it was merely that in the presence of this foreign condition he was a simple child of the earlier plains. He picked up his starboard revolver, and, placing both weapons in their holsters, he went away. His feet made funnel-shaped tracks in the heavy sand.

A DOUBLE-DYED DECEIVER
BY O. HENRY *(The Texan)*

O. Henry (William Sydney Porter, 1862–1910), the master of the surprise-ending short story, created two memorable Western despera-does: the Cisco Kid, who underwent a metamorphosis in the 1950s television series starring Duncan Renaldo and Leo Carrillo and became a dashing "Robin Hood of the Old West"; and the Llano Kid, the "villainous hero" of both the story "A Double-Dyed Deceiver" (1905) and the early Gary Cooper screen adaptation of it, The Texan *(1930). Curiously, there is even a blending of the two characters in an obscure 1939 film with Tito Guizar and Alan Mowbray: its title is* The Llano Kid, *but it is loosely based on the exploits of the Cisco Kid.*

The trouble began in Laredo. It was the Llano Kid's fault, for he should have confined his habit of manslaughter to Mexicans. But the Kid was past twenty; and to have only Mexicans to one's credit at twenty is to blush unseen on the Rio Grande border.

It happened in old Justo Valdo's gambling house. There was a poker game at which sat players who were not all friends, as happens often where men ride in from afar to shoot Folly as she gallops. There was a row over so small a matter as a pair of queens; and when the smoke had cleared away it was found that the Kid had committed an indiscretion, and his adversary had been guilty of a blunder. For, the unfortunate combatant, instead of being a Greaser, was a high-blooded youth from the cow ranches, of about the Kid's own age and possessed of friends and champions. His blunder in missing the Kid's right ear only a six-teenth of an inch when he pulled his gun did not lessen the indiscre-tion of the better marksman.

The Kid, not being equipped with a retinue, nor bountifully supplied with personal admirers and supporters—on account of a rather umbrageous reputation, even for the border—considered it not incompatible with his indisputable gameness to perform that judicious tractional act known as "pulling his freight."

Quickly the avengers gathered and sought him. Three of them overtook him within a rod of the station. The Kid turned and showed his teeth in that brilliant but mirthless smile that usually preceded his deeds of insolence and violence, and his pursuers fell back without making it necessary for him even to reach for his weapon.

But in this affair the Kid had not felt the grim thirst for encounter that usually urged him on to battle. It had been a purely chance row, born of the cards and certain epithets impossible for a gentleman to brook that had passed between the two. The Kid had rather liked the slim, haughty, brown-faced young chap whom his bullet had cut off in the first pride of manhood. And now he wanted no more blood. He wanted to get away and have a good long sleep somewhere in the sun on the mesquit grass with his handkerchief over his face. Even a Mexican might have crossed his path in safety while he was in this mood.

The Kid openly boarded the north-bound passenger train that departed five minutes later. But at Webb, a few miles out, where it was flagged to take on a traveller, he abandoned that manner of escape. There were telegraph stations ahead; and the Kid looked askance at electricity and steam. Saddle and spur were his rocks of safety.

The man whom he had shot was a stranger to him. But the Kid knew that he was of the Coralitos outfit from Hidalgo; and that the punchers from that ranch were more relentless and vengeful than Kentucky feudists when wrong or harm was done to one of them. So, with the wisdom that has characterized many great fighters, the Kid decided to pile up as many leagues as possible of chaparral and pear between himself and the retaliation of the Coralitos bunch.

Near the station was a store; and near the store, scattered among the mesquits and elms, stood the saddled horses of the customers. Most of them waited, half asleep, with sagging limbs and drooping heads. But one, a long-legged roan with a curved neck, snorted and pawed the turf. Him the Kid mounted, gripped with his knees, and slapped gently with the owner's own quirt.

If the slaying of the temerarious card-player had cast a cloud over the Kid's standing as a good and true citizen, this last act of his veiled his

figure in the darkest shadows of disrepute. On the Rio Grande border if
you take a man's life you sometimes take trash; but if you take his
horse, you take a thing the loss of which renders him poor, indeed, and
which enriches you not—if you are caught. For the Kid there was no
turning back now.

With the springing roan under him he felt little care or uneasiness.
After a five-mile gallop he drew in to the plainsman's jogging trot, and
rode northeastward toward the Nueces River bottoms. He knew the
country well—its most tortuous and obscure trails through the great
wilderness of brush and pear, and its camps and lonesome ranches
where one might find safe entertainment. Always he bore to the east;
for the Kid had never seen the ocean, and he had a fancy to lay his
hand upon the mane of the great gulf, the gamesome colt of the
greater waters.

So after three days he stood on the shore at Corpus Christi, and
looked out across the gentle ripples of a quiet sea.

Captain Boone, of the schooner *Flyaway*, stood near his skiff, which
one of his crew was guarding in the surf. When ready to sail he had
discovered that one of the necessaries of life, in the parallelogrammatic
shape of plug tobacco, had been forgotten. A sailor had been dispatched for the missing cargo. Meanwhile the captain paced the sands,
chewing profanely at his pocket store.

A slim, wiry youth in high-heeled boots came down to the water's
edge. His face was boyish, but with a premature severity that hinted at
a man's experience. His complexion was naturally dark; and the sun
and wind of an outdoor life had burned it to a coffee brown. His hair
was as black and straight as an Indian's; his face had not yet been
upturned to the humiliation of a razor; his eyes were a cold and steady
blue. He carried his left arm somewhat away from his body, for pearl-
handled .45s are frowned upon by town marshals, and are a little bulky
when packed in the left armhole of one's vest. He looked beyond Captain Boone at the gulf with the impersonal and expressionless dignity of
a Chinese emperor.

"Thinkin' of buyin' that'ar gulf, buddy?" asked the captain, made
sarcastic by his narrow escape from the tobaccoless voyage.

"Why, no," said the Kid gently, "I reckon not. I never saw it before.
I was just looking at it. Not thinking of selling it, are you?"

"Not this trip," said the captain. "I'll send it to you C.O.D. when I

get back to Buenas Tierras. Here comes that capstanfooted lubber with
the chewin'. I ought to've weighed anchor an hour ago."

"Is that your ship out there?" asked the Kid.

"Why, yes," answered the captain, "if you want to call a schooner a
ship, and I don't mind lyin'. But you better say Miller and Gonzales,
owners, and ordinary plain, Billy-be-damned old Samuel K. Boone,
skipper."

"Where are you going to?" asked the refugee.

"Buenas Tierras, coast of South America—I forgot what they called
the country the last time I was there. Cargo—lumber, corrugated iron,
and machetes."

"What kind of a country is it?" asked the Kid, "—hot or cold?"

"Warmish, buddy," said the captain. "But a regular Paradise Lost for
elegance of scenery and be-yooty of geography. Ye're wakened every
morning by the sweet singin' of red birds with seven purple tails, and
the sighin' of breezes in the posies and roses. And the inhabitants never
work, for they can reach out and pick steamer baskets of the choicest
hothouse fruit without gettin' out of bed. And there's no Sunday and
no ice and no rent and no troubles and no use and no nothin'. It's a
great country for a man to go to sleep with, and wait for somethin' to
turn up. The bananys and oranges and hurricanes and pineapples that
ye eat comes from there."

"That sounds to me!" said the Kid, at last betraying interest.
"What'll the expressage be to take me out there with you?"

"Twenty-four dollars," said Captain Boone; "grub and transporta-
tion. Second cabin. I haven't got a first cabin."

"You've got my company," said the Kid, pulling out a buckskin bag.
With three hundred dollars he had gone to Laredo for his regular
"blowout." The duel in Valdos's had cut short his season of hilarity, but
it had left him with nearly two hundred dollars for aid in the fight that
it had made necessary.

"All right, buddy," said the captain. "I hope your ma won't blame
me for this little childish escapade of yours." He beckoned to one of
the boat's crew. "Let Sanchez lift you out to the skiff so you won't get
your feet wet."

Thacker, the United States consul at Buenas Tierras, was not yet
drunk. It was only eleven o'clock; and he never arrived at his desired

state of beatitude—a state where he sang ancient maudlin vaudeville songs and pelted his screaming parrot with banana peels—until the middle of the afternoon. So, when he looked up from his hammock at the sound of a slight cough, and saw the Kid standing in the door of the consulate, he was still in a condition to extend the hospitality and courtesy due from the representative of a great nation. "Don't disturb yourself," said the Kid easily. "I just dropped in. They told me it was customary to light at your camp before starting in to round up the town. I just came in on a ship from Texas."

"Glad to see you, Mr.—," said the consul.

The Kid laughed.

"Sprague Dalton," he said. "It sounds funny to me to hear it. I'm called the Llano Kid in the Rio Grande country."

"I'm Thacker," said the consul. "Take that cane-bottom chair. Now if you've come to invest, you want somebody to advise you. These dingies will cheat you out of the gold in your teeth if you don't understand their ways. Try a cigar?"

"Much obliged," said the Kid, "but if it wasn't for my corn shucks and the little bag in my back pocket I couldn't live a minute." He took out his "makings," and rolled a cigarette.

"They speak Spanish here," said the consul. "You'll need an interpreter. If there's anything I can do, why, I'd be delighted. If you're buying fruit lands or looking for a concession of any sort, you'll want somebody who knows the ropes to look out for you."

"I speak Spanish," said the Kid, "about nine times better than I do English. Everybody speaks it on the range where I come from. And I'm not in the market for anything."

"You speak Spanish?" said Thacker thoughtfully. He regarded the Kid absorbedly.

"You look like a Spaniard, too," he continued. "And you're from Texas. And you can't be more than twenty or twenty-one. I wonder if you've got any nerve."

"You got a deal of some kind to put through?" asked the Texan, with unexpected shrewdness.

"Are you open to a proposition?" said Thacker.

"What's the use to deny it?" said the Kid. "I got into a little gun frolic down in Laredo and plugged a white man. There wasn't any

Mexican handy. And I come down to your parrot-and-monkey range just for to smell the morning-glories and marigolds. Now, do you *sabe?*"

Thacker got up and closed the door.

"Let me see your hand," he said.

He took the Kid's left hand, and examined the back of it closely.

"I can do it," he said excitedly. "Your flesh is as hard as wood and as healthy as a baby's. It will heal in a week."

"If it's a fist fight you want to back me for," said the Kid, "don't put your money up yet. Make it gun work, and I'll keep you company. But no barehanded scrapping, like ladies at a tea-party, for me."

"It's easier than that," said Thacker. "Just step here, will you?"

Through the window he pointed to a two-story white-stuccoed house with wide galleries rising amid the deep-green tropical foliage on a wooded hill that sloped gently from the sea.

"In that house," said Thacker, "a fine old Castilian gentleman and his wife are yearning to gather you into their arms and fill your pockets with money. Old Santos Urique lives there. He owns half the gold-mines in the country."

"You haven't been eating loco weed, have you?" asked the Kid.

"Sit down again," said Thacker, "and I'll tell you. Twelve years ago they lost a kid. No, he didn't die—although most of 'em here do from drinking the surface water. He was a wild little devil, even if he wasn't but eight years old. Everybody knows about it. Some Americans who were through here prospecting for gold had letters to Señor Urique, and the boy was a favourite with them. They filled his head with big stories about the States; and about a month after they left, the kid disappeared, too. He was supposed to have stowed himself away among the banana bunches on a fruit steamer, and gone to New Orleans. He was seen once afterward in Texas, it was thought, but they never heard anything more of him. Old Urique has spent thousands of dollars having him looked for. The madam was broken up worst of all. The kid was her life. She wears mourning yet. But they say she believes he'll come back to her some day, and never gives up hope. On the back of the boy's left hand was tattooed a flying eagle carrying a spear in his claws. That's old Urique's coat of arms or something that he inherited in Spain."

The Kid raised his left hand slowly and gazed at it curiously.

"That's it," said Thacker, reaching behind the official desk for his bottle of smuggled brandy. "You're not so slow. I can do it. What was I consul at Sandakan for? I never knew till now. In a week I'll have the eagle bird with the frog-sticker blended in so you'd think you were born with it. I brought a set of the needles and ink just because I was sure you'd drop in some day, Mr. Dalton."

"Oh, hell," said the Kid. "I thought I told you my name!"

"All right, 'Kid,' then. It won't be that long. How does Señorito Urique sound, for a change?"

"I never played son any that I remember of," said the Kid. "If I had any parents to mention they went over the divide about the time I gave my first bleat. What is the plan of your round-up?"

Thacker leaned back against the wall and held his glass up to the light.

"We've come now," said he, "to the question of how far you're willing to go in a little matter of the sort."

"I told you why I came down here," said the Kid simply.

"A good answer," said the consul. "But you won't have to go that far. Here's the scheme. After I get the trademark tattooed on your hand I'll notify old Urique. In the meantime I'll furnish you with all of the family history I can find out, so you can be studying up points to talk about. You've got the looks, you speak the Spanish, you know the facts, you can tell about Texas, you've got the tattoo mark. When I notify them that the rightful heir has returned and is waiting to know whether he will be received and pardoned, what will happen? They'll simply rush down here and fall on your neck, and the curtain goes down for refreshments and a stroll in the lobby."

"I'm waiting," said the Kid. "I haven't had my saddle off in your camp long, pardner, and I never met you before; but if you intend to let it go at a parental blessing, why, I'm mistaken in my man, that's all."

"Thanks," said the consul. "I haven't met anybody in a long time that keeps up with an argument as well as you do. The rest of it is simple. If they take you in only for a while it's long enough. Don't give 'em time to hunt up the strawberry mark on your left shoulder. Old Urique keeps anywhere from $50,000 to $100,000 in his house all the time in a little safe that you could open with a shoe buttoner. Get it. My skill as a tattooer is worth half the boodle. We go halves and catch a tramp steamer for Rio Janeiro. Let the United States go to pieces if it can't get along without my services. *Que dice, señor?*"

"It sounds to me!" said the Kid, nodding his head. "I'm out for the dust."

"All right, then," said Thacker. "You'll have to keep close until we get the bird on you. You can live in the back room here. I do my own cooking, and I'll make you as comfortable as a parsimonious Government will allow me."

Thacker had set the time at a week, but it was two weeks before the design that he patiently tattooed upon the Kid's hand was to his notion. And then Thacker called a *muchacho*, and dispatched this note to the intended victim:

EL SEÑOR DON SANTOS URIQUE,
   La Casa Blanca,

MY DEAR SIR:

I beg permission to inform you that there is in my house as a temporary guest a young man who arrived in Buenas Tierras from the United States some days ago. Without wishing to excite any hopes that may not be realized, I think there is a possibility of his being your long-absent son. It might be well for you to call and see him. If he is, it is my opinion that his intention was to return to his home, but upon arriving here, his courage failed him from doubts as to how he would be received.   Your true servant,

                                   THOMPSON THACKER.

Half an hour afterward—quick time for Buenas Tierras—Señor Urique's ancient landau drove to the consul's door, with the barefooted coachman beating and shouting at the team of fat, awkward horses.

A tall man with a white moustache alighted, and assisted to the ground a lady who was dressed and veiled in unrelieved black.

The two hastened inside, and were met by Thacker with his best diplomatic bow. By his desk stood a slender young man with clear-cut, sunbrowned features and smoothly brushed black hair.

Señora Urique threw back her heavy veil with a quick gesture. She was past middle age, and her hair was beginning to silver, but her full, proud figure and clear olive skin retained traces of the beauty peculiar to the Basque province. But, once you had seen her eyes, and comprehended the great sadness that was revealed in their deep shadows and hopeless expression, you saw that the woman lived only in some memory.

She bent upon the young man a long look of the most agonized questioning. Then her great black eyes turned, and her gaze rested upon his left hand. And then with a sob, not loud, but seeming to shake the room, she cried *"Hijo mío!"* and caught the Llano Kid to her heart.

A month afterward the Kid came to the consulate in response to a message sent by Thacker.

He looked the young Spanish *caballero*. His clothes were imported, and the wiles of the jewellers had not been spent upon him in vain. A more than respectable diamond shone on his finger as he rolled a shuck cigarette.

"What's doing?" asked Thacker.

"Nothing much," said the Kid calmly. "I eat my first iguana steak today. They're them big lizards, you *sabe?* I reckon, though, that frijoles and side bacon would do me about as well. Do you care for iguanas, Thacker?"

"No, nor for some other kinds of reptiles," said Thacker.

It was three in the afternoon, and in another hour he would be in his state of beatitude.

"It's time you were making good, sonny," he went on, with an ugly look on his reddened face. "You're not playing up to me square. You've been the prodigal son for four weeks now, and you could have had veal for every meal on a gold dish if you'd wanted it. Now, Mr. Kid, do you think it's right to leave me out so long on a husk diet? What's the trouble? Don't you get your filial eyes on anything that looks like cash in the Casa Blanca? Don't tell me you don't. Everybody knows where old Urique keeps his stuff. It's U. S. currency, too; he don't accept anything else. What's doing? Don't say 'nothing' this time."

"Why, sure," said the Kid, admiring his diamond, "there's plenty of money up there. I'm no judge of collateral in bunches, but I will undertake for to say that I've seen the rise of $50,000 at a time in that tin grub box that my adopted father calls his safe. And he lets me carry the key sometimes just to show me that he knows I'm the real little Francisco that strayed from the herd a long time ago."

"Well, what are you waiting for?" asked Thacker angrily. "Don't you forget that I can upset your apple-cart any day I want to. If old Urique knew you were an impostor, what sort of things would happen to you? Oh, you don't know this country, Mr. Texas Kid. The laws here have got mustard spread between 'em. These people here'd stretch you out like a frog that had been stepped on, and give you about fifty sticks at every corner of the plaza. And they'd wear every stick out, too. What was left of you they'd feed to alligators."

"I might as well tell you now, pardner," said the Kid, sliding down low on his steamer chair, "that things are going to stay just as they are. They're about right now."

"What do you mean?" asked Thacker, rattling the bottom of his glass on his desk.

"The scheme's off," said the Kid. "And whenever you have the pleasure of speaking to me address me as Don Francisco Urique. I'll guarantee I'll answer to it. We'll let Colonel Urique keep his money. His little tin safe is as good as the time-locker in the First National Bank of Laredo as far as you and me are concerned."

"You're going to throw me down, then, are you?" said the consul.

"Sure," said the Kid cheerfully. "Throw you down. That's it. And now I'll tell you why. The first night I was up at the colonel's house they introduced me to a bedroom. No blankets on the floor—a real room, with a bed and things in it. And before I was asleep, in comes this artificial mother of mine and tucks in the covers. 'Panchito,' she says, 'my little lost one, God has brought you back to me. I bless His name forever.' It was that, or some truck like that, she said. And down comes a drop or two of rain and hits me on the nose. And all that stuck by me, Mr. Thacker. And it's been that way ever since. And it's got to stay that way. Don't you think that it's for what's in it for me, either, that I say so. If you have any such ideas, keep 'em to yourself. I haven't had much truck with women in my life, and no mothers to speak of, but here's a lady that we've got to keep fooled. Once she stood it; twice she won't. I'm a low-down wolf, and the devil may have sent me on this trail instead of God, but I'll travel it to the end. And now, don't forget that I'm Don Francisco Urique whenever you happen to mention my name."

"I'll expose you to-day, you—you double-dyed traitor," stammered Thacker.

The Kid arose and, without violence, took Thacker by the throat with a hand of steel, and shoved him slowly into a corner. Then he drew from under his left arm his pearl-handled .45 and poked the cold muzzle of it against the consul's mouth.

"I told you why I come here," he said, with his old freezing smile. "If I leave here, you'll be the reason. Never forget it, pardner. Now, what is my name?"

"Er—Don Francisco Urique," gasped Thacker.

From outside came a sound of wheels, and the shouting of some one, and the sharp thwacks of a wooden whipstock upon the backs of fat horses.

The Kid put up his gun, and walked toward the door. But he turned again and came back to the trembling Thacker, and held up his left hand with its back toward the consul.

"There's one more reason," he said slowly, "why things have got to stand as they are. The fellow I killed in Laredo had one of them same pictures on his left hand."

Outside, the ancient landau of Don Santos Urique rattled to the door. The coachman ceased his bellowing. Señora Urique, in a voluminous gay gown of white lace and flying ribbons, leaned forward with a happy look in her great soft eyes.

"Are you within, dear son?" she called, in the rippling Castilian.

"Madre mía, yo vengo [mother, I come]," answered the young Don Francisco Urique.

MASSACRE

BY JAMES WARNER BELLAH

(Fort Apache)

No one has written better stories of the life of frontier soldiers or given more historical accuracy to the oft-used (and oft-misused) theme of battle between the U.S. Cavalry and the Indian nations than James Warner Bellah (1899–1976). And his 1947 story "Massacre," a fictional rendering of the Little Big Horn destruction of General George Armstrong Custer and his troops, is perhaps the most accomplished of all his works of this type. It was filmed as Fort Apache *in 1948, the first of director John Ford's cavalry trilogy starring John Wayne and adapted from Bellah stories; the other two films are* She Wore a Yellow Ribbon *(1949), from "Big Hunt" and "Command," and* Rio Grande *(1950), based on "Mission with No Record." Ford also directed yet another film taken from a Bellah work:* Sergeant Rutledge *(1960), from the* Saturday Evening Post *serial of the same title.*

The wind was out of the east, and there can be a great restlessness of soul in the east wind—a ghost shuffle of unfulfilled promise. Flintridge Cohill awakened quickly all over, and lay quite still from long habit, until it came back to him that he was safe in his own quarters at Fort Starke. He snaked out a hand to his repeater and pressed the ring-back release. The watch struck three quarters of an hour past three o'clock. And as the soft bell sang in the darkness, Flint was a little boy again, watching his father, the captain, come angrily up the path to their quarters at Sackets Harbor, seven years before Sumter, push open the door and fling his cap to the rosewood table in the hall. "Molly, they've finally got Grant. He's resigned . . . for the good of the service!" Why should those things come back years later? Some friend of his father's. Some captain out at Fort Humboldt. A brother officer who had fought at Contreras and Chapultepec with his father.

Flint sat upright in bed. "Good God, I'll bet that was General Grant!" he said out loud, and he snorted. "And at a quarter before four in the morning twenty years later, what difference does it make if it was?" Then he heard the distant staccato of feet running.

Someone's boots pounding the headquarters' duckboards. The sound bounced clearly across the parade ground to the row, on the east wind. In a moment, Fire Call would sound or someone would bawl for the corporal of the guard. Cohill flung out of bed and went out on his lean-to veranda. There was a carriage standing across the parade ground in the darkness by headquarters. A carriage with restless horses and dry axles.

It'll be twenty years more before I get within shooting distance of general officer's stars—like Grant and the Old Man—and by that time I won't care. It won't be nearly as important as making captain, in a few more years. But I'd like to be a general before I die—the best damned general in the world at the right time and the right place! It's only the middle of the month and that's a paymaster's wagon over there. I can see the glass glint silver in the starlight like a sheet of bucket-flung water.

Cohill was pulling on cold breeches and stiff boots, and his teeth were chattering in the east wind; he was running fast and silently through the living darkness of the parade ground, with somewhere in the cellars of his mind the nasty-sounding name of Custis Meacham, Indian agent at White River. What are those tricks of association?

Feet raced toward him. He pivoted with flung arms, bending down to silhouette whoever it was against the lighter darkness of the sky. "Brailey?"

Brailey came toward him. "Mr. Cohill, sir, I got orders to call you and Mr. Sitterding and Mr. Topliff. You're wanted at post headquarters, sir."

And Cohill said, "What's the paymaster's wagon got to do with it, Brailey?"

Brailey said, "The new post commander arrived in the wagon. Drove all night from Indian Wells."

Owen Thursday was a tall man, dried out to leather and bone and sinew. Whatever he was doing, he moved about incessantly, not with nerves, but with primeval restlessness; not with impatience, but with an echo of lost destiny. Brevet Major General Thursday, of Clarke's Corps —Thursday of Cumberland Station and of Sudler's Mountain, at twenty-six. Now a major of cavalry at thirty-eight, back in the slow Army runway again, with the flame of glory burning low on his horizon ("I don't know what you were in the habit of doing under similar circumstances when you commanded your division, major, but as long as you have a battalion in my regiment, you will—") for it is far worse to go up and come back again than it ever is not to go up at all. And the cities of the world should always be a vision. For few men can walk their streets and come back to live at peace with their souls in the quietude of their own villages.

"Lieutenant Cohill, sir"—the dark was alive and prowling, like a large cat. There was cool dampness in it, and the faint whisper of threat. A horse whinnied in screaming soprano. Close to, when the team moved the paymaster's wagon, its glass windows flashed black, like polished ebony in the starlight.

"You got here damned fast, Cohill. Where's the acting post commander? Do you all sleep with the covers over your heads at Fort Starke?"

There were booted feet on the veranda boards of headquarters. Inside, someone cursed persistently over the lighting of a lamp. Bitter wood smoke fanned low from a chimney lip and stained the smell of the white dawn air to gray. "Your father, General Cohill, asked me to convey his affection to you, Cohill, when I left Washington."

"Thank you, general."

"Not 'general,' " Thursday said sharply. "A man is what he's paid for. I'm paid in the rank of major."

"Yes, sir. I remembered you as General Thursday."

Then Joplyn came sprinting down the duckboards and braked himself to a quick stop. "Captain Joplyn, sir, acting in command."

"Joplyn," Thursday said, "I've come all the way in from Indian Wells on the whip and two wheels. Mr. Meacham, the agent at White River, wants a show of strength up there at once. He's afraid Stone Buffalo will get out of hand without it."

"Stone Buffalo has been out of hand for months. He is trying to see how far Meacham's religious sentiment will let him go, sir. And Meacham is the biggest fool west of Kansas City and the biggest liar. I'll get a half company off by reveille. I'll take it up myself."

"I call it to your attention that Mr. Meacham is an agent of the United States Government. You will get two companies and an escort wagon train off before reveille, Captain Joplyn. And I'll take them up to White River myself. I've had the officer of the guard send a runner to knock out Mr. Sitterding and Mr. Topliff. Mr. Cohill has already reported in. I'd like all three of them with me, for I know their names and records from department files. And I suggest you keep an officer at headquarters in future—on night duty—until I get back to take over command formally. I don't like daylight soldiers."

"Yes, sir." Joplyn turned sharp about to Flint Cohill with no change of voice, no strain in his manner. "Mr. Cohill, pass the word at once to A and B. Turn them to. Full field equipment, and three hundred rounds of carbine ammunition per man. You will take eight escort wagons, rations and forage for fifteen days, and half of C as mounted wagon guards."

"That is a lot of ammunition . . . for men who are supposed to be trained to shoot," Major Thursday said. "One hundred rounds per man should be ample for any emergency."

"One hundred rounds of carbine ammunition per man, Mr. Cohill. Fifty rounds for revolving pistols per pistol. Sitterding commands A. Topliff, B. You command the escort train. It is twenty minutes after four. How soon can you move out, Mr. Cohill?"

"Reveille is five-forty-five. We can pass the head of the column through the main gate at five-thirty, sir. When Topliff and Sitterding get here, will you tell them I shall be forming the train in the area in front of the cavalry stables? They can find me there. Their first sergeants will know everything you've told me . . . Brailey, follow me on the double as runner." Flint Cohill then turned sharp about to Thursday. "Have you anything additional, sir?"

"Yes, I've several things. I've a few ideas of my own on how Indians should be dealt with. I shall want colors and a proper color guard, guidons and trumpeters. Have the men bring their polishing kits and button sticks and boot blacking. A little more military dignity and decorum out here, and a little less cowboy manners and dress, will engender a lot more respect for the Army. I'll meet you here to take over command, Cohill, as the column passes. You will act as adjutant, in addition to your other duties. Officers' Call in the saddle on the march for further orders as soon as the tail clears the post. Questions?"

"Nothing, sir."

"Move out."

The sun in August is a molten saber blade. It will burn the neckline and the back of a hand to blistered uselessness as you watch it. It sears the lower lip into stiff scar tissue and sweats up shirts and beltlines into noisome sogginess while you stand still. The column was headed due north to make a crossing of the upper reaches of the Paradise, girths frothed white, saddles hot damp, hat brims low, and the blue of trousers and shirts faded out to Southern gray with the dust silt that blanketed everything except eyeballs and the undersides of tongues.

Owen Thursday rode alone, off to the right of the leading files, where he could turn and look down the strung-out length with the faint echo in his eyes of larger columns he had commanded—of regiments of infantry with colors and field music; of artillery rolling inexorably in its heavy dust, hames taut and chains growling, wheels slithering in ruts with the protesting sound of cracking balk ends; of cavalry flank guards flung far out on his right and left by battalion.

All of which dissolved into a hundred and nine officers and men and eight escort wagons—as big a detachment as Mr. Cohill or Mr. Topliff or Mr. Sitterding had ever taken on the warpath in all their service.

"Mr. Cohill!"

Flint kneed out of column and put his horse to the gallop and rode in on Major Thursday's near side.

Thursday said, "Move down the column and have every man crease his hat fore and aft as a fedora. The front of the brim may be snapped downward as eye protection, but all the rest of the brim will be turned up. The hat will sit squarely on the head. Look at them, Mr. Cohill! They look like scratch farmers on market day! The hat is a uniform, not a subject for individual whimsical expression!"

Thursday had a point ahead and flankers out on either side and a tiny rear guard with a warning mission only, but somehow it seemed more like a maneuver—a problem—than it did a march into hostile territory. D'Arcy Topliff, heading up B, never knew where the thought came from. But it was there suddenly from something he'd read years before or heard someone say: The major has fewer years left to live than he has lived already, and when that knowledge hits a man's mind, he can break easily. He must hurry then, for his time is shortening. He must seek short cuts. And, seeking them, he may destroy the worth of his decisions, the power of his judgment. Only a solid character with a fine sense of balance can face the fewer years as they shrink ahead, and go on into them with complacent courage, all the way to the Door.

Flint Cohill, with the wagons and head down to the dust, thought, *Damn it, this isn't a ceremonial detail of the First City Troop turned out for a governor's funeral. He's got the men disliking him from the start, deliberately, for picayune cause.*

And then Flint remembered a name brought into conversation at a reception once, and he likewise remembered old General Malcolm Hamilton's grave bow.

"Madame, only four officers in the Army know the facts of that incident, but none of them will talk as long as the colonel's widow lives."

Three days north of Fort Starke, the detachment went into bivouac on the high ground above the headwaters of Crazy Man Creek, which is the south branch of White River, and a little under thirty miles from the agency. The commanding officer sent Clay Sitterding on ahead to scout and contact Custis Meacham, the agent.

Clay rode back in, about sundown. "Stone Buffalo is camped at the junction of White River and Crazy Man, sir, in the chevron the fork makes. His camp is about a week old. From three hundred to three hundred and fifty people, all told. Most of them warriors and dog soldiers. No women and children. It's a war camp. There are scouting parties all the way along between us."

"You contacted Meacham, Mr. Sitterding?"

"I did, sir. He professes to have Stone Buffalo's complete confidence. Stone Buffalo has attempted to have himself accepted as medicine chief as well as war chief of all his nation. Running Calf contested the claim and took the Red Hill people and left the reservation. Stone Buffalo followed him to force him back into the fold. Mr. Meacham sent for us to stop the two factions from warring, but the last four days seem to have settled the argument peaceably."

Major Thursday's lip thinned. "In other words, as soon as the Indians knew troops were on the way, they decided to behave."

"That could be it, sir. Stone Buffalo would like to smoke with you. Mr. Meacham requests it. I strongly advise against letting Indians into our camp. It will not be advisable to let them know any more about our strength than they do now."

"When I want advice from my officers, Mr. Sitterding, I ask for it. Will you remember that, please?"

The smell of an Indian is resinous and salty and rancid. It is the wood smoke of his tepee and the fetidity of his breath that comes of eating body-hot animal entrails. It is his uncured tobacco and the sweat of his unwashed body. It is animal grease in his hair and old leather and fur, tanned with bird lime and handed down unclean from ancestral bodies long since gathered to the Happy Lands.

Major Thursday saw their impassive Judaic faces, their dignity, their reserve. He felt the quiet impact of their silence, but being new to the game, he had no way of knowing that they drew all of it on as they drew on their trade-goods blankets—to cover a childish curiosity and the excitability of terriers. Stone Buffalo. Black Dog. Pony that Runs. Running Calf. Eagle Claw. Chiefs of tribes in the sovereign nation of Stone Buffalo—a nation under treaty of peace with the United States. A nation, in effect, held as prisoners of war, so that it would keep that peace.

Custis Meacham was painfully nearsighted and frighteningly short of breath. It was necessary for him to gasp wide-mouthed when he spoke. His hands were damp in the palms and restless. His fingernails were concave, like the bowls of small blue spoons. He sat with the skirts of his greasy Prince Albert draped across his pendulous abdomen.

The pipe went solemnly around to the left, each man pulling it red until his cheeks ached, drawing in its raw smoke until his lungs were stifled.

Custis Meacham coughed himself red-eyed and completely breathless. "Oh, dear," he said. "I can't stand to be near them when they smoke. I trust that you don't indulge in the vice for pleasure, Mr. Thursday?"

"I do, constantly," Thursday said. "And I am Major Thursday, Mr. Meacham, not Mr. Thursday."

"God bless you, I pay no attention whatever to military titles. I don't believe in titles of any kind. You can see from their faces and actions, as they pass the pipe, that they have settled all their troubles peaceably among themselves. Thanks be to God. You can take all your soldiers straight back tomorrow. What is your church, please?"

Owen Thursday looked long at Custis Meacham. He said, "You put in a request for this detachment, but that does not put you in command of it. Any further action on your part will be made through the same channel you used for the original request—direct to departmental headquarters. I am a back-slidden Presbyterian, Mr. Meacham. I intend to remain one."

"You cannot tell me what to do." Custis Meacham's voice was shrill. "I am quite used to the way the Army does things! When I was secretary of the International Bible Association, I once told General Scott—"

Flint Cohill touched the major's arm. "Stone Buffalo is going to speak, sir," and, after a moment, Stone Buffalo rose. He talked and for a great many minutes Cohill said nothing.

Then he said, "All he has said so far is that he is a very, very brave man." Thursday nodded, and Stone Buffalo talked on for many more minutes. Cohill said, "He says now that he is also a very great hunter—he and his whole tribe." Again Thursday nodded, and Stone Buffalo told how the railroads and the white hunters had killed off the buffalo, and how he alone, as medicine chief, could bring them back again.

Suddenly Cohill whispered, "I don't like any of it, sir. He's covering up for time. This is an insolent attempt at reconnaissance, I believe."

"Stop it then." Thursday's voice was hard.

"It will have to run out—protocol requires it—you cannot stop him now until he is finished. That would be a grave insult."

"Is there anyone at Fort Starke who recognizes an order when it is given?"

Cohill rose to his feet. Stone Buffalo stopped talking in vibrant anger. Major Thursday leaned forward. "Cohill, no preliminary nonsense with him, no ceremonial phrasing. Straight from the shoulder as I tell you, do you hear me? They are recalcitrant swine. They must feel it."

Cohill stood there, white-faced. He said, "I hear you, sir. What shall I tell them?"

"Tell them I find them without honor or manhood. Tell them it is written on sacred paper that they will remain on their reservation. That they have broken this promise puts them beneath fighting men's contempt, makes them turkey-eating women. Tell them they are not talking to me, but to the United States. Tell them the United States orders them to leave here at once. They will break camp at dawn and return to the reservation, for I move in to their camp site at daylight," and Major Thursday turned his back and stalked off into the darkness, calling sharply for the officer of the guard.

Clay Sitterding, D'Arcy Topliff and Flint Cohill squatted in the white mists, gulping their steaming coffee. The morning was a gaunt old woman in the shadows, standing there wrapped in a shawl, seeing what she would not see again. A thin old woman with sadness in her face, and courage and the overpowering knowledge of life's inevitable defeat.

Ten years and better had passed under the bridges of Sitterding, Topliff and Cohill. Ten knowledgeable years of hard and bitter learning. They could have talked. "I told him not to receive them, not to smoke with them last night, and he shut me up." They could have said, "One hundred rounds of ammunition instead of three!" But you learn not to talk before you can ever learn other things. Behind them in the mists there was the movement of many men, but not enough men now, because the shock action of cavalry at one to three is suicidal madness without surprise. Who cares what you have commanded before, or what people think of you, or what other wars you have fought in? In war it is always what happens now! What happens next! Who commands here . . . now!

Sitterding finished his bitter coffee and for one brief instant he could feel the harsh winds of March on his face—the winds that howl up the Hudson River Valley and cut across the parade ground at the Academy like canister fired at zero elevation. There had been a time when the melting heat of Starke had made him forget the chilled wine of those Eastern winds.

D'Arcy Topliff said, "I wish I'd married the one rich woman I ever met! I'd be a banker in St. Louis this morning, and still in bed."

Cohill tried to laugh, but some ancient instinct within him had dried up the wells of his laughter. The curtain was down across the back of his mind, shutting him off from all he had been, so that he could only move forward. Some men are fortunate that way.

"Here we go," he said quietly, and with both hands he pressed briefly on the shoulders of the other two. "Just remember that the escort train is in mobile reserve, and if you get a fight, save me a piece."

You have seen it so often in the Jonathan Redfield print. The powder-blue trace of Crazy Man Creek against the burnt yellow grass on the rising ground behind. The dead of Company A stripped naked and scalped, their heads looking like faces screaming in beards. Major Thursday, empty gun in hand, dying gloriously with what is left of Company B, in an attempt to rally and save the colors, but this is how it happened. *This is how it happened:*

The column moved out with the mists of the morning still cold, moved out in a long breath of saddle soap on still-stiffened leather, rough wool, not yet sweat-damp, and the thin brown of gun oil. Dog-faced cavalry, the like of which has passed from the knowledge of the world. Up the gently sloping rise from the bivouac to the ridge line above Crazy Man Creek. Across the hogback ridge, outlined against the spreading yellow light that rimmed the eastern horizon. Guidons, booted carbine butts, hats creased fore and aft, backs arched and colors flying. There are cowpokes who will tell you solemnly that sometimes when a murderous thunderstorm howls down the valley, you can see them again crossing that ridge. That you can hear the brass scream of the charge echoing. But that is not so, for soldiers pass once only, and all that they ever leave behind is memory. "Close up the intervals! Close up!"

The point crossed the ridge first and wound on down the slope where the trail weaves onto high and rock-strewn ground before it reaches the ford. The point went on through and forded Crazy Man and signaled back from the other side to Lieutenant Sitterding at the head of A. All clear.

Sitterding gave the word, and A crossed the ridge and started down, with B, under D'Arcy Topliff, three hundred yards behind and echeloned three hundred yards to the left, west, rear. Which was by explicit order of Owen Thursday. So much for the creek side of the ridge. On the bivouac side, there was still Flintridge Cohill and the wagon train and the mounted guards from C. Flintridge Cohill was held up as soon as he started . . . by a broken linchpin.

Owen Thursday, sitting his horse high on the sky line, was the only man who could see the entire command. He sat there against the whitening dawn as if he had chosen that position to sit on and wait for it.

Company A rode on slowly down into the defile, breakfasts still warm in stomachs, saddles softening to the butt, muscles limbering up to the new day's work. Then unbelievably there was a sudden ring of fire in their faces and on both flanks. One hundred and eighty degrees of fire—half the horizon around—splintered around them like dry and rotted timber, tearing around them like grommets ripped from heavy cloth. Clay Sitterding and forty-two men were down. Half their mounts, reeling, galloping, were thrashing back over them, trying to get out and up the slope again.

Flint Cohill, blind to the sight of it because the ridge line masked it, knew it desperately for what it might be. He stared into his farrier sergeant's face.

He said, "Sergeant Magee, fix that pin and hold the train here on my order!"

And he spurred furiously toward the ridge top. Almost it was as if Owen Thursday were trying to escape facing him. He seemed to wait until he could wait no longer, until Cohill was almost to him, then he sank his rowels into his horse and plunged him headlong down the opposite side toward the Valley of the Shadow. But not soon enough, for Cohill saw what he was going to do. Cohill saw it. With no further reconnaissance and no clear idea of what he was up against, with no brief withdrawal to reform, with all of A lying dead now in the defile for everyone to see, Thursday screamed to Topliff to deploy B and to hit the sides of the defile at the gallop as foragers.

Cohill turned his back. "Magee," he shouted through cupped hands, "get the wagons up here fast!"

Then Cohill turned again, and this time he saw that murderous ring of fire from the rocks, half a full circle round, and there were tears within him that would never, as long as he lived, quite leave him again. In that moment he knew that the train and the mounted guards were all that there was left; that he alone on an open ridge line was all that remained of the sovereign dignity of the United States for hundreds of miles around. But he was saying it this way—he was saying it out loud, "D'Arcy's gone . . . and Clay's gone . . . but no man gets off this ridge line . . . no man!"

"Sergeant Magee, take the wagon boxes from the beds! Put one here! . . . Put one twenty full paces to the left! . . . One down there where you're standing, and one here to the right! All hands turn to, to dig rifle pits between the boxes! Turn in all canteens! Corral all animals on the rope, down the backslope!"

It's not always in the book. It's a hundred thousand years. It's a heritage and a curse and the white man's burden. It's Cannae and Agincourt and Wagram and Princeton, and it's the shambles of Shiloh. With Flint Cohill it was thirty-one men on a hog-back ridge and the thought in his angry mind that he'd never live now to be a general officer, but he'd die the best damned first lieutenant of cavalry that the world could find to do the job that morning!

Lying on the ridge top, searching the ghastly valley below with his glasses, Flint saw the last of it—an officer and three men and the colors on their broken staff. He couldn't swear to it, but it looked like Clay Sitterding and old Sergeant Shattuck and Aiken and Sergeant Ershick. Only for a minute before they went down under the final rush. Then Stone Buffalo's warriors were overrunning the dead of both A and B, pincushioning the bodies with arrows. Scalping. Lopping off a foot and the right hand, so that the spirits, too, would suffer mutilation and never fight again. Then the Indians withdrew to consider the ridge top, and, by the dust presently, they were commencing to ring it, to cut it off from water, to wither it for the kill.

Cohill called young Brailey over and squatted down with him. "Brailey, you're a show-off and a braggart, and I never thought I'd have the right job for you. But I have. Take the best horse on the picket line. Make Fort Starke. Tell 'em where we are, and tell 'em we may still be alive if they hurry. I'm making you corporal, but you'll never draw a dime of pay if we're dead when you get back. Move out and make it so."

Shortly after that, Cohill saw the tiny group far below, struggling painfully up the draw. Six men, crawling, dragging two, stumbling. Hatless and bleeding. Stopping exhausted, faces downward; starting up the slow way once again. Cohill finally got down to them. D'Arcy Topliff, hit four times and barely breathing. Glastonby of the red hair, from A. "Sir, we didn't have a chance!"—crying every time he tried to speak. Pointing back helplessly. Cursing, with the tears greasing the filth of his cheeks. "Get Mr. Topliff to the ridge top, Glastonby." And there were Moore and Stonesifer and Coyne, out of B, dragging Bittendorfer with them. Shocked speechless. Bleeding. Obeying like whipped beasts. "Go on up, all of you, straight up the draw."

Cohill said that, because at that moment he saw the seventh man, still far below them. "And tell Sergeant Magee I'll be along in a few minutes . . . a few minutes behind you," and he scrambled on down the draw until he was crouched beside Owen Thursday.

"Cohill, sir."

Thursday turned and looked at him as if he had never seen him before in his life. The light was gone from his eyes and the pride was dead in him at last. All of his days the ghost of today had ridden with him, mocking his pride, pointing the finger of scorn at his personal ambition. General Thursday, of Clarke's Corps, of Cumberland Station, of Sudler's Mountain, with luck and the devil to help and a hero's crown for the snatching!

But today, the ghost was come alive at the cost of seventy-two men lying dead, through the ignorance that is pride's handmaiden, the stubbornness that is ambition's mistress.

"I am dug in on the ridge top," Cohill said, "with the wagon boxes loopholed, and rifle pits. I have thirty-seven men, one officer and one man wounded. I have water and ammunition—"

"Get ready to move out at once," Thursday said. "We must try to cut back into Fort Starke." But his voice broke.

Flint Cohill shook his head. "Stone Buffalo is already ringing the position. We cannot leave that ridge top. If we try, we'll be cut to ribbons before we've gone ten miles."

"Get ready to move out, Mr. Cohill!" The voice was a high and broken whine.

"I've sent a courier to Starke, sir. I believe he'll get through. I believe Captain Joplyn can get here in five days. I can hold until then. Besides, we've no other choice! General—" Cohill said it deliberately, but there was no defiance in it, no indictment. He was almost pleading. "General, there are two dead companies down there—all the friends I've had in the world for years." He snagged his hand gun from his holster, spun it until it was butt first toward Thursday, then he thrust it out and held it. "You don't have to tell me again, but A and B are all present or accounted for, and so am I! I'll move out to your order, but only under arrest, sir! Only under arrest!"

Thursday rose slowly to his feet, Cohill's gun in hand. "I've had all I can have," he said softly; "this is where the road stops at last." His eyes were completely empty as Flint looked into them. The light was gone forever. "Mr. Cohill, your ridge top. I'm going back down. Good luck."

"Mr. Sitterding can't talk, sir, nor can Shattuck nor Ershick nor

Aiken, and you have my word of honor that I won't . . . ever . . . for the good of the service." Flint whispered it almost.

And that is how they found Owen Thursday when the flying column from Starke relieved Cohill's party on the fifth day.

He was dead with the little group that had defended the colors— dead beside Sitterding, Shattuck, Ershick and Aiken—shot in the right ear, with the gun held so close that the contract surgeon couldn't have missed knowing that the major had squeezed off the trigger himself. But Flintridge Cohill got there first, for there are ways of living that are finer than the men who try to live them, and a regiment has honor that no man may usurp as his personal property. Glory is a jade of the streets who can be bought for a price by anyone who wants her. Thursday wanted her but his pockets were empty, so Cohill lent him the two dollars for posterity. Cohill took his own gun from Thursday's dead hand. He threw out the cylinder and jerked the five ball cartridges and the one empty case into his left hand. He spun the gun far out into Crazy Man Creek.

The five ball cartridges, he dropped one by one as he moved away, but the empty cartridge case he always carried with him for the rest of his life, for fingering it in his pocket always gave him courage in moments when he needed it—when the way was dark and decisions not easy.

And it was Cohill, years later, who reconstructed the scene for Jonathan Redfield to paint. "Major Thursday," he said, "was a very gallant officer. We found him dead with the little group that defended the colors—with Lieutenant Sitterding and Sergeant Shattuck and Ershick and Private Aiken. No man could have wished for more."

But even when he was very old, Cohill always looked sharply at anyone who said, "for the good of the service," and he always said, "What exactly does that mean to you, sir?"

THE TIN STAR
BY JOHN M. CUNNINGHAM
(High Noon)

High Noon *(1952) is on everyone's list of Great Western Films and ranks number one on many. Not nearly so famous is the short story on which it is based, John M. Cunningham's "The Tin Star" (1947)—a story that, in its own deceptively simple fashion, is every bit as memorable as the film. (The same is true of the model for Gary Cooper's Will Kane, Sheriff Doane of an unnamed western Montana town.) Cunningham is the author of many first-rate Western stories, another of which also became the basis for a film,* Day of the Bad Man *(1958), starring Fred MacMurray, and of two excellent novels,* Warhorse *and* Starfall.

Sheriff Doane looked at his deputy and then down at the daisies he had picked for his weekly visit, lying wrapped in newspaper on his desk. "I'm sorry to hear you say that, Toby. I was kind of counting on you to take over after me."

"Don't get me wrong, Doane," Toby said, looking through the front window. "I'm not afraid. I'll see you through this shindig. I'm not afraid of Jordan or young Jordan or any of them. But I want to tell you now. I'll wait till Jordan's train gets in. I'll wait to see what he does. I'll see you through whatever happens. After that, I'm quitting."

Doane began kneading his knuckles, his face set against the pain as he gently rubbed the arthritic, twisted bones. He said nothing.

Toby looked around, his brown eyes troubled in his round, olive-skinned face. "What's the use of holding down a job like this? Look at you. What'd you ever get out of it? Enough to keep you eating. And what for?"

Doane stopped kneading his arthritic hands and looked down at the

star on his shirt front. He looked from it to the smaller one on Toby's.
"That's right," he said. "They don't even hang the right ones. You risk
your life catching somebody, and the damned juries let them go so they
can come back and shoot at you. You're poor all your life, you got to do
everything twice, and in the end they pay you off in lead. So you can
wear a tin star. It's a job for a dog, son."

Toby's voice did not rise, but his eyes were a little wider in his round,
gentle face. "Then why keep on with it? What for? I been working for
you for two years—trying to keep the law so sharp-nosed money-grab-
bers can get rich, while we piddle along on what the county pays us.
I've seen men I used to bust playing marbles going up and down this
street on four-hundred-dollar-saddles, and what've I got? Nothing. Not
a damned thing."

There was a little smile around Doane's wide mouth. "That's right,
Toby. It's all for free. The headaches, the bullets and everything, all for
free. I found that out long ago." The mock-grave look vanished. "But
somebody's got to be around and take care of things." He looked out of
the window at the people walking up and down the crazy boardwalks.
"I like it free. You know what I mean? You don't get a thing for it.
You've got to risk everything. And you're free inside. Like the larks.
You know the larks? How they get up in the sky and sing when they
want to? A pretty bird. A very pretty bird. That's the way I like to feel
inside."

Toby looked at him without expression. "That's the way you look at
it. I don't see it. I've only got one life. You talk about doing it all for
nothing, and that gives you something. What? What've you got now,
waiting for Jordan to come?"

"I don't know yet. We'll have to wait and see."

Toby turned back to the window. "All right, but I'm through. I
don't see any sense in risking your neck for nothing."

"Maybe you will," Doane said, beginning to work on his hands
again.

"Here comes Mettrick. I guess he don't give up so easy. He's still got
that resignation in his hand."

"I guess he doesn't," Doane said. "But I'm through listening. Has
young Jordan come out of the saloon yet?"

"No," Toby said, and stepped aside as the door opened. Mettrick
came in. "Now listen, Doane," he burst out, "for the last time—"

"Shut up, Percy," Doane said. "Sit down over there and shut up or get out."

The flare went out of the mayor's eyes. "Doane," he moaned, "you are the biggest—"

"Shut up," Doane said. "Toby, has he come out yet?"

Toby stood a little back from the window, where the slant of golden sunlight, swarming with dust, wouldn't strike his white shirt.

"Yes. He's got a chair. He's looking this way, Doane. He's still drinking. I can see a bottle on the porch beside him."

"I expected that. Not that it makes much difference." He looked down at the bunch of flowers.

Mettrick, in the straight chair against the wall, looked up at him, his black eyes scornful in his long, hopeless face.

"Don't make much difference? Who the hell do you think you are, Doane? God? It just means he'll start the trouble without waiting for his stinking brother, that's all it means." His hand was shaking, and the white paper hanging listlessly from his fingers fluttered slightly. He looked at it angrily and stuck it out at Doane. "I gave it to you. I did the best I could. Whatever happens, don't be blaming me, Doane. I gave you a chance to resign, and if—" He left off and sat looking at the paper in his hand as though it were a dead puppy of his that somebody had run a buggy over.

Doane, standing with the square, almost chisel-pointed tips of his fingers just touching the flowers, turned slowly, with the care of movement he would have used around a crazy horse. "I know you're my friend, Percy. Just take it easy, Percy. If I don't resign, it's not because I'm ungrateful."

"Here comes Staley with the news," Toby said from the window. "He looks like somebody just shot his grandma."

Percy Mettrick laid his paper on the desk and began smoothing it out ruefully. "It's not as though it were dishonorable, Doane. You should have quit two years ago, when your hands went bad. It's not dishonorable now. You've still got time."

He glanced up at the wall clock. "It's only three. You've got an hour before he gets in . . . you can take your horse . . ." As he talked to himself, Doane looking slantwise at him with his little smile, he grew more cheerful. "Here." He jabbed a pen out at Doane. "Sign it and get out of town."

The smile left Doane's mouth. "This is an elective office. I don't have to take orders, even if you are mayor." His face softened. "It's simpler than you think, Percy. When they didn't hang Jordan, I knew this day would come. Five years ago, I knew it was coming, when they gave him that silly sentence. I've been waiting for it."

"But not to commit suicide," Mettrick said in a low voice, his eyes going down to Doane's gouty hands. Doane's knobby, twisted fingers closed slowly into fists, as though hiding themselves; his face flushed slightly. "I may be slow, but I can still shoot."

The mayor stood up and went slowly over to the door.

"Goodby, Doane."

"I'm not saying goodby, Percy. Not yet."

"Goodby," Mettrick repeated, and went out of the door.

Toby turned from the window. His face was tight around the mouth. "You should have resigned like he said, Doane. You ain't a match for one of them alone, much less two of them together. And if Pierce and Frank Colby come, too, like they was all together before—"

"Shut up, shut up," Doane said. "For God's sake, shut up." He sat down suddenly at the desk and covered his face with his hands. "Maybe the pen changes a man." He was sitting stiff, hardly breathing.

"What are you going to do, Doane?"

"Nothing. I can't do anything until they start something. I can't do a thing. . . . Maybe the pen changes a man. Sometimes it does. I remember—"

"Listen, Doane," Toby said, his voice, for the first time, urgent. "It maybe changes some men, but not Jordan. It's already planned, what they're going to do. Why else would young Jordan be over there, watching? He's come three hundred miles for this."

"I've seen men go in the pen hard as rock and come out peaceful and settle down. Maybe Jordan—"

Toby's face relapsed into dullness. He turned back to the window listlessly. Doane's hands dropped.

"You don't think that's true, Toby?"

Toby sighed. "You know it isn't so, Doane. He swore he'd get you. That's the truth."

Doane's hands came up again in front of his face, but this time he was looking at them, his big gray eyes going quickly from one to the other, almost as though he were afraid of them. He curled his fingers slowly into fists, and uncurled them slowly, pulling with all his might, yet slowly. A thin sheen on his face reflected the sunlight from the floor. He got up.

"Is he still there?" he asked.

"Sure, he's still there."

"Maybe he'll get drunk. Dead drunk."

"You can't get a Jordan that drunk."

Doane stood with feet apart, looking at the floor, staring back and forth along one of the cracks. "Why didn't they hang him?" he asked the silence in the room.

"Why didn't they hang him?" he repeated, his voice louder.

Toby kept his post by the window, not moving a muscle in his face, staring out at the man across the street. "I don't know," he said. "For murder, they should. I guess they should, but they didn't."

Doane's eyes came again to the flowers, and some of the strain went out of his face. Then suddenly his eyes closed and he gave a long sigh, and then, luxuriously, stretched his arms. "Good God!" he said, his voice easy again. "It's funny how it comes over you like that." He shook his head violently. "I don't know why it should. It's not the first time. But it always does."

"I know," Toby said.

"It just builds up and then it busts."

"I know."

"The train may be late."

Toby said nothing.

"You never can tell," Doane said, buckling on his gun belt. "Things may have changed with Jordan. Maybe won't even come. You never can tell. I'm going up to the cemetery as soon as we hear from Staley."

"I wouldn't. You'd just tempt young Jordan to start something."

"I've geen going up there every Sunday since she died."

"We'd best both just stay in here. Let them make the first move."

Feet sounded on the steps outside and Doane stopped breathing for a second. Staley came in, his face pinched, tight and dead, his eyes on the floor. Doane looked him over carefully.

"Is it on time?" he asked steadily.

Staley looked up, his faded blue eyes distant, pointed somewhere over Doane's head. "Mr. Doane, you ain't handled this thing right. You should of drove young Jordan out of town." His hand went to his chest and he took off the deputy's badge.

"What are you doing?" Doane asked sharply.

"If you'd of handled it right, we could have beat this," Staley said, his voice louder.

"You know nobody's done nothing yet," Toby said softly, his gentle brown eyes on Staley. "There's nothing we can do until they start something."

"I'm quitting, Mr. Doane," Staley said. He looked around for someplace to put the star. He started for the desk, hesitated, and then awkwardly, with a peculiar diffidence, laid the star gently on the window sill.

Doane's jaw began to jut a little. "You still haven't answered my question. Is the train on time?"

"Yes. Four ten. Just on time." Staley stood staring at Doane, then swallowed. "I saw Frank Colby. He was in the livery putting up his horse. He'd had a long ride on that horse. I asked him what he was doing in town—friendly like." He ducked his head and swallowed again. "He didn't know I was a deputy, I had my star off." He looked up again. "They're all meeting together, Mr. Doane. Young Jordan, and Colby and Pierce. They're going to meet Jordan when he comes in. The same four."

"So you're quitting," Doane said.

"Yes, sir. It ain't been handled right."

Toby stood looking at him, his gentle eyes dull. "Get out," he said, his voice low and tight.

Staley looked at him, nodded and tried to smile, which was too weak to last. "Sure."

Toby took a step toward him. Staley's eyes were wild as he stood against the door. He tried to back out of Toby's way.

"Get out," Toby said again, and his small brown fist flashed out. Staley stepped backward and fell down the steps in a sprawling heap, scrambled to his feet and hobbled away. Toby closed the door slowly. He stood rubbing his knuckles, his face red and tight.

"That didn't do any good," Doane said softly.

Toby turned on him. "It couldn't do no harm," he said acidly, throwing the words into Doane's face.

"You want to quit, too?" Doane asked, smiling.

"Sure, I want to quit," Toby shot out. "Sure. Go on to your blasted cemetery, go on with your flowers, old man—" He sat down suddenly on the straight chair. "Put a flower up there for me, too."

Doane went to the door. "Put some water on the heater, Toby. Set out the liniment that the vet gave me. I'll try it again when I get back. It might do some good yet."

He let himself out and stood in the sunlight on the porch, the flowers drooping in his hand, looking against the sun across the street at the dim figure under the shaded porch.

Then he saw the two other shapes hunkered against the front of the saloon in the shade of the porch, one on each side of young Jordan, who sat tilted back in a chair. Colby and Pierce. The glare of the sun beat back from the blinding white dust and fought shimmering in the air.

Doane pulled the brim of his hat farther down in front and stepped slowly down to the board sidewalk, observing carefully from squinted eyes, and just as carefully avoiding any pause which might be interpreted as a challenge.

Young Jordan had the bottle to his lips as Doane came out. He held it there for a moment motionless, and then, as Doane reached the walk, he passed the bottle slowly sideward to Colby and leaned forward, away from the wall, so that the chair came down softly. He sat there, leaning forward slightly, watching while Doane untied his horse. As Doane mounted, Jordan got up. Colby's hand grabbed one of his arms. He shook it off and untied his own horse from the rail.

Doane's mouth tightened and his eyes looked a little sad. He turned his horse, and holding the flowers so the jog would not rattle off the petals, headed up the street, looking straight ahead.

The hoofs of his horse made soft, almost inaudible little plops in the deep dust. Behind him he heard a sudden stamping of hoofs and then the harsh splitting and crash of wood. He looked back. Young Jordan's horse was up on the sidewalk, wild-eyed and snorting, with young Jordan leaning forward half out of the saddle, pushing himself back from the horse's neck, back off the horn into the saddle, swaying insecurely. And as Jordan managed the horse off the sidewalk Doane looked quickly forward again, his eyes fixed distantly ahead and blank.

He passed men he knew, and out of the corner of his eye he saw their glances slowly follow him, calm, or gloomy, or shrewdly speculative. As he passed, he knew their glances were shifting to the man whose horse was softly coming behind him. It was like that all the way up the street. The flowers were drooping markedly now.

The town petered out with a few Mexican shacks, the road dwindled to broad ruts, and the sage was suddenly on all sides of him, stretching away toward the heat-obscured mountains like an infinite multitude of gray-green sheep. He turned off the road and began the slight ascent up the little hill whereon the cemetery lay. Grasshoppers shrilled invisibly in the sparse, dried grass along the track, silent as he came by, and shrill again as he passed, only to become silent again as the other rider came.

He swung off at the rusty barbed wire Missouri gate and slipped the loop from the post, and the shadow of the other slid tall across his path and stopped. Doane licked his lips quickly and looked up, his grasp tightening on the now sweat-wilted newspaper. Young Jordan was sitting his horse, open-mouthed, leaning forward with his hands on the pommel to support himself, his eyes vague and dull. His lips were wet and red, and hung in a slight smile.

A lark made the air sweet over to the left, and then Doane saw it, rising into the air. It hung in the sun, over the cemetery. Moving steadily and avoiding all suddenness, Doane hung his reins over the post.

"You don't like me, do you?" young Jordan said. A long thread of saliva descended from the corner of his slackly smiling mouth.

Doane's face set into a sort of blank preparedness. He turned and started slowly through the gate, his shoulders hunched up and pulled backward.

Jordan got down from the saddle, and Doane turned toward him slowly. Jordan came forward straight enough, with his feet apart, braced against staggering. He stopped three feet from Doane, bent forward, his mouth slightly open.

"You got any objections to me being in town?"

"No," Doane said, and stood still.

Jordan thought that over, his eyes drifting idly sideways for a moment. Then they came back, to a finer focus this time, and he said, "Why not?" hunching forward again, his hands open and held away from the holsters at his hips.

Doane looked at the point of his nose. "You haven't done anything, Jordan. Except get drunk. Nothing to break the law."

"I haven't done nothing," Jordan said, his eyes squinting away at one of the small, tilting tombstones. "By God, I'll do something. Whadda I got to do?" He drew his head back, as though he were farsighted, and squinted. "Whadda I got to do to make you fight, huh?"

"Don't do anything," Doane said quietly, keeping his voice even. "Just go back and have another drink. Have a good time."

"You think I ain't sober enough to fight?" Jordan slipped his right gun out of its holster, turning away from Doane. Doane stiffened. "Wait, mister," Jordan said.

He cocked the gun. "See that bird?" He raised the gun into the air, squinting along the barrel. The bright nickel of its finish gleamed in the sun. The lark wheeled and fluttered. Jordan's arm swung unsteadily in a small circle.

He pulled the trigger and the gun blasted. The lark jumped in the air, flew away about twenty feet, and began circling again, catching insects.

"Missed 'im," Jordan mumbled, lowering his arm and wiping sweat off his forehead. "Damn it, I can't see!" He raised his arm again. Again the heavy blast cracked Doane's ears. Down in the town, near the Mexican huts, he could see tiny figures run out into the street.

The bird didn't jump this time, but darted away out of sight over the hill.

"Got him," Jordan said, scanning the sky. His eyes wandered over the graveyard for a moment, looking for the bird's body. "Now you see?" he said, turning to Doane, his eyes blurred and watering with the sun's glare. "I'm going down and shoot up the damned town. Come down and stop me, you old —"

He turned and lurched sideways a step, straightened himself out and walked more steadily toward his horse, laughing to himself. Doane turned away, his face sick, and trudged slowly up the hill, his eyes on the ground.

He stopped at one of the newer graves. The headstone was straight on this one. He looked at it, his face changing expression. "Here lies Cecelia Doane, born 1837, died 1885, the loyal wife . . ."

He stooped and pulled a weed from the side of the grave, then pulled a bunch of withered stems from a small green funnel by the headstone, and awkwardly took the fresh flowers out of the newspaper. He put the flowers into the funnel, wedging them firmly down into the bottom, and set it down again. He stood up and moved back, wiping sweat from his eyes.

A sudden shout came from the gate, and the sharp crack of a quirt. Doane turned with a befuddled look.

Jordan was back on his horse, beating Doane's. He had looped the reins over its neck so that it would run free. It was tearing away down the slope headed back for town.

Doane stood with his hat in his hand, his face suddenly beet red. He took a step after Jordan, and then stood still, shaking a little. He stared fixedly after him, watching him turn into the main road and toward the main street again. Then, sighing deeply, he turned back to the grave. Folding the newspaper, he began dusting off the heavy slab, whispering to himself. "No, Cissie. I could have gone. But, you know—it's my town."

He straightened up, his face flushed, put on his hat, and slapping the folded paper against his knee, started down the path. He got to the Missouri gate, closed it, and started down the ruts again.

A shot came from the town, and he stopped. Then there were two more, sharp spurts of sound coming clear and definite across the sage. He made out a tiny figure in a blue shirt running along a sidewalk.

He stood stock-still, the grasshoppers singing in a contented chorus all around him in the bright yellow glare. A train whistle came faint from off the plain, and he looked far across it. He made out the tiny trailed plume of smoke.

His knees began to quiver very slightly and he began to walk, very slowly, down the road.

Then suddenly there was a splatter of shots from below. The train whistle came again, louder, a crying wail of despair in the burning, brilliant, dancing air.

He began to hurry, stumbling a little in the ruts. And then he stopped short, his face open in fear. "My God, my empty horse, those shots—Toby, no!" He began to run, shambling, awkward and stumbling, his face ashen.

From the end of the street, as he hobbled panting past the tight-shut Mexican shanties, he could see a blue patch in the dust in front of the saloon, and shambled to a halt. It wasn't Toby, whoever it was, lying there face down: face buried in the deep, pillowing dust, feet still on the board sidewalk where the man had been standing.

The street was empty. None of the faces he knew looked at him now. He drew one of his guns and cocked it and walked fast up the walk, on the saloon side.

A shot smashed ahead of him and he stopped, shrinking against a store front. Inside, through the glass door, he could see two pale faces in the murk. Blue powder smoke curled out from under the saloon porch ahead of him.

Another shot smashed, this time from his office. The spurt of smoke, almost invisible in the sunlight, was low down in the doorway. Two horses were loose in the street now, his own, standing alert up past the saloon, and young Jordan's, half up on the boardwalk under one of the porches.

He walked forward, past young Jordan's horse, to the corner of the saloon building. Another shot slammed out of his office door, the bullet smacking the window ahead of him. A small, slow smile grew on his mouth. He looked sideways at the body in the street. Young Jordan lay with the back of his head open to the sun, crimson and brilliant, his bright nickel gun still in his right hand, its hammer still cocked, unfired.

The train whistle moaned again, closer.

"Doane," Toby called from the office door, invisible. "Get out of town." There was a surge of effort in the voice, a strain that made it almost a squeal. "I'm shot in the leg. Get out before they get together."

A door slammed somewhere. Doane glanced down between the saloon and the store beside it. Then he saw, fifty yards down the street, a figure come out of another side alley and hurry away down the walk toward the station. From the saloon door another shot slammed across the street. Toby held his fire.

Doane peered after the running figure, his eyes squinting thoughtfully. The train's whistle shrieked again like the ultimatum of an approaching conqueror at the edge of town, and in a moment the ground under his feet began to vibrate slightly and the hoarse roar of braking wheels came up the street.

He turned back to young Jordan's horse, petted it around the head a moment and then took it by the reins close to the bit. He guided it across the street, keeping its body between him and the front of the saloon, without drawing fire, and went on down the alley beside his office. At the rear door he hitched the horse and went inside.

Toby was on the floor, a gun in his hand, his hat beside him, peering out across the sill. Doane kept low, beneath the level of the window, and crawled up to him. Toby's left leg was twisted peculiarly and blood leaked steadily out from the boot top onto the floor. His face was sweating and very pale, and his lips were tight.

"I thought he got you," Toby said, keeping his eyes on the saloon across the street. "I heard those shots and then your horse came bucketing back down the street. I got Jordan. Colby got me in the leg before I got back inside."

"Never mind about that. Come on, get on your feet if you can and I'll help you on the horse in back. You can get out of town and I'll shift for myself."

"I think I'm going to pass out. I don't want to move. It won't hurt no worse getting killed than it does now. The hell with the horse! Take it yourself."

Doane looked across the street, his eyes moving over the door and the windows carefully, inch by inch.

"I'm sorry I shot him," Toby said. "It's my fault. And it's my fight now, Doane. Clear out."

Doane turned and scuttled out of the back. He mounted the horse and rode down behind four stores. He turned up another alley, dashed across the main street, down another alley, then back up behind the saloon.

He dismounted, his gun cocked in his hand. The back door of the place was open and he got through it quickly, the sound of his boot heels dimmed under the blast of a shot from the front of the saloon. From the dark rear of the room, he could see Pierce, crouched behind the bar, squinting through a bullet hole in the stained-glass bottom half of the front window.

There was a bottle of whisky standing on the bar beside Pierce; he reached out a hand and tilted the bottle up to his mouth, half turning toward Doane as he did so. Pierce kept the bottle to his lips, pretending to drink, and, with his right hand invisible behind the bar, brought his gun into line with Doane.

The tip of Pierce's gun came over the edge of the bar, the rest of him not moving a hair, and Doane, gritting his teeth, squeezed slowly and painfully on his gun trigger. The gun flamed and bucked in his hand, and he dropped it, his face twisting in agony. The bottle fell out of Pierce's hand and spun slowly on the bar. Pierce sat there for a moment before his head fell forward and he crashed against the edge of the bar and slipped down out of sight.

Doane picked up his gun with his left hand and walked forward to the bar, holding his right hand like a crippled paw in front of him. The bottle had stopped revolving. Whisky inside it, moving back and forth, rocked it gently. He righted it and took a short pull at the neck, and in a moment the pain lines relaxed in his face. He went to the batwing doors and pushed one of them partly open.

"Toby!" he called.

There was no answer from across the street, and then he saw the barrel of a revolver sticking out of his office door, lying flat, and behind it one hand, curled loosely and uselessly around the butt.

He looked down the street. The train stood across it. A brakeman moved along the cars slowly, his head down. There was nobody else in sight.

He started to step out, and saw then two men coming up the opposite walk, running fast. Suddenly one of them stopped, grabbing the other by the arm, and pointed at him. He stared back for a moment, seeing Jordan clearly now, the square, hard face unchanged except for its pallor, bleak and bony as before.

Doane let the door swing to and continued to watch them over the top of it. They talked for a moment. Then Colby ran back down the street—well out of effective range—sprinted across it and disappeared. Down the street the engine, hidden by some buildings, chuffed angrily, and the cars began to move again. Jordan stood still, leaning against the front of a building, fully exposed, a hard smile on his face.

Doane turned and hurried to the back door. It opened outward. He slammed and bolted it, then hurried back to the front and waited, his gun ready. He smiled as the back door rattled, turned, fired a shot at it and listened. For a moment there was no sound. Then something solid hit it, bumped a couple of times and silence came again.

From the side of the building, just beyond the corner where Pierce's body lay, a shot crashed. The gun in the office door jumped out of the hand and spun wildly. The hand lay still.

He heard Jordan's voice from down the street, calling, the words formed slowly, slightly spaced.

"Is he dead?"

"Passed out," Colby called back.

"I'm going around back to get him. Keep Doane inside." Jordan turned and disappeared down an alley.

Doane leaned across the bar, knocked bottles off the shelves of the back bar and held his pistol on the corner of the wall, about a foot above the floor.

"Pierce," he said.

"Throw out your guns," Pierce answered.

Doane squinted at the corner, moved his gun slightly and fired. He heard a cry of pain, then curses; saw the batwing doors swing slightly. Then he turned and ran for the back door. He threw back the bolt and pushed on the door. It wouldn't give. He threw himself against it. It gave a little at the bottom. Colby had thrown a stake up against it to keep him locked in.

He ran back to the front.

Across the street, he could see somebody moving in his office, dimly, beyond the window. Suddenly the hand on the floor disappeared.

"Come on out, you old ——," Pierce said, panting. "You only skinned me." His voice was closer than before, somewhere between the door and the corner of the building, below the level of the stained glass.

Then Doane saw Toby's white shirt beyond the window opposite. Jordan was holding him up, and moving toward the door. Jordan came out on the porch, hugging Toby around the chest, protecting himself with the limp body. With a heave he sent Toby flying down the steps, and jumped back out of sight. Toby rolled across the sidewalk and fell into the street, where he lay motionless.

Doane looked stupidly at Toby, then at young Jordan, still lying with his feet cocked up on the sidewalk.

"He ain't dead, Doane," Jordan called. "Come and get him if you want him alive." He fired through the window. Dust jumped six inches from Toby's head. "Come on out, Doane, and shoot it out. You got a chance to save him." The gun roared again, and dust jumped a second time beside Toby's head, almost in the same spot.

"Leave the kid alone," Doane called. "This fight's between you and me."

"The next shot kills him, Doane."

Doane's face sagged white and he leaned against the side of the door. He could hear Pierce breathing heavily in the silence, just outside. He pushed himself away from the door and drew a breath through clenched teeth. He cocked his pistol and strode out, swinging around. Pierce fired from the sidewalk, and Doane aimed straight into the blast and pulled as he felt himself flung violently around by Pierce's bullet.

Pierce came up from the sidewalk and took two steps toward him, opening and shutting a mouth that was suddenly full of blood, his eyes wide and wild, and then pitched down at his feet.

Doane's right arm hung useless, his gun at his feet. With his left hand he drew his other gun and stepped out from the walk, his mouth wide open, as though he were gasping for breath or were about to scream, and took two steps toward Toby as Jordan came out of the office door, firing. The slug caught Doane along the side of his neck, cutting the shoulder muscle, and his head fell over to one side. He staggered on, firing. He saw Toby trying to get up, saw Jordan fall back against the building, red running down the front of his shirt, and the smile gone.

Jordan stood braced against the building, holding his gun in both hands, firing as he slid slowly down. One bullet took Doane in the stomach, another in the knee. He went down, flopped forward and dragged himself up to where Toby lay trying to prop himself up on one elbow. Doane knelt there like a dog, puking blood into the dust, blood running out of his nose, but his gray eyes almost indifferent, as though there were one man dying and another watching.

He saw Jordan lift his gun with both hands and aim it toward Toby, and as the hammer fell, he threw himself across Toby's head and took it in the back. He rolled off onto his back and lay staring into the sky.

Upside down, he saw Toby take his gun and get up on one elbow, level it at Jordan and fire, and then saw Toby's face, over his, looking down at him as the deputy knelt in the street.

They stayed that way for a long moment, while Doane's eyes grew more and more dull and the dark of his blood in the white dust grew broader. His breath was coming hard, in small sharp gasps.

"There's nothing in it, kid," he whispered. "Only a tin star. They don't hang the right ones. You got to fight everything twice. It's a job for a dog."

"Thank you, Doane."

"It's all for free. You going to quit, Toby?"

Toby looked down at the gray face, the mouth and chin and neck crimson, the gray eyes dull. Toby shook his head. His face was hard as a rock.

Doane's face suddenly looked a little surprised, his eyes went past Toby to the sky. Toby looked up. A lark was high above them, circling and fluttering, directly overhead. "A pretty bird," Doane mumbled. "A very pretty bird."

His head turned slowly to one side, and Toby looked down at him and saw him as though fast asleep.

He took Doane's gun in his hand, and took off Doane's star, and sat there in the street while men slowly came out of stores and circled about them. He sat there unmoving, looking at Doane's half-averted face, holding the two things tightly, one in each hand, like a child with a broken toy, his face soft and blurred, his eyes unwet.

After a while the lark went away. He looked up at the men, and saw Mettrick.

"I told him he should have resigned," Mettrick said, his voice high. "He could have taken his horse—"

"Shut up," Toby said. "Shut up or get out." His eyes were sharp and his face placid and set. He turned to another of the men. "Get the doc," he said. "I've got a busted leg. And I've got a lot to do."

The man looked at him, a little startled, and then ran.

MY BROTHER DOWN THERE
BY STEVE FRAZEE
(Running Target)

"My Brother Down There" is pure, nail-biting suspense—a contemporary Western that deals with a manhunt in the Colorado wilderness and its immediate and long-range effects on both the hunters and the hunted. When the novelette first appeared, in 1953, it was awarded first prize in an annual contest sponsored by Ellery Queen's Mystery Magazine *and was anthologized in Martha Foley's* Best American Short Stories: 1953. *The film version,* Running Target, *was produced in 1956, and shortly afterward a novel-length expansion of the story appeared under that title. Several other films have been made from the excellent (and underrated) works of Steve Frazee (b. 1909), including* Many Rivers to Cross *(1955; from the novel of the same title),* Wild Heritage *(1958; based on the novel* Smoke in the Valley), *and* Gold of the Seven Saints *(1961; adapted from the novelette "Singing Sands").*

Now there were three left. Here was the fourth, doubled up on his side at the edge of the meadow grass where the wind had scattered pine needles. His face was pinched and gray. Big black wood ants were backing away from the blood settling into the warm soil.

Jaynes turned the dead man over with his foot. "Which one is this?"

Holesworth, deputy warden of the State Penitentiary, gave Jaynes an odd look.

"Joseph Otto Weyerhauser," he said. "Lifer for murder."

Deputy Sheriff Bill Melvin was standing apart from the rest of the posse. He had been too deep in the timber to take part in the shooting. He watched the little green State patrol plane circling overhead. It was a windless day. The voice of the mountains spoke of peace and summer.

Joseph Otto Weyerhauser. Spoken that way, the words gave dignity to the fugitive who lay now on the earth in the pale green uniform that had been stolen from the wash lines of a little filling station a hundred miles away.

Sid Jaynes was a beefy man with dark eyes that glittered. Jaynes had not known who the convict was and he had not cared. The green pants and shirt, when Weyerhauser tried to run across the head of the little meadow, had been enough for him.

"He played it like a fool," Jaynes said. "He could have stayed in the timber."

"You made twelve-fifty with each one of those shots, Jaynes." The deputy warden's voice ran slowly and deliberately.

"Let the State keep their twenty-five bucks," Jaynes said. "I didn't come along for that." His rifle was a beautiful instrument with a telescopic sight. The dead man lay beside a sawed-off shotgun and a .38 pistol taken from a guard he had slugged with a bar of soap in a sock. "Why didn't he stay in the timber, the damn fool?"

"They're all city boys," Warden Holesworth said. "He was heading for the highway."

It put you on the wrong side of your job to make a comparison between the dead man's short-range weapons and the rifles of the posse, Deputy Bill Melvin thought. Weyerhauser had been one of four prison escapees. He had taken his big chance with the others, and here the chance had ended.

That was all there was to it; but Melvin wished he did not have to look at Weyerhauser or hear any more from Jaynes, who was always the first man to reach the sheriff's office when the word went out that a manhunt was on. Jaynes, who ran a garage, never came when help was needed to find a lost hunter or a wrecked plane.

Sheriff Rudd spoke. Sheriff Rudd was a veteran of the open-range days of men and cattle. He stood like a rifle barrel, tall and spare. His face was bony, with a jutting nose.

"There's three more," the sheriff said. "All tougher than Weyerhauser." He squinted at the green plane, now circling lower in the trough of the mountains. "Call that flyer, Melvin. He's buzzing around this basin like a bee in a washtub. Tell him to get up in the air.

Tell him about this and have him call the patrol station over the hill and see if anything has popped there."

Deputy Melvin started back to the horse with the radio gear. Jaynes called, "Ask him if he's spotted any of the other three."

Melvin paid no attention.

"One twenty, ground party, Stony Park."

"Ground party, go ahead."

"Get some altitude. You're making Sheriff Rudd nervous."

"What does Rudd think I am? There's a hell of a wind up here. What happened?"

"We got Weyerhauser. Dead. Call Scott and Studebaker on the road blocks."

"Stand by," the pilot said.

Melvin leaned against the mare. She moved a little, cropping grass, switching her tail at deer flies unconcernedly, while Melvin listened to the plane call across the mountains. Jaynes's sleeping bag was on the crosspieces of the pack saddle, put there to protect the radio from branches.

Jaynes walked over. "Has he spotted—?"

"I didn't ask," said Melvin.

"Why not?"

"He would have said so if he had."

"Well, it won't hurt to ask. Maybe—"

"Go collect your twenty-five bucks, Jaynes."

"What do you mean by that?"

Jaynes did not understand. He never would.

"Ground party, One twenty," the pilot said. "Negative on all road blocks and patrol cars."

"Thanks, One twenty. Call Studebaker again and have an ambulance meet us at the big spring, east side of Herald Pass, at one this afternoon."

"Okay." The plane began to climb. Melvin watched until it gained altitude and shot away across the timbered hump of Herald Pass.

"That's a hell of a note," Jaynes complained. "Guys like me come out here, taking time off from our business just to do what's right, and you don't even ask whether he's spotted the others or not."

Melvin pulled the canvas cover back over the radio. "Four times twenty-five makes a hundred, Jaynes. What are you going to buy with all that money?"

"I give it to the Red Cross, don't I!"

"You mean that first twenty-five you knocked down—that little forger? I remember him, Jaynes. He came out of a railroad culvert trying to get his hands up, scared to death, and you cut loose."

Jaynes was puzzled, not angry. He said, "You talk funny for a deputy sheriff, Melvin. You sound like you thought there was something nice about these stinking cons. What are we supposed to do with them?"

Melvin went back to the posse. Deputy Warden Holesworth had searched the dead man. On the ground was a pile. Candy bars, smeary and flattish from being carried in pockets; seven packs of cigarettes.

"One down and three to go," Jaynes said. "Where do we head now, Sheriff?"

Sheriff Rudd looked around the group. Two or three of the men sitting in the grass had already lost stomach. Rudd named them and said, "Take that sorrel that's started to limp and pack Weyerhauser up to the highway."

"At the big spring on the east side," Melvin said. "There'll be an ambulance there at one o'clock."

"I've got to get back myself," the deputy warden said. "Tomorrow I'll send a couple of guards out. We can fly in Blayden's hounds from up north—"

"I don't favor hounds," the sheriff said. "Keep your guards, too, Holesworth. The last time you sent guards we had to carry 'em out. You keep 'em sitting in those towers too much."

"That's what they get paid for, not for being Indian guides and cross-country men. To hell with you." They grinned at each other. Then Holesworth gave Jaynes another speculative glance and helped lift Weyerhauser on to the lame horse.

That left seven in the posse. They divided the cigarettes. Small ants went flying when someone gave the pile of candy bars a kick. One chocolate bar, undisturbed by the boot, was melting into the earth beside the other stain.

Two days later Sheriff Rudd cut the trail of three men whose heelprints showed *P* marks in the center. Rudd swung down and studied the tracks, and then he took the saddle off his gelding.

"What's the stall?" Jaynes asked. "That's the track of our meat, Rudd."

"A day and a half old, at least. Give your horse a rest." The sheriff sat down on a log and began to fill his pipe.

Melvin walked beside the footprints for several steps. He saw the wrapper of a candy bar lying on the ground. Four days on candy and desperation. The poor devils. Poor devils, hell; the candy had been stolen from the filling station where they had slugged a sixty-year-old man, the desperation was their own, and they were asking for the same as Weyerhauser.

Melvin looked up at the gray caps of the mountains. They ran here in a semicircle, with only one trail over them, and that almost unknown. If these tracks with the deep-cut marks in the heels continued up, the fugitives would be forced to the forgotten road that led to Clover Basin. From there the trail went over the spine at thirteen thousand feet.

It was a terrible climb for men living on candy bars. Melvin went back to the resting posse, saying nothing.

"Clover Basin, maybe?" Sheriff Rudd asked.

Melvin nodded.

"Why haven't the damn search planes seen them?" Jaynes asked.

"There's trees and rocks, and the sound of a plane engine carries a long way ahead." Bud Pryor was a part-time deputy, here now because he had been called to go. He was a barrel-chested man who could stop a barroom fight by cracking heads together, but he didn't care much for riding the mountains. And he didn't care at all for Jaynes.

"Any other stupid questions, sharpshooter?" Bud Pryor asked Jaynes.

The sheriff got up. "Let's go."

They rode into the first of the great fields of golden gaillardia at the lower end of Clover Basin. The buildings of the Uncle Sam Mine hung over the slope at the upper end like gray ghosts. Rudd stopped his horse. The others crowded up behind him.

Motion started at the highest building and sent small points out on the slide-rock trail. "Hey!" Jaynes cried. Both he and Melvin put glasses on the tiny figures scrambling over the flat gray stones. Two men in green uniforms. Two men who ran and fell and crawled upward toward the harsh rise of Clover Mountain.

Jaynes let his binoculars fall on the cord around his neck. He raised his rifle, sighting through the 'scope. Some sort of dedication lay in his glittering eyes, some drive that made Melvin look away from him and glance at the sheriff.

Rudd, however, without the aid of glasses, was watching the fleeing men on the eternal stones of Clover Mountain.

Jaynes kicked his horse ahead. "Come on!"

"Get off and lead that horse a while, Jaynes," the sheriff said. "You've knocked the guts out of him already the last few days."

"There they are!" Jaynes gestured with his rifle.

"And there they go." Rudd got down and began to lead his horse.

"Now what the hell!" Jaynes twisted his face. "They're getting away —farther out of range every second!"

"They're a mile airline. It'll take us the best part of two hours to reach the mine," Sheriff Rudd said with weary patience. "And then it will be dark. Go on, Jaynes, if you want to, but leave that horse behind."

"It's mine."

"You'll leave it behind, I said."

Jaynes looked through his 'scope and cursed.

"Three came in here," Bud Pryor said. "Go on up and kick that third one out, Jaynes. He's there."

"How do you know?" Jaynes's voice was not large.

Pryor's thick lips spread in a grin. He was still sweating from the last steep hill where they had led the horses. "Gets chilly mighty quick in these high places, don't it?"

Rudd started on, leading his horse. It was dusk when they closed in on the bunkhouse of the Uncle Sam Mine, working around from the rocks and coming closer in short rushes to the toe of the dump. Jaynes and Melvin went up the dump together until their heads were nearly level with the rusted rails that still held rotting chocks.

"I'll cover you from here," Jaynes said. "This 'scope gathers light so a man can't miss."

Melvin raised his head above the dump. An evening wind drove grouse feathers across the yellow waste toward him. He saw a rat scurry along the ledge of a broken window and then sit still, looking out. Inside, two or three others squealed as they raced across the floor.

Melvin scrabbled on up and walked into the bunkhouse. Two rats carrying grouse bones ducked through holes in the floor. One half of the roof was caved in but the other end, where the stove sat with its pipe reduced to lacy fragility, was still a shelter.

The stove was warm.

Here, for a time, three men had stayed. They were city-bred, and so this man-made shell seemed the natural place to take shelter. No outdoorsman would have sought the rat-fouled place, but the escaped prisoners must have received some small comfort from it.

Instinctively they had huddled inside this pitiful ruin for the security that all pursued mankind must seek. And now, caught by the dusk and the silence, looking through a window at the mighty sweep of the high world, Bill Melvin was stirred by a feeling for the fugitives that sprang from depths far below the surface things called logic and understanding.

"What's in there?" Jaynes called.

Melvin stepped outside. "Nothing."

Jaynes cursed. He climbed to the dump level and stared at the dim slide-rock trail. He fondled his rifle.

Pryor's voice came from the lower buildings, high-pitched and clear, running out to the walls of the great basin and echoing back with ghostly mockery. "Nothing in any of these, Sheriff!"

"Let's get on the trail!" Jaynes yelled.

"Come down here," Sheriff Rudd said, and both their voices ran together on the darkening rocks around them.

Melvin and Jaynes rejoined the others. Melvin was dead-weary now, but Jaynes kept looking at the slide-rock, fretting.

"We can't get horses over that slide-rock at night," Rudd said. "And maybe not in daylight. We'll camp here tonight."

"And all that time they'll be moving," Jaynes objected. "Are you sure you want to catch them, Sheriff?"

"They'll be feeling their way down the worst switchbacks in these hills," Rudd said. "On empty stomachs."

"Like hell!" Jaynes said. "They've been living like kings on grouse."

"One grouse," Melvin said.

"They must be getting fat." Rudd pointed to the floor of the basin. "We'll camp down there and give the horses a chance to graze."

"And make this climb again in the morning," Jaynes said disgustedly.

Dew was gathering on the grass when they picketed the horses. All the chill of the high-country night seemed to have gathered in the enormous black hole. They ate almost the last of their food at a fire built from scrubby trees.

Jaynes cleaned his rifle before he ate. He rubbed the stock and admired the weapon, standing with the firelight glittering in his eyes.

"What will that pretty thing do that a good Krag won't?" Bud Pryor asked.

Jaynes smiled and let the answer gleam in the reflection of the flames.

"Somebody will have to start out tomorrow for grub," the sheriff said. "How about it, Jaynes?"

"I can live on the country," Jaynes said.

"Yeah." The sheriff unrolled his sleeping bag. "One hour each on guard tonight. Not at the fire, either. Stay out by the horses. I'll take it from three till dawn."

Jaynes peered into the darkness. "You think the third one is around in the rocks, huh?"

"I think the horses can get all tangled up. The third man went over the hill a long time ago," Rudd said.

"How do you know that?" Jaynes asked.

"Because I'm betting it was Marty Kaygo. He's the toughest and the smartest. He wouldn't sit in that eagle's nest up there, hoping nobody comes after him."

"Kaygo, huh? What was he in for?" Jaynes stared toward the gloomy crest of the mountain.

"He killed two cops." Rudd took off his boots, pulled his hat down tightly, and got into his sleeping bag. "He killed them with one shot each." The sheriff was asleep a few moments later.

Jaynes set his rifle on his sleeping bag and began to eat. "Who are the other two?"

"Don't you even know their names?" Melvin asked.

"What's the difference if I don't?"

Maybe Jaynes was right. It had to be done, one way or another; names merely made it harder. "Sam Castagna and Ora L. Strothers," Melvin said. "Castagna used to blow up rival gamblers for a syndicate. Strothers specialized in holding up banks."

"Ora L. That's nice and gentle, a con having a name like that," Jaynes said.

"Don't you give him the right to have a name?" Melvin asked. "Don't you give him the right to be a human being?"

Jaynes looked blank at the anger in Melvin's voice. "What is it with you, anyway? You and Rudd both talk like it was a crime to send those bastards rolling in the grass."

Rolling in the grass. That was exactly what had happened to Weyerhauser when Jaynes's second shot ripped through his belly.

Melvin walked away from the fire suddenly, into the cold dark layers of the night. The possemen were sacking out. Jaynes squatted near the fire alone, eating, a puzzled expression on his face. Bud Pryor, stripped down to long underwear and his boots, came over and stood beside the flames for a few minutes, warming his hands.

Dislike of Jaynes and a sort of wonder mingled on Pryor's fleshy face. He parted his thick lips as if to speak. But then he left the fire and settled into his sleeping bag, grunting.

The night was large and silent. Up toward the knife edge of Clover Mountain two men had scrambled across the rocks, crawling where slides had filled the trail. Two men running for their lives.

Melvin kept seeing it over and over.

Castagna's sentence had been commuted to life just two days short of the gas chamber. Strothers had never killed a man, but he was cold and ruthless. Marty Kaygo, who must have gone across the hill before the others, was in debt to the law 180 years. This was his third escape from prison.

They were all no good, predators against society. But . . . In the solemn night, with the tremendous peace of the mountains upon him, Bill Melvin stared uneasily at the line which must run from crime to punishment.

Ordinarily, he did not allow himself to be disturbed like this; but Jaynes, scraping the last of his supper from a tin plate, had kicked over the little wall that divided what men must do from what they think.

"I'll take the first watch," Melvin said.

Jaynes came out from the fire. He spoke in a low voice. "It's only nine o'clock. Barker's got a flashlight. We could slip up on the slide-rock trail—there's patches of snow there—and see for sure if they all three crossed."

"Why?"

"If one is still here, he'll try to slip out of the basin tonight. We could lay out in that narrow place and nail him dead to rights."

"I'll take the first watch." Melvin walked deeper into the night, trembling from high-altitude fatigue, mouthing the sickening aftertaste of Jaynes's presence.

"Why not, Melvin?"

"Go to bed!"

Sometimes a healthy man does not sleep well at great altitudes, and so it was with Melvin this night. When Jaynes relieved him, Melvin heard the beefy hunter going down the basin past the horses. He knew that Jaynes would make for a place where he could command the narrow entrance to the basin, and that he would lie there, patiently, his rifle ready.

Melvin wondered if his eyes would glitter in the dark.

Jaynes stayed his watch, and the watch of the man he did not waken for relief.

Dawn slid across the peaks. Light was there when dew and gloom were still heavy in the basin. The sheriff and Pryor cooked the last of the bacon and opened the last two cans of beans.

Jaynes saddled up and led his horse toward the fire before he ate. "What kind of rifle was it this—what was his name, Kaygo?—stole at the filling station?"

"A .30–06," Rudd said. There were pouches under his eyes this morning, and he looked his years. He stared through the smoke at Jaynes. "New one. He took five boxes of shells, too, Jaynes. They're hunting cartridges."

"I've got a few expanding noses myself," Jaynes said. "Let's get started."

Rudd spat to one side. "You're like a hog going to war."

Bud Pryor laughed. The other manhunters stared at Jaynes or at the ground. They seemed ashamed now, Melvin thought, to be a part of this thing. Or a part of Jaynes.

Pryor said explosively, "I'll go in after chow today, Sheriff. Me and Jaynes."

"No!" Jaynes said. "I can live on the country. Me and Melvin can keep going when the rest of you have to run for a restaurant."

Rudd said to Pryor, "You and Barker, then. It's closer now to Scott than it is to Studebaker, so we'll split up after we cross the hill. Try the radio again, Melvin. Maybe nobody will have to go in."

"No contact," Melvin said, later. "When we get to the top, we can reach out and make it."

They took the slide-rock trail from the dump at the side of the bunkhouse. In passing, Melvin noticed that the grouse feathers were almost entirely blown away.

Seventy years before, jack trains had used the trail; but now the years had slid into it. The posse led their horses. Sparks from steel shoes in the stretches where the ledge still showed drill marks; a clattering and a scramble, with the horses rolling their eyes when they had to cross the spills of dry-slippery rocks.

In the snowbanks, the tracks of three men; and one man had gone about a day before the others.

There lay the ridge, half a mile ahead. On the left, where they traveled, the mountain ran down wildly to ledges where no human being would ever set foot.

They lost the little radio mare. She slipped and fell and then she was threshing over and the slide-rock ran with her. She struck a ledge and was gone. The rocks kept spilling down a thousand feet below.

Rudd patted the neck of his frightened gelding. "There went a damn good little mare."

Jaynes said, "They don't exactly give those radios away, either. My sleeping bag cost sixty-two bucks."

They came out on the wedge-top and went down three switchbacks to let the horses take a blow out of the wind. A dozen lakes were winking in the sunlight. The mountains on this side ran in a crazy pattern. Every major range in the United States runs north and south, with one exception; but from the pinpoints where a man must stand, the north-south coursing is often lost or does not exist at all.

There was no highway in sight, no smoke, just the vast expanse of timber with the gray-sharp slopes above and the shine of beaver meadows where little streams lay separated from each other by ridges eight thousand feet high.

"A regiment could hide out down there all summer," Rudd said. "But these guys will most likely keep running downhill, hoping to hit a highway sooner or later."

Jaynes's rifle was in his hands, as usual when he was on foot. He pointed with it. "I know every inch of that country. I've fished and hunted all through it."

"Don't be a fool," Sheriff Rudd said. "I rode that country before you were born, and I discovered a new place every time I went out. And I could do the same for a hundred years." Rudd shook his head. "Every inch of it . . . !"

Jaynes said, "I can find any tenderfoot that tries to hide out down there." He patted the stock of his rifle.

"Goddamn you, Jaynes! I'm sick of you!" Melvin cried. "Keep your mouth shut!"

Jaynes was surprised. "Now what did I say? Have you got a biting ulcer or something, Melvin?"

"Let's go on down," Rudd said.

Melvin's stomach held a knot that eased off slowly. For a moment he had seen the land without a man in it, forgetting even himself as he stood there on the mountain. But Jaynes would never let a man forget himself for long.

In the middle of the morning the green plane came over and circled them. The pilot was calling, Melvin knew, but they had no way now to listen or call back. After a while the plane soared away over the green timber and drifted on toward Scott.

They struck the timber. Fallen trees lay across the trail, slowing the horses. There were still three men ahead.

"Planes, radios, horses—what the hell good are they?" Jaynes said irritably. "In the end it comes down to men on foot closing in on each other."

"Like you closed in on the Uncle Sam bunkhouse, huh?" Pryor asked. "Hand to hand, tooth and toenail."

"Strip down to a breechclout, Jaynes," Rudd said. "I'll give you my knife and you can go after Kaygo properly."

Barker said, "Yeah, why don't you do that, Jaynes? You big-mouthed bastard, you."

Barker had little imagination. He was a sullen man who would kill the fugitives as quickly as Jaynes. All that motivated Barker now, Melvin thought, was a desire to transfer the cause of his hunger and weariness to another human being. Jaynes had already been marked by him as a target.

"I don't understand you guys, so help me," Jaynes said.

Melvin felt a flash of pity for him; the man really did not understand. What made Jaynes tick probably was as obscure as the forces that had sent the men he so greatly wanted to kill into a life of crime. Somebody ought to be able to figure it out. . . .

The big buck flashed across the narrow lane in a split second. The smaller one that followed an instant later was going just as fast. Jaynes broke its neck with one shot.

The thought of fresh liver relieved some of Melvin's dislike of Jaynes. "Nice shooting, Jaynes."

"Thanks."

"I'll eat that thing without skinning it," Bud Pryor said. He had his knife out already and was trotting ahead.

Jaynes sat on a log and cleaned his rifle while Pryor and Melvin dressed the buck. Jaynes had merely glanced at it and turned away.

"He's larded up like first-class, grass-fed beef," Pryor said. "Lucky shot, Jaynes."

"I seldom miss a running target." Jaynes spoke absently, looking ahead at the trees.

Pryor sent Melvin a helpless look. "It sure looked lucky to me."

"No luck at all," said Jaynes. "It's simple if you have the eye for it."

Pryor made a motion with his knife as if to cut his own throat. He and Melvin laughed. For a few moments Jaynes was no problem to them.

"Sling it on a horse," Sheriff Rudd said. "We can eat when we get to Struthers' sawmill set."

"Struthers? That's one of the men we want," Jaynes said.

"Different spelling," Rudd said. "Jumbo Struthers has been dead for forty years, and the sawmill hasn't run for fifty-two years."

"We could dig him up," Pryor said, grinning, "so Jaynes could shoot him."

For the first time Jaynes showed anger. "Why do you keep digging at me? What are we out here for, anyway? You act like there was something wrong in what we're doing!"

"We're here to bring back three men, dead *or* alive," Rudd said. "Let's go."

The trail expanded into a logging road, with live trees trying to close it out and dead trees trying to block it. Mosquitoes came singing in from a marsh on the left. Already tormented by the snags on fallen timber, the horses shook their heads as the insects buzzed their ears. Pryor kept swinging his hat at blowflies settling on the carcass of the deer. "The good old summertime," he said. "How'd you get me out here, Sheriff?"

"You were getting fat, so you volunteered."

The small talk irritated Jaynes. "We're not making much time," he said. Later, after a delay to lever aside a tangle of dead jackpines, he went ahead in a stooping posture for several steps. "One of the boys ain't doing so good all at once."

Melvin studied the tracks. One man had started to drag his leg; a second one was helping him. The third track was still older than these two. Farther down the road a punch mark appeared in the soil. One man was using a short pole as a cane.

Jaynes wanted to race away on the trail. "We'll have that one before long!"

"Hold up." The sheriff stopped to fill his pipe. "I'd say the fellow twisted a muscle or sprained his ankle trying to jump that tangle we just cleared out. The other one will leave him, that's sure."

"The old ranger lean-to in Boston Park must be pretty close," Jaynes said. "Half a mile, I'd say."

"About a mile," Rudd said.

Melvin knew about it, the big lean-to sometimes used by fishermen and hunters. Man had made it, and the fact would seem important to the men ahead. Considering the tracks of the injured fugitive, Melvin wondered whether the convict would last to Boston Park.

"If he's bunged up as bad as it looks, he's likely ready to quit," Rudd said.

"He won't give up," Jaynes said. "He'll make a stand."

The sheriff narrowed his eyes at Jaynes. "Why will he, if he's hurt?"

"If he's been left at that lean-to, he's the loneliest man in the world right now," Melvin put in.

"Yeah?" Jaynes kept edging ahead. "I'm not walking up on that hut to find out how lonely he is."

"Nobody is," Rudd said. "When we get close, two men will take the horses. The rest of us will cut off into the timber and come in from all sides of the lean-to. He may not be there at all."

The lean-to was set between two trees on high ground, clear of the swamp that edged the beaver ponds. Generations of outdoorsmen had piled boughs along the sides and on top until the shelter was a rust-brown mass. That it had not been burned by a careless match long ago spoke tersely of the nature of the men who came far into the mountains.

Melvin and Sheriff Rudd came to the edge of the trees a hundred yards apart. They waited for Pryor, on the right. Barker and Jaynes were to ease out of the trees on the left, Barker to cover the back of the shelter, Jaynes to prevent escape farther to the left.

There had been a fire recently among the blackened stones before the lean-to. Fine ashes stirred there, lifting to a little wind that rolled across the beaver ponds and whispered through the tall swamp grass.

Melvin saw Pryor come to the edge of the trees and signal with his hand. Barker slipped to the cover of a windfall behind the shelter. He wagged his rifle.

Inside the lean-to a man cleared his throat.

Melvin sank to one knee behind a log.

The sheriff said, "Come out of there! You're boxed. Walk out with your hands up!"

"I can't walk," a voice replied.

"Come out of there. We'll rip that place apart with bullets if I have to ask again."

The brittle needles scraped against each other. A chunky man whose face was black with beard came on hands and knees from the hut. He was wearing a soiled, torn green uniform, too small for him. One pants leg was gone below the knee.

"Toss your pistol away," Rudd ordered.

"No gun." The man clawed against one of the trees. He pulled himself erect. "No gun, you stinking, dirty—" He started to fall and made a quick grab at the crosspiece of the shelter.

A rifle blasted from the edge of the timber beyond Barker. The man at the lean-to fell. He was dead, Melvin was sure. "Watch him! Watch him!" Jaynes called. "It's just his arm!"

Melvin and the sheriff walked in then. The man had been shot through the left hand, a thick hand, by a soft-nosed hunting bullet. The palm was torn away and the fingers were spread like the spokes of a shattered wheel. The man rolled on his side and put his broken hand under his arm.

"My leg is cracked before." He cursed. "Now look at it!" The leg was really broken now; it had twisted under when the man fell. Melvin searched him and found two packs of cigarettes.

Barker came around the hut. Jaynes arrived on the run. "I could just see his arm when he grabbed for his gun!"

"He grabbed, all right," Sheriff Rudd said. "To keep from falling on a busted leg."

"Oh!" Jaynes stared down. "It looked to me like—"

"Shut up." Rudd yelled at the timber where the two men were holding the horses. "Bring 'em on!" There was a first-aid kit on Melvin's horse.

"Which one is this?" Jaynes asked.

"Sam Castagna." Suspected of seven murders, convicted of one, sentence commuted to life. "Where's Strothers, Sam?"

"Run out on me." With his face against the brown needles Castagna tried to spit explosively. It merely dribbled from his mouth and hung in his black beard. He cursed in Italian, glaring up at Jaynes.

Barker said, "No gun anywhere around the hut. They had two sawed-offs and two .38 pistols, besides the rifle Kaygo swiped at the filling station."

The horses came in at the trot. Pryor circled the swamp and plodded through the grass. He looked at the wounded man. "Castagna, huh? Nice boy who likes to put bombs on carstarters. The other two are still going down the trail, Sheriff."

"Straight to a highway," Rudd said. "Let's patch him up and move on."

"I'm going to eat here," Pryor said, "if you have to leave me. I'm going to beat the blowflies to some of that deer." He began to build a fire.

Melvin and Barker made splints for Castagna's broken leg. They wrapped his hand. He watched them stolidly. When they pulled his leg, he ground his teeth and sweated. Melvin got him a drink of water afterward.

"Thanks," Castagna held the cup in a trembling hand, slopping part of the water down his chin and into the thick black hairs at the base of his neck.

"Where's Strothers and Kaygo, Castagna?" Jaynes asked.

Castagna looked hungrily at the meat Pryor was roasting on a green limb. He lay back on the ground and closed his eyes. There was a depression under his head and it caused his face to tilt straight into the sun. Melvin took off his coat and rolled it under the wounded man's head.

They squatted around the fire, roasting cutlets chopped from the loin with a hand ax, too hungry to bother with a frying pan. Blood from half-raw meat ran down their chins when they chewed.

None of us is far removed from the wolf, Melvin thought; but there is a difference between men like Rudd and Sam Castagna. There has to be. Yet where was the difference between Castagna and Jaynes, who cleaned his rifle before he ate?

Melvin glanced at the gleaming weapon, laid carefully aside on the dry grass. He felt an urge to hurl the rifle far out into the beaver pond.

Sheriff Rudd ground his meat moodily. "I never used to stop when I was on the chase. We stop to gorge ourselves while a desperate man keeps going. The difference is he *has* to get away and we don't *have* to catch him."

"Him? Who do you mean?" Jaynes asked. "Why don't we have to catch him?"

"Oh, hell," Rudd said. "Gimme the salt, Barker."

"I don't understand what—" Jaynes said.

"Before we leave here, Jaynes, you throw into that pond every damn hunting bullet you got," Rudd said. "I'm going to watch you do it."

They all looked at Jaynes. He could not grasp the reason for their hostility. "Shells cost money. I'll use that old coffee can over there and bury them under the lean-to. Next fall I'll be through here hunting."

"Do that then," Rudd said. "Every damn soft-nose you got." But Rudd seemed to find no satisfaction in the trifling victory.

He knew he was only scratching at the surface, Melvin thought.

The sheriff twisted around toward Castagna. "Some deer meat, Sam?"

"Yeah. Yeah, let me try it." Castagna ate greedily, and then he lost everything before they could get him onto a horse.

The green plane was cruising southwest of them. A few minutes later it came over Boston Park, dipping low. It went southwest again, circling six or seven times.

"Uh-huh," Rudd said.

"He must be over the Shewalter Meadows," Jaynes said. "That's all down-timber between here and there."

"Not if you know the way from the sawmill set." Rudd swung up. "Catch Castagna there if he starts to fall."

There were still two sets of mantracks down the logging road. Just before they reached the sawmill site they found a sawed-off shotgun laid across a log, pointing toward one of the sawdust piles near the creek. Under it an arrow mark scratched in the black soil pointed in the same direction.

"Now that's a cute trick," Jaynes said. He sighted through his 'scope at the sawdust piles, age-brown mounds blending into the wilderness. He was suspicious, but he was confused.

"It reads to me that Strothers wants to quit, and wants to be sure we know it," Rudd said.

"Suppose he's still got the pistol? Suppose it's Kaygo?" Jaynes asked.

"Most likely Kaygo is over there where the plane was circling," Melvin said. Kaygo had left the others at the Uncle Sam Mine. The sheriff, at least, was sure of that, and Melvin had accepted it. Still, he did not like the quiet of the sawdust piles, warm and innocent-looking out there by the creek.

Rudd said, "Come on, Melvin. The rest of you stay here. Take Castagna off the horse and let him lay down a while."

"I'd better—" Jaynes said.

"Stay right here," the sheriff said.

Rudd and Melvin leaped the creek and tramped upon the spongy surface of the sawdust piles. In a little hollow of the shredded wood they found their man, asleep.

His blond whiskers were short and curly. The sun had burned his face. His green shirt, washed recently in the stream, was spread near him and now it was dry. His heavy prison shoes were set neatly together near his feet.

"Strothers, all right," Rudd said. "Wake up!"

The man was snoring gently. He jerked a little but he did not rouse until Rudd tossed one of the shoes on his stomach. Strothers opened his eyes and yawned.

"What kept you so long?" he asked.

Cold and deadly, the bulletins had read; he had never killed a man, but he had always entered banks prepared to kill. He had studied law, and later, engineering. It was said that he could have been successful in either. Now he sat on a pile of sawdust in the wilderness, ready to go back to the isolation cells.

"Local yokels, eh? I didn't think those lazy bastards of guards would come this far. Got anything to smoke, Constable?"

"Where's Kaygo?" the sheriff asked.

Strothers yawned again. He felt his feet. "Talk about blisters!" He began to put on his shoes. "Why, Marty left us at a rat hole on the side of a cliff day before yesterday."

"We know that," Rudd said.

"That's why I mentioned it." Strothers reached toward his shirt.

"Hold it!" Melvin picked up the shirt. There was no weight in it, nothing under it. He tossed it to Strothers, who rose and began to put it on.

"Where's the other .38?" Rudd asked mildly.

"The other? So you got Weyerhauser. Can I have a smoke?"

Melvin lit a cigarette and tossed it to Strothers. The sheriff and his deputy glanced quickly at each other.

"I don't know who's got it," Strothers said. The horses were coming out of the timber.

He saw Castagna. "Did you ask Sam?"

The sheriff's eyes were tight. He spoke easily, "Sam's clean. You look clean. So Kaygo's got it. Why'd you give up, Strothers?"

"Too much of nothing here. No future." Strothers grinned, dragging on his cigarette, watching the horses from the corners of his eyes. The surface was smooth, but there was steel savagery underneath. Castagna was a bully who had graduated to bombs on starters and bundles of dynamite against the bedroom walls of gambling kings; Strothers was everything the long F.B.I. reports said.

"You could have given up with Castagna," Melvin said.

"That two-bit character! I play it alone." Strothers puffed his smoke. "Do I get some chow?"

"Yeah," Rudd said. "Half-done venison."

"Raw will be fine, Constable."

"Walk on over toward the horses," Rudd said. "When I say stop— stop."

"Sure, Constable. Just don't stall. I want to get home as soon as possible. I'm doing some leather work that can't be neglected."

Not the usual bravado of a petty criminal—Strothers was too coldly intelligent for that. He was spreading it on lightly for another purpose. He wouldn't have much luck with Rudd, Melvin knew. Let him find it out.

Strothers limped ahead of them. "When my last blister broke, that was when I decided to hell with it."

"Right there, Strothers," Rudd said, when they were twenty feet from the horses. With the exception of Jaynes, the posse was relaxed. The first heat of the chase had been worn from them, and this third easy victory coming toward them was nothing to cause excitement.

Rudd nodded at Melvin, making a circle with his finger in the air. Melvin walked wide around Strothers and freed his lariat from the saddle.

"The great big Strothers, he comes easy," Castagna said sullenly.

Strothers ignored Castagna; his eyes were on the rope in Melvin's hands. Barker and the others looked at Strothers dully, but Jaynes sensed what they did not. He pushed his 'scope sight down and raised his rifle.

"Never mind!" Rudd said sharply, standing several paces behind Strothers. "Put that rifle down, Jaynes. Drop your pants, Strothers."

Strothers smiled. "Now look, Constable . . ." He was watching the loop in Melvin's hand.

And that was when Rudd stepped in and slammed Strothers to the ground with the butt of his rifle. Melvin drove in quickly then. Strothers was enough for the two of them for a while, but they got his arms tied behind him at last.

The little automatic, flat, fully loaded, was tied with strips of green cloth from Castagna's pants leg to the inside of Strothers's thigh. Castagna cursed bitterly, clinging to the saddle horn with his one good hand.

"Why didn't you search him right at first?" Jaynes demanded angrily.

"It takes more steam out of them to let them go right up to where it looks like it's going to work," the sheriff said. "Build a fire, Pryor. We may as well eat again before we split up."

Strothers chewed his meat with good appetite. He had struggled like a wolf, but that was done now and his intelligence was at work again. "What tipped it, Constable—the cigarettes?"

"Partly," Rudd said. "You wouldn't have left both packs with Sam unless you figured to be with him soon. That wasn't too much, but I knew you would never go back down the river and let them say Ora L. Strothers was caught asleep and gave up without a fight. You really were asleep, too—on purpose."

"Sure. I got the nerve for things like that. It made it look real." Strothers's good nature was back, but he was not thinking of his words. His mind, Melvin knew, was thinking far ahead now, to another plan, setting himself against walls and locks and ropes and everything that could be used to restrain a man physically, pitting his fine mind against all the instruments of the thing called society.

There was a lostness in him that appalled Melvin. Strothers was a cold wind running from a foggy gorge back in the dawn age of mankind. The wind could never warm or change or remain confined. Compared to Strothers, Sam Castagna was just a lumbering animal that knocked weaker animals out of the way.

"You would have taken Castagna with you, if you could have knocked a couple of us off and got to the horses?" Melvin asked.

"Sure," Strothers said. "We planned it that way."

That was talk to be repeated in the prison yard, to be passed along the corridors of the cell block. Talk to fit the code. But not to feed the vanity of Ora L. Strothers, because it was a lie. Let Castagna, lying feverishly on the ground in Melvin's jacket, believe what Strothers said. Castagna had been left behind to build up the illusion that desperate men would surrender without a fight. That he was injured and had to be left was not primary in Strothers's mind; it was merely helpful coincidence.

"Which one of us was to 've been first?" Melvin asked.

Strothers wiped his lips. "You, I thought. Then I changed my mind." He glanced at Jaynes.

"Yeah," Jaynes said. "I read you like a book. I wish you had tried something, Strothers."

The two men stared at each other. The antagonism that separated them was as wide as the sky.

"I'll bet you're the one shot Sam," Strothers said. "Did you shoot Joe Weyerhauser, too?"

Jaynes did not answer. Watching him, Melvin thought: He lacks the evil power of Strothers's intelligence, and he lacks the strength of natural good. He doesn't know what he is, and he knows it.

Strothers smiled. "I've taken half a million from the banks and never had to shoot a man. You, Snake Eyes, you're just a punk on the other side because you don't have the guts and brains of men like me. How about it?"

Jaynes leaped up. His wasp voice broke when he cursed Strothers. He gripped his rifle and stood with the butt poised to smash into Strothers's face.

"Whoa there, Jaynes!" Sheriff Rudd said, but it was not he who stopped the rifle. With his legs tied and one arm bound behind his back, Strothers looked at Jaynes and smiled, and Jaynes lowered his rifle and walked away. After a few steps he turned toward the creek and went there, pretending to drink.

Barker and Pryor stared at Strothers. "Don't call *me* any of your names," Barker growled.

Strothers looked at him as he might have glanced at a noisy child; and then he forgot them all. His mind was once more chewing facts and plans, even as his strong teeth chewed meat.

If this man had been led by Marty Kaygo, what kind of man was Kaygo? thought Melvin.

Rudd said, "I'll take everybody in but you and Jaynes, Melvin. Do you feel up to staying on the trail?"

There was no place where a plane could set down to pick up Castagna. Two and a half days out, Melvin estimated. Rudd would need five men to keep an eye on Strothers day and night. They were out of food, too.

"All right," Melvin said.

Jaynes had overheard. He came back from the creek. "I'm staying, too."

Strothers smiled.

"I'll send the green plane over Shewalter Meadows three days from now," Rudd said. "With grub. Now what else will you need?"

"Send me another coat," Melvin said. "Send Jaynes another sleeping bag. We both better have packs, too."

The sheriff nodded. He put Strothers on a horse and tied him there. They lifted Castagna to the saddle again. He was going to suffer plenty before they reached the highway. Castagna looked at Melvin and said thickly, "Thanks for the coat."

Strothers smiled at Melvin from the corner of his eyes. The smile said: Chump!

A hundred yards down the creek a logging road took off to the left, and there went the tracks of Marty Kaygo. Melvin and Jaynes walked into second-growth timber. The sounds of the horses died away. Under his belt Melvin was carrying the pistol he had taken from Strothers.

Jaynes said, "I damn near smashed that Strothers's ugly face for him."

"Uh-huh."

"You can't hit a man tied up like that, not even a pen bird."

"No."

"Of course not," Jaynes said.

The road began to angle to the right, along a ridge.

"This won't take us straight to where the plane spotted Kaygo," Jaynes said. "Let's cut into the timber."

"I'm staying with his tracks. I don't know what that plane was circling over."

The road turned down the ridge again, on the side away from Shewalter Meadows. Kaygo's tracks were still there, but Jaynes was mightily impatient. "I'm going straight over the ridge," he said.

"Go ahead."

"Where will I meet you then?"

"At the Meadows."

"You sure?" Jaynes asked doubtfully.

"This old road runs into one hell of a swamp before long. I'm betting he went to the Meadows, but I'm going to follow his trail all the way."

They separated. Melvin was glad. He wanted to reduce the chase to the patient unwinding of a trail, to an end that was nothing more than law and duty; and he could not think of it that way so long as Jaynes was with him.

Where the swamp began, Kaygo had turned at once up the ridge. There was something in that which spoke of the man's quality, of an ability to sense the lie of a country. Most city men would have blundered deep into the swamp before deciding to turn.

Jaynes was right about down-timber on the ridge, fire-killed trees that had stood for years before rot took their roots and wind sent them crashing. Melvin went slowly. Kaygo had done the same, and before long Melvin noticed that the man had traveled as a woodsman does, stepping over nothing that could be walked around.

Kaygo would never exhaust himself in blind, disorderly flight. What kind of man was he?

Going down the west side of the ridge, Melvin stopped when a grouse exploded from the ground near a rotting spruce log. He drew the pistol and waited until he saw two others near the log, frozen in their protective coloration. He shot one through the head, and five more flew away.

Now an instrument of the law had broken the law for a second time during this chase; but there were, of course, degrees of breakage. A man like Strothers no doubt could make biting comments on the subject.

Melvin pulled the entrails from the bird and went on, following Kaygo's trail. The man had an eye for terrain, all right. He made few mistakes that cost him time and effort, and that was rare in any man crossing unfamiliar, wooded country.

A woodsman at some time in his life? Melvin went back over Kaygo's record. Thirty-five years old. Sixteen of those years spent in reformatories and prisons. An interesting talker. Athletic. Generally armed, considered extremely dangerous. Approach with caution. The record fell into the glib pattern of the words under the faces on the bulletin board in Rudd's office.

Gambles heavily. If forced to work, seeks employment as clerk in clothing store . . . There was nothing Melvin could recall to indicate that Kaygo had ever been five miles from pavement.

The sun was getting low and the timber was already gathering coolness in its depths when Melvin came out on a long slope that ran down to the Meadows, two miles away.

Where the sun still lay on a bare spot near a quartz outcrop Melvin stopped, puzzled by what he saw. The mark of the steel butt-plate of Kaygo's rifle and the imprint of his shoes, one flat, the other showing no heel print, said that Kaygo had squatted near the ant hill; four cigarette butts crushed into the ground said that he had been here for some time.

Coolness had diminished activity of the ants, but they were still seething in and out of their dome of sand and pine needles; and Kaygo had squatted there for perhaps an hour to watch.

It was Melvin's experience that some perverseness in man causes him to step upon ant hills or to kick them in passing. This one was undisturbed. Kaygo had watched and gone away. Melvin had done the same thing many times.

What if I have and what if he did also? he asked himself. Does that change what I have to do? But as he went on, Melvin kept wondering what Kaygo had thought as he squatted beside the ant hill.

Near dusk Melvin lost the trail where the wide arm of a swamp came up from the drainage basin of the Meadows. But Kaygo was headed that way, Melvin was sure. One gentle turn too far to the left, back there on the long slope, would have sent Kaygo into the ragged canyons near the lower end of the Meadows.

He must have spotted the place from the top of Clover Mountain; but seeing from the heights and finding from a route through timber-choked country are two different things.

Kaygo had a fine sense of distance and direction, though. I can grant him that, Melvin thought, without feeling anything else about him to impede my purpose. The purpose—and Melvin wondered why he had to keep restating it—was to bring Marty Kaygo out, dead or alive.

On the edge of Shewalter Meadows, where the grass stood waist-high to a man all over the flooded ground and the beaver runs that led to the ponds out in the middle, Melvin stopped behind a tree and scanned the open space. There was only half-light now, but that was enough.

Beavers were making ripples in the ponds and trout were leaping for their evening feeding. The Meadows lay in a great dog-leg, and the upper part was cut from Melvin's view by spruce trees and high willows. The best windfalls for sleeping cover were up there, and that was where Jaynes would be, undoubtedly.

Let him stay there tonight alone. Sooner or later Melvin would have to rejoin him, and that would be soon enough. Melvin went back into the timber and cooked his grouse. He ate half of it and laid the rest in the palm of a limb, head-high.

The night came in with a gentle rush. He dozed off on top of his sleeping bag, to awaken chilled and trembling some time later. The night was windless, the ground stony. Melvin built up the fire and warmed himself by it before getting into his sleeping bag.

Dead or alive. The thought would not submerge.

One Kaygo was a vagueness written on a record; Melvin had learned of another Kaygo today. They made a combination that would never give up.

If Melvin had been here just to fish and loaf, to walk through the dappled fall of sunshine in the trees, and—yes, to be caught away from himself while watching the endless workings of an ant hill; to see the sun come and go on quietness; to see the elk thrusting their broad muzzles underwater to eat; to view all the things that are simple and understandable . . . then, he knew, he would be living for a while as man was meant to live.

You are Bill Melvin, a deputy sheriff. He is a man called Kaygo, an escaped murderer.

Dead or alive . . .

He came from dreamless sleep when the log ends of the fire were no longer flaming but drizzling smoke across a bed of coals. He felt the presence near him by the rising of the hackles on his neck, from deep memories forgotten by the human race.

Carefully, not breaking the even tenor of his breathing, he worked one hand up to the pistol on the head shield of the sleeping bag.

The man was squatted by the fire with a rifle across his knees. His hair was curling brown that caught a touch of redness from the glow of embers. The light outlined a sandy beard, held steady on wide cheekbones, and lost itself in the hollows under massive brow arches. The man's trousers were muddy, at least as high as the knees, where the fabric was strained smooth by his position. They might have been any color. But there was no doubt that the shirt was green.

The face by itself was enough.

It was Marty Kaygo.

He was eating what was left of Melvin's grouse.

He turned the carcass in his hands, gnawing, chewing; and all the while his face was set toward the shadows where Melvin lay.

Slowly Melvin worked the pistol along the edge of the ground until, lying on his side, he raised it just a trifle. The front sight was a white bead that lined across the coals to Kaygo's chest. Melvin's thumb pushed the safety down.

Long rifle cartridges, just a spot of lead that could sing over space and kill. Kaygo, the cop-killer. Speak to him, tell him to put up his hands and let his rifle fall. If he swung the rifle to fire, the pistol could sing and kill.

From where came the whisper that fire and food must be shared even with a deadly enemy? From the jungle all around that might pull them both beneath its slime an instant later?

The sabre-tooth and the great reptiles were out there in the night. And men were men together, if only for a moment. The jungle was not gone, merely changed.

Melvin let the pistol rest upon the ground.

Marty Kaygo rose. He was not a tall man. Even in his prison shoes he moved lightly as he stepped to a tree and replaced the carcass of the grouse. He grinned, still looking toward where Melvin lay.

And then he was gone.

Melvin lay a long time before he fell asleep again.

When he rose in the bitter cold of morning, he went at once to the dead fire. There were the tracks. He took the grouse from the limb. One leg was untouched.

Staring out to where the first long-slanting rays of the sun were driving mist from the beaver ponds and wet grass, Melvin held the chilled grouse in his hands.

What's the matter with me?

The truth was, Jaynes was Melvin and Melvin was Jaynes, great developments of the centuries; and Kaygo did not fit where they belonged. But . . .

Melvin shivered.

He went out of the timber into the sunshine, and he sat down to let it warm him while he ate the rest of the grouse. There before him, leading through the gray mud out toward the wickerwork of the beaver dams, were the tracks of Kaygo. He had crossed the boggy ground by night, walking the beaver dams above deep water, returning the same way. It was not an easy feat even in daytime.

I wish I could talk to him, Melvin thought. I wish . . .

The shot was a cracking violation of the wilderness quiet. It came from somewhere around the dog-leg of the Meadows.

Melvin went back to the camp site and got his gear.

Before he turned the dog-leg, he saw Jaynes coming toward him. Jaynes stopped and waited.

"What the hell happened to you, Melvin?" There was blood on Jaynes's shirt.

"I followed his trail, just as I said I would. You shoot a deer?"

"Yeah. That's one thing there's plenty of here. Kaygo's around. I saw his tracks in the upper part of the Meadows last night. We'll get him. I know every inch—"

"Let's get at the deer."

They roasted meat, and then Jaynes was impatient to be off.

"Just hold your steam," said Melvin. "We've got another two days before the plane drops chow, so we're going to start drying some of this meat."

"There's lots of deer."

"We'll dry some of this. We don't know where that plane will drop our supplies, or what they'll be like when we get to them. And you're not going to shoot a deer every day, Jaynes."

They cut the meat in thin strips and laid it on the gray twigs of a fallen tree until the branches were festooned with dangling brown meat. Camp-robber birds were there at once, floating in, snatching.

"How you going to stop that?" Jaynes asked.

"By staying here. I'm going to do some smoking with a willow fire, too. Take a turn around the Meadows. See what you can find out. You know every inch of the land."

"I'll do that." Jaynes took his rifle and strode away.

He was back at noon. "Where'd you camp, Melvin?"

Melvin told him.

"Well, he was there, this morning. He crossed the swamp and went back the same way. He's in the timber on this side somewhere. He's getting smart now about covering his tracks."

"What's he eating?" Melvin asked cleverly.

"I don't know, and I don't care. He slept one night under a windfall. Where'd he learn that, Melvin?" Jaynes was worried.

"I think it must come to him naturally. He's probably enjoying more freedom right now than he's had in his whole life."

Jaynes grunted. He eyed the tree that was serving as a drying rack. "Hey! Do you suppose we could pull him in with that?" He looked all around at the fringe of trees. "Say we go down into the timber on the other side and then circle back to that little knob over there . . .

About 325 yards." Jaynes rubbed the oily sheen of his rifle barrel. "One shot, Melvin."

"You think he's hungry enough to try it?"

"He must be."

"The birds will scatter our meat."

"Part of a lousy deer, or one jailbird! What's the matter with you, Melvin?"

The venison was not going to cure before the plane came in and Melvin knew it. He had stalled long enough.

They went a half-mile beside the lower Meadows. On the way Jaynes stepped sidewise to jump into an ant hill and twist his feet; and then he went on, stamping ants loose from his shoes. "He must be hungry enough by now."

They went back through the timber and crept behind a log on the little hill across the field from their camp. The smoky birds were having a merry time with the meat.

Now Jaynes was patient. His eyes caught every movement across the park, and his position did not seem to strain his muscles. They stayed until the shadows lowered cold upon their backs. It was then that they heard the rifle-shot somewhere in the lower Meadows, two miles away.

"He's got his own meat." Melvin laughed.

Jaynes rose. "What's so damn funny about it?"

Melvin had wrapped his undershirt around a venison haunch, but the blowflies had got to it anyway. He brushed the white larva away.

They roasted meat and ate in silence.

Marty Kaygo was still around Shewalter Meadows. They cut his sign the next day, and they found where he had killed the deer. The convict was here, and it seemed that he intended to stay.

Jaynes was infuriated. And he was speechless for a while when they returned to camp that night and found that Kaygo had stolen Melvin's sleeping bag.

"Who are the tenderfeet around here?" Melvin laughed again.

"You don't act like you want to catch him! By God, I do, and I'll stay here all summer to do it, if necessary!"

"To catch him?"

"To kill him! I'm going to gut-shoot him for this little trick!"

"You would have, anyway." There was no humor now in Kaygo's stealing the sleeping bag.

The plane came in on the afternoon of the third day. Clouds were scudding across the peaks and the pilot was in a hurry to beat out a local storm. He banked sharply to look down at the two men standing in the open dryness of the upper Meadows.

He went on east, high above the timber. They saw him fighting a tricky wind. On the next bank he kicked out the box. The parachute became a white cone. Lining out with a tailwind boosting him, the pilot sped away toward Scott.

"If he had any brains he'd've stayed to make sure we got it," Jaynes said. "Typical State employee."

A great wind-front flowing in from the mountains struck them with a chill that spoke of the rain soon to follow. Melvin watched the plane bouncing jerkily in downdrafts above the canyons. "The pilot's all right, Jaynes."

"Look at that thing drift!"

They knew for sure after another few moments that the box would not land in the upper Meadows. Melvin said, "Wouldn't it be something if it lit right at Kaygo's feet?"

"Big fine joke, huh?"

They trotted across the creek and down along the edge of the Big Shewalter to keep the 'chute in sight. They were a long way from it when they saw it splash into the water near the opposite side of the flooded area. An instant later the rain boiled down on them.

"I hope they had sense enough to put the stuff in cans." Jaynes turned up the collar of his jacket.

The ponds were dancing froth now. Through the mist they saw Kaygo run from the timber and wade out after the box.

Jaynes dropped to one knee. He pushed his 'scope down and began to click the sight-adjustment. "Eight hundred yards," he muttered. His rifle bellowed with the thunder on the mountains. "Where'd I hit?"

"I couldn't tell."

The first hard blast of rain was sweeping on. Jaynes fired again, and this time Melvin saw the bullet strike the water to the left of Kaygo, chest-deep now, towing the box to shore with the shroud-lines of the chute.

"About five feet to the left," Melvin said.

Kaygo sprawled into the grass when the next shot came.

"That did it," Melvin said.

"No! He ducked."

Kaygo raised up. Skidding the box over wet grass and mud, he reached timber while Jaynes tried two more shots. Over that distance, through wind and rain, Jaynes had performed well—but Kaygo was still free.

Kaygo's boldness was worth applause, but Melvin felt only a bleak apathy. The end had been delayed, that was all.

"Come on!" Jaynes said.

"Across that open swamp? No, thanks. We'll work through the timber."

"He's got our stuff!"

"He's got a rifle, too."

The box had been fastened with wing-nuts, easy to tap loose. The packs Melvin had asked for were gone, and the jacket, and about three-fourths of the food, Melvin estimated. The sleeping bag had been unrolled. Rain was filtering through the pines on a manila envelope containing a note.

They peered into the gloom of the wet forest. It was no time to press Kaygo hard, and they both knew it.

While Jaynes raged, Melvin read the note.

"Rudd started in at noon today with big posse. He says not to take any chances. He says there were *two* .22 pistols and a hunting knife taken from the filling station."

"That's a big help!" Jaynes cursed the weather, the pilot, and the stupidity of circumstance.

"I told you on Clover Mountain I was sick of you, Jaynes. Now shut up! You're lucky Kaygo didn't slice your sleeping bag to pieces or throw it into the water."

"I'm fed up with you, too, Melvin! You didn't even try to shoot a while ago. You act like the stinking louse is your brother!"

My brother. The thought plowed through Melvin, leaving a fresh wake. It was not fashionable to speak of men as brothers; you killed your brother, just like anybody else.

They plodded toward camp, carrying the cans of food in their hands. The labels began to soak off. Melvin finished the job on the cans he was holding.

"That's smart," Jaynes said. "Now what's in them?"

"You're right, they're no good to us any more. A hungry man has to know what he's getting." Melvin began to hurl the cans into a beaver pond, until Jaynes pleaded with him.

"Then shut your mouth for a while!" Melvin cried.

They went on to camp through a cold rain that soaked into Melvin's soul.

"Soup!" Jaynes said later, when they sat under a dripping tree before a smoking fire. "Kaygo's back in the timber having hot coffee and canned chicken."

Jaynes could not destroy everything, for he had the unrealized power to give laughter. Melvin began to laugh while Jaynes stared at him angrily. Was it the sound of laughter, as well as the smell of fire, that caused the monsters of the long-ago jungle to raise their heads in fear?

"I said I'd get Kaygo if it took all summer. You sit here and laugh some more, Melvin. *I'll get him!*"

They found the second pack the next morning, empty, hanging on a tree. "He's cached part of the grub somewhere," Jaynes growled. "He couldn't have put it all in one pack. Smart! He did it in the rain, and now we can't backtrack him."

But they could trail him in the fresh dampness. Kaygo had realized that, too; he had gone far south of the Meadows, and on a rocky ridge they lost his trail. The ridge was a great spur that ran down from Spearhead Mountain, bucking through lesser cross-ridges arrogantly. The lower end of it, Melvin knew, was not eight miles from the highway.

"Maybe he's clearing out," Jaynes said. "He read that note about Rudd. He knows he's going to get it. He's headed for the highway now. Somebody else will get him, after all we've done!"

"Pathetic, ain't it?" Melvin looked at Spearhead Mountain. "Maybe he went that way. He likes mountains."

"What do you mean?"

"Nothing you'd understand. He's gone toward Spearhead, Jaynes."

"The highway! I'm going after him, Melvin. If I don't cut his trail by the time I hit Bandbox Creek, I'll come back. Don't sneak off this time and camp by yourself. He could have walked right in on you that night."

"Yes, he could have killed me, I suppose."

Jaynes's eyes narrowed. "Those tracks beside your fire the next morning—one of yours was on top of one of his, Melvin. He sneaked in while you were asleep, didn't he? And you were ashamed to mention it to me! It's a wonder he didn't take your rifle and sleeping bag right from under you. I'll mention that to Rudd when he gets here."

"You do that, Jaynes." Harlan Rudd had shared food and fire with outlaws in the old days, and he was not ashamed to talk about it now that he was sheriff. "Get out of my sight, Jaynes, before I forget I'm a brother to you, too!"

"Brother?" Jaynes gave Melvin a baffled look before he started down the ridge.

There was something Kaygo could not have known about this ridge: It appeared to be the natural route to Spearhead, but higher up it was a jumble of tree-covered cliffs.

Melvin stayed on it only until he found where Kaygo had slipped from his careful walking on rocks and left a mark which he had tried to smooth away. Then Melvin left the ridge and took a roundabout, but faster, route toward Spearhead.

He went too rapidly. In mid-afternoon he saw Kaygo far below him, between two curving buttresses of the mountain. The fugitive was not pushing himself.

While Melvin watched through his glasses, Kaygo removed the stolen pack and lay down in a field of columbines, pillowing his head on the stolen sleeping bag. The wind was cold on Melvin's sweating skin as he hugged his vantage point behind the rocks.

Jaynes might have made a shot from here; he would have tried, although the range was four hundred yards greater than yesterday across the Big Shewalter. Melvin knew his own rifle would do no more than scare Kaygo down the hill.

Like hunting sheep, he thought. You have to wait and try to make them blunder into you.

Kaygo lay there for an hour. He was not asleep. He moved occasionally, but mostly he lay there looking at the sky and clouds.

He was wallowing in freedom; that was it. Damn him! He would not do what fugitives are supposed to do. He insisted on acting like a man enjoying life.

My brother down there, Melvin thought. Yes, and I'll kill him when he comes near enough on the saddle of the mountain.

Kaygo rose at last, but he did not go. He stretched his arms to the sky, as if he would clutch a great section of it. Then he sat down and smoked a cigarette.

The sweat was tight and dry on Melvin. The wind scampered through his clothing. Of course I have to kill him, he told himself. He's found something he loves so much he won't be taken from it any other way.

Kaygo went up at last. Melvin slipped behind the rib of the mountain and climbed steadily. The wind was growing quiet now. There was a sullen heaviness in the air. It would rain again today.

Melvin was far ahead when he took a position among rocks that overlooked the saddle. He could see Kaygo, still in no hurry, coming up the harder way, coming over a red iron dike that had made the notch on Spearhead back when man clutched his club and splashed toward refuge as the clamor broke out in the forest.

It was his job. Society paid him, Melvin reminded himself. Climb faster Marty Kaygo. You will have your chance to go back where you belong, and when you refuse the job will be done quickly.

The air grew heavily quiet. Melvin blinked when he heard a tiny snap and saw a blue spark run along his rifle barrel. He rubbed his hand against his woolen shirt. His palm crackled with pinpoint sparks and the fibers of the sleeve tried to follow the hand away. He stroked his hair and heard the little noises and felt the hair rising.

All this was not uncommon on the heights in summer when a storm was making, but Melvin had never experienced it before. It gave him a weird sensation.

Kaygo came into the saddle when the air was fully charged. He jumped when blue light ran along his rifle barrel. He was then two hundred yards away from Melvin. He would have to pass much closer. Kaygo stared in wonder at his rifle, and then at the leaden sky.

He held up his hunting knife. Sparks played upon the point. Kaygo laughed. He raised both knife and rifle and watched the electricity come to them.

A little later he discovered steel was not necessary to draw static from the swollen air. Kaygo's fingers, held aloft, drew sparks. He did a dance upon the rocks, shouting his wonder and pleasure. Strange balls of light ran along the iron dike and the air was filled with a sterile odor.

This day on Spearhead Mountain, Marty Kaygo roared with joy.

Melvin had never heard laughter run so cleanly. Laughter from the littered caves above the slime; laughter from the tree-perch safe from walking beasts; laughter challenging the brutes . . .

It did not last. The rain came just after the first whistling surge of wind. The bursting air cleared.

Kaygo trotted easily for shelter, his head lowered against the pelt of ice. He came straight toward the rocks where Melvin lay. There was a clatter somewhere behind Melvin, granite slipping on granite, but he had no time to wonder.

"Kaygo!" he yelled. "Drop it!"

The man threw up his head as he ran and he brought the rifle up, not hesitating.

My brother, Melvin thought. That held him one split second longer, with his finger on the trigger and his sights on Kaygo's chest.

Another rifle roared behind him. Kaygo's legs jerked as he tried to keep running. He went down and his hands reached out for the wet stones. That was all.

Jaynes came limping through the rocks. "I hurt my knee, but I got him, rain and all!"

Melvin could not rise for a moment. He felt frozen to the rock.

At last he came up, slowly.

"You were right," Jaynes said. "He took the hard way. After I left you I got to thinking that was what he would do."

They went across the stones to Kaygo. Jaynes turned him over. "Heart. I said I didn't miss running shots, not very often." That was all the interest he had in Marty Kaygo; and now that vanished, too.

Jaynes slipped the pack from the dead man's back. "Steal our chow, would he! Grab your sleeping bag and let's get out of here. Rudd and the others can take care of the chores now. Four for four, Melvin."

"You're counting Strothers?"

"I wish that big-mouth had tried something."

The rain was the coldest that ever fell on Melvin. He unrolled the sleeping bag and covered Kaygo with it, weighting the sides with stones.

Jaynes started to protest, but near the end he helped. "I guess even Kaygo deserves something. He wasn't a bad-looking character at that, was he?"

All this time Melvin had not looked at Jaynes. Now he picked up Jaynes's rifle. Deliberately, Melvin began to smash it against a rock. He splintered the stock and the forestock. He bent the bolt and he battered the 'scope until it was a twisted tube hanging by one mount, and he continued to beat the breech against the rock until the front sight ripped his palm and the impacts numbed his wrists.

He dropped the rifle then and stood breathing hard.

Jaynes had cursed loudly at first, but then he had stopped. The hard glitter was gone from his eyes.

Now, in the voice of a man who lives with splinters in his soul, Jaynes said, "By God, you're going to buy me a new rifle, Melvin. What's the matter with you, anyway?"

Melvin said nothing. Then together they started down the rain-soaked mountain . . .

THREE-TEN TO YUMA
BY ELMORE LEONARD
(3:10 to Yuma)

*Several of the fine novels and stories of Elmore Leonard (b. 1925)
have been the basis for films, among them the classic* Hombre *(1967;
from the novel of the same title),* Valdez Is Coming *(1971; also from the
novel of the same title), and* The Tall T *(1957; from the story entitled
"The Hostage"). The film version of* 3:10 to Yuma *(1957) certainly
ranks with* Hombre *as a Western classic; and the short story—one of
Leonard's early efforts, having been first published in 1953, the year
before his maiden novel,* The Bounty Hunters, *appeared—is every bit as
well crafted and powerful. You'll not soon forget this tense tale of a
deputy marshal named Scallen who undertakes the deadly job of deliver-
ing a killer to the Yuma penitentiary.*

He had picked up his prisoner at Fort Huachuca shortly after midnight
and now, in a silent early morning mist, they approached Contention.
The two riders moved slowly, one behind the other.

Entering Stockman Street, Paul Scallen glanced back at the open
country with the wet haze blanketing its flatness, thinking of the long
night ride from Huachuca, relieved that this much was over. When his
body turned again, his hand moved over the sawed-off shotgun that was
across his lap and he kept his eyes on the man ahead of him until they
were near the end of the second block, opposite the side entrance of
the Republic Hotel.

He said just above a whisper, though it was clear in the silence, "End
of the line."

The man turned in his saddle, looking at Scallen curiously, "The
jail's around on Commercial."

"I want you to be comfortable."

Scallen stepped out of the saddle, lifting a Winchester from the boot, and walked toward the hotel's side door. A figure stood in the gloom of the doorway, behind the screen, and as Scallen reached the steps the screen door opened.

"Are you the marshal?"

"Yes, sir." Scallen's voice was soft and without emotion. "Deputy, from Bisbee."

"We're ready for you. Two-oh-seven. A corner . . . fronts on Commercial." He sounded proud of the accommodation.

"You're Mr. Timpey?"

The man in the doorway looked surprised. "Yeah, Wells Fargo. Who'd you expect?"

"You might have got a back room, Mr. Timpey. One with no windows." He swung the shotgun on the man still mounted. "Step down easy, Jim."

The man, who was in his early twenties, a few years younger than Scallen, sat with one hand over the other on the saddle horn. Now he gripped the horn and swung down. When he was on the ground his hands were still close together, iron manacles holding them three chain lengths apart. Scallen motioned him toward the door with the stubby barrel of the shotgun.

"Anyone in the lobby?"

"The desk clerk," Timpey answered him, "and a man in a chair by the front door."

"Who is he?"

"I don't know. He's asleep . . . got his brim down over his eyes."

"Did you see anyone out on Commercial?"

"No . . . I haven't been out there." At first he had seemed nervous, but now he was irritated, and a frown made his face pout childishly.

Scallen said calmly, "Mr. Timpey, it was your line this man robbed. You want to see him go all the way to Yuma, don't you?"

"Certainly I do." His eyes went to the outlaw, Jim Kidd, then back to Scallen hurriedly. "But why all the melodrama? The man's under arrest—already been sentenced."

"But he's not in jail till he walks through the gates at Yuma," Scallen said. "I'm only one man, Mr. Timpey, and I've got to get him there."

"Well, dammit . . . I'm not the law! Why didn't you bring men with you? All I know is I got a wire from our Bisbee office to get a hotel room and meet you here the morning of November third. There weren't any instructions that I had to get myself deputized a marshal. That's your job."

"I know it is, Mr. Timpey," Scallen said, and smiled, though it was an effort. "But I want to make sure no one knows Jim Kidd's in Contention until after train time this afternoon."

Jim Kidd had been looking from one to the other with a faintly amused grin. Now he said to Timpey, "He means he's afraid somebody's going to jump him." He smiled at Scallen. "That marshal must've really sold you a bill of goods."

"What's he talking about?" Timpey said.

Kidd went on before Scallen could answer. "They hid me in the Huachuca lock-up 'cause they knew nobody could get at me there . . . and finally the Bisbee marshal gets a plan. He and some others hopped the train in Benson last night, heading for Yuma with an army prisoner passed off as me." Kidd laughed, as if the idea were ridiculous.

"Is that right?" Timpey said.

Scallen nodded. "Pretty much right."

"How does he know all about it?"

"He's got ears and ten fingers to add with."

"I don't like it. Why just one man?"

"Every deputy from here down to Bisbee is out trying to scare up the rest of them. Jim here's the only one we caught," Scallen explained— then added, "Alive."

Timpey shot a glance at the outlaw. "Is he the one who killed Dick Moons?"

"One of the passengers swears he saw who did it . . . and he didn't identify Kidd at the trial."

Timpey shook his head. "Dick drove for us a long time. You know his brother lives here in Contention. When he heard about it he almost went crazy." He hesitated, and then said again, "I don't like it."

Scallen felt his patience wearing away, but he kept his voice even when he said, "Maybe I don't either . . . but what you like and what I like aren't going to matter a whole lot, with the marshal past Tucson by now. You can grumble about it all you want, Mr. Timpey, as long as you keep it under your breath. Jim's got friends . . . and since I have to haul him clear across the territory, I'd just as soon they didn't know about it."

Timpey fidgeted nervously. "I don't see why I have to get dragged into this. My job's got nothing to do with law enforcement . . ."

"You have the room key?"

"In the door. All I'm responsible for is the stage run between here and Tucson—"

Scallen shoved the Winchester at him. "If you'll take care of this and the horses till I get back, I'll be obliged to you . . . and I know I don't have to ask you not to mention we're at the hotel."

He waved the shotgun and nodded and Jim Kidd went ahead of him through the side door into the hotel lobby. Scallen was a stride behind him, holding the stubby shotgun close to his leg. "Up the stairs on the right, Jim."

Kidd started up, but Scallen paused to glance at the figure in the arm chair near the front. He was sitting on his spine with limp hands folded on his stomach and, as Timpey had described, his hat low over the upper part of his face. *You've seen people sleeping in hotel lobbies before*, Scallen told himself, and followed Kidd up the stairs. He couldn't stand and wonder about it.

Room 207 was narrow and high-ceilinged, with a single window looking down on Commercial Street. An iron bed was placed the long way against one wall and extended to the right side of the window, and along the opposite wall was a dresser with wash basin and pitcher and next to it a rough-board wardrobe. An unpainted table and two straight chairs took up most of the remaining space.

"Lay down on the bed if you want to," Scallen said.

"Why don't you sleep?" Kidd asked. "I'll hold the shotgun."

The deputy moved one of the straight chairs near to the door and the other to the side of the table opposite the bed. Then he sat down, resting the shotgun on the table so that it pointed directly at Jim Kidd sitting on the edge of the bed near the window.

He gazed vacantly outside. A patch of dismal sky showed above the frame buildings across the way, but he was not sitting close enough to look directly down onto the street. He said, indifferently, "I think it's going to rain."

There was a silence, and then Scallen said, "Jim, I don't have anything against you personally . . . this is what I get paid for, but I just want it understood that if you start across the seven feet between us, I'm going to pull both triggers at once—without first asking you to stop. That clear?"

Kidd looked at the deputy marshal, then his eyes drifted out the window again. "It's kinda cold, too." He rubbed his hands together and the three chain links rattled against each other. "The window's open a crack. Can I close it?"

Scallen's grip tightened on the shotgun and he brought the barrel up, though he wasn't aware of it. "If you can reach it from where you're sitting."

Kidd looked at the window sill and said without reaching toward it, "Too far."

"All right," Scallen said, rising. "Lay back on the bed." He worked his gun belt around so that now the Colt was on his left hip.

Kidd went back slowly, smiling. "You don't take any chances, do you? Where's your sporting blood?"

"Down in Bisbee with my wife and three youngsters," Scallen told him without smiling, and moved around the table.

There were no grips on the window frame. Standing with his side to the window, facing the man on the bed, he put the heel of his hand on the bottom ledge of the frame and shoved down hard. The window banged shut and with the slam he saw Jim Kidd kicking up off of his back, his body straining to rise without his hands to help. Momentarily, Scallen hesitated and his finger tensed on the triggers. Kidd's feet were on the floor, his body swinging up and his head down to lunge from the bed. Scallen took one step and brought his knee up hard against Kidd's face.

The outlaw went back across the bed, his head striking the wall. He lay there with his eyes open looking at Scallen.

"Feel better now, Jim?"

Kidd brought his hands up to his mouth, working the jaw around. "Well, I had to try you out," he said. "I didn't think you'd shoot."

"But you know I will the next time."

For a few minutes Kidd remained motionless. Then he began to pull himself straight. "I just want to sit up."

Behind the table, Scallen said, "Help yourself." He watched Kidd stare out the window.

Then, "How much do you make, Marshal?" Kidd asked the question abruptly.

"I don't think it's any of your business."

"What difference does it make?"

Scallen hesitated. "A hundred and fifty a month," he said, finally, "some expenses, and a dollar bounty for every arrest against a Bisbee ordinance in the town limits."

Kidd shook his head sympathetically. "And you got a wife and three kids."

"Well, it's more than a cowhand makes."

"But you're not a cowhand."

"I've worked my share of beef."

"Forty a month and keep, huh?" Kidd laughed.

"That's right, forty a month," Scallen said. He felt awkward. "How much do you make?"

Kidd grinned. When he smiled he looked very young, hardly out of his teens. "Name a month," he said. "It varies."

"But you've made a lot of money."

"Enough. I can buy what I want."

"What are you going to be wanting the next five years?"

"You're pretty sure we're going to Yuma."

"And you're pretty sure we're not," Scallen said. "Well, I've got two train passes and a shotgun that says we are. What've you got?"

Kidd smiled. "You'll see." Then he said right after it, his tone changing, "What made you join the law?"

"The money," Scallen answered, and felt foolish as he said it. But he went on, "I was working for a spread over by the Pantano Wash when Old Nana broke loose and raised hell up the Santa Rosa Valley. The army was going around in circles, so the Pima County marshal got up a bunch to help out and we tracked Apaches almost all spring. The marshal and I got along fine, so he offered me a deputy job if I wanted it." He wanted to say that he had started for seventy-five and worked up to the one hundred and fifty, but he didn't.

"And then someday you'll get to be marshal and make two hundred."

"Maybe."

"And then one night a drunk cowhand you've never seen will be tearing up somebody's saloon and you'll go in to arrest him and he'll drill you with a lucky shot before you get your gun out."

"So you're telling me I'm crazy."

"If you don't already know it."

Scallen took his hand off the shotgun and pulled tobacco and paper from his shirt pocket and began rolling a cigarette. "Have you figured out yet what my price is?"

Kidd looked startled, momentarily, but the grin returned. "No, I haven't. Maybe you come higher than I thought."

Scallen scratched a match across the table, lighted the cigarette, then threw it to the floor, between Kidd's boots. "You don't have enough money, Jim."

Kidd shrugged, then reached down for the cigarette. "You've treated me pretty good. I just wanted to make it easy on you."

The sun came into the room after a while. Weakly at first, cold and hazy. Then it warmed and brightened and cast an oblong patch of light between the bed and the table. The morning wore on slowly because there was nothing to do and each man sat restlessly thinking about somewhere else, though it was a restlessness within and it showed on neither of them.

The deputy rolled cigarettes for the outlaw and himself and most of the time they smoked in silence. Once Kidd asked him what time the train left. He told him shortly after three, but Kidd made no comment.

Scallen went to the window and looked out at the narrow rutted road that was Commercial Street. He pulled a watch from his vest pocket and looked at it. It was almost noon, yet there were few people about. He wondered about this and asked himself if it was unnaturally quiet for a Saturday noon in Contention . . . or if it were just his nerves . . .

He studied the man standing under the wooden awning across the street, leaning idly against a support post with his thumbs hooked in his belt and his flat-crowned hat on the back of his head. There was something familiar about him. And each time Scallen had gone to the window—a few times during the past hour—the man had been there.

He glanced at Jim Kidd lying across the bed, then looked out the window in time to see another man moving up next to the one at the post. They stood together for the space of a minute before the second man turned a horse from the tie rail, swung up and rode off down the street.

The man at the post watched him go and tilted his hat against the sun glare. And then it registered. With the hat low on his forehead Scallen saw him again as he had that morning. The man lying in the arm chair . . . as if asleep.

He saw his wife, then, and the three youngsters and he could almost feel the little girl sitting on his lap where she had climbed up to kiss him good-bye, and he had promised to bring her something from Tucson. He didn't know why they had come to him all of a sudden. And after he had put them out of his mind, since there was no room now, there was an upset feeling inside as if he had swallowed something that would not go down all the way. It made his heart beat a little faster.

Jim Kidd was smiling up at him. "Anybody I know?"

"I didn't think it showed."

"Like the sun going down."

Scallen glanced at the man across the street and then to Jim Kidd. "Come here." He nodded to the window. "Tell me who your friend is over there."

Kidd half rose and leaned over looking out the window, then sat down again. "Charlie Prince."

"Somebody else just went for help."

"Charlie doesn't need help."

"How did you know you were going to be in Contention?"

"You told that Wells Fargo man I had friends . . . and about the posses chasing around in the hills. Figure it out for yourself. You could be looking out a window in Benson and seeing the same thing."

"They're not going to do you any good."

"I don't know any man who'd get himself killed for a hundred and fifty dollars." Kidd paused. "Especially a man with a wife and young ones . . ."

Men rode to town in something less than an hour later. Scallen heard the horses coming up Commercial, and went to the window to see the six riders pull to a stop and range themselves in a line in the middle of the street facing the hotel. Charlie Prince stood behind them, leaning against the post.

Then he moved away from it, leisurely, and stepped down into the street. He walked between the horses and stopped in front of them just below the window. He cupped his hands to his mouth and shouted, *"Jim!"*

In the quiet street it was like a pistol shot.

Scallen looked at Kidd, seeing the smile that softened his face and was even in his eyes. Confidence. It was all over him. And even with the manacles on, you would believe that it was Jim Kidd who was holding the shotgun.

"What do you want me to tell him?" Kidd said.

"Tell him you'll write every day."

Kidd laughed and went to the window, pushing it up by the top of the frame. It raised a few inches. Then he moved his hands under the window and it slid up all the way.

"Charlie, you go buy the boys a drink. We'll be down shortly."

"Are you all right?"

"Sure I'm all right."

Charlie Prince hesitated. "What if you don't come down? He could kill you and say you tried to break . . . Jim, you tell him what'll happen if we hear a gun go off."

"He knows," Kidd said, and closed the window. He looked at Scallen standing motionless with the shotgun under his arm. "Your turn, Marshal."

"What do you expect me to say?"

"Something that makes sense. You said before I didn't mean a thing to you personally—what you're doing is just a job. Well, you figure out if it's worth getting killed for. All you have to do is throw your guns on the bed and let me walk out the door and you can go back to Bisbee and arrest all the drunks you want. Nobody's going to blame you with the odds stacked seven to one. You know your wife's not going to complain . . ."

"You should have been a lawyer, Jim."

The smile began to fade from Kidd's face. "Come on—what's it going to be?"

The door rattled with three knocks in quick succession. Abruptly the room was silent. The two men looked at each other and now the smile disappeared from Kidd's face completely.

Scallen moved to the side of the door, tip-toeing in his high-heeled boots, then pointed his shotgun toward the bed. Kidd sat down.

"Who is it?"

For a moment there was no answer. Then he heard, "Timpey."

He glanced at Kidd who was watching him. "What do you want?"

"I've got a pot of coffee for you."

Scallen hesitated. "You alone?"

"Of course I am. Hurry up, it's hot!"

He drew the key from his coat pocket, then held the shotgun in the crook of his arm as he inserted the key with one hand and turned the knob with the other. The door opened—and slammed against him, knocking him back against the dresser. He went off balance, sliding into the wardrobe, going down on his hands and knees, and the shotgun clattered across the floor to the window. He saw Jim Kidd drop to the floor for the gun . . .

"Hold it!"

A heavyset man stood in the doorway with a Colt pointing out past the thick bulge of his stomach. "Leave that shotgun where it is." Timpey stood next to him with the coffeepot in his hand. There was coffee down the front of his suit, on the door and on the flooring. He brushed at the front of his coat feebly, looking from Scallen to the man with the pistol.

"I couldn't help it, Marshal—he made me do it. He threatened to do something to me if I didn't."

"Who is he?"

"Bob Moons . . . you know, Dick's brother . . ."

The heavyset man glanced at Timpey angrily. "Shut your damn whining." His eyes went to Jim Kidd and held there. "You know who I am, don't you?"

Kidd looked uninterested. "You don't resemble anybody I know."

"You didn't have to know Dick to shoot him!"

"I didn't shoot that messenger."

Scallen got to his feet, looking at Timpey. "What the hell's wrong with you?"

"I couldn't help it. He forced me."

"How did he know we were here?"

"He came in this morning talking about Dick and I felt he needed some cheering up, so I told him Jim Kidd had been tried and was being taken to Yuma and was here in town . . . on his way. Bob didn't say anything and went out, and a little later he came back with the gun."

"You damn fool." Scallen shook his head wearily.

"Never mind all the talk." Moons kept the pistol on Kidd. "I would've found him sooner or later. This way, everybody gets saved a long train ride."

"You pull that trigger," Scallen said, "and you'll hang for murder."

"Like he did for killing Dick . . ."

"A jury said he didn't do it." Scallen took a step toward the big man. "And I'm damned if I'm going to let you pass another sentence."

"You stay put or I'll pass sentence on you!"

Scallen moved a slow step nearer. "Hand me the gun, Bob."

"I'm warning you—get the hell out of the way and let me do what I came for."

"Bob, hand me the gun or I swear I'll beat you through that wall."

Scallen tensed to take another step, another slow one. He saw Moons' eyes dart from him to Kidd and in that instant he knew it would be his only chance. He lunged, swinging his coat aside with his hand and when the hand came up it was holding a Colt. All in one motion. The pistol went up and chopped an arc across Moons' head before the big man could bring his own gun around. His hat flew off as the barrel swiped his skull and he went back against the wall heavily, then sank to the floor.

Scallen wheeled to face the window, thumbing the hammer back. But Kidd was still sitting on the edge of the bed with the shotgun at his feet.

The deputy relaxed, letting the hammer ease down. "You might have made it, that time."

Kidd shook his head. "I wouldn't have got off the bed." There was a note of surprise in his voice. "You know, you're pretty good . . ."

At two-fifteen Scallen looked at his watch, then stood up, pushing the chair back. The shotgun was under his arm. In less than an hour they would leave the hotel, walk over Commercial to Stockman and then up Stockman to the station. Three blocks. He wanted to go all the way. He wanted to get Jim Kidd on that train . . . but he was afraid.

He was afraid of what he might do once they were on the street. Even now his breath was short and occasionally he would inhale and let the air out slowly to calm himself. And he kept asking himself if it was worth it.

People would be in the windows and the doors though you wouldn't see them. They'd have their own feelings and most of their hearts would be pounding . . . and they'd edge back of the door frames a little more. The man out on the street was something without a human nature or a personality of its own. He was on a stage. The street was another world.

Timpey sat on the chair in front of the door and next to him, squatting on the floor with his back against the wall, was Moons. Scallen had unloaded Moons' pistol and placed it in the pitcher behind him. Kidd was on the bed.

Most of the time he stared at Scallen. His face bore a puzzled expression, making his eyes frown, and sometimes he would cock his head as if studying the deputy from a different angle.

Scallen stepped to the window now. Charlie Prince and another man were under the awning. The others were not in sight.

"You haven't changed your mind?" Kidd asked him seriously.

Scallen shook his head.

"I don't understand you. You risk your neck to save my life, now you'll risk it again to send me to prison."

Scallen looked at Kidd and suddenly felt closer to him than any man he knew. "Don't ask me, Jim," he said, and sat down again.

After that he looked at his watch every few minutes.

At five minutes to three he walked to the door, motioning Timpey aside, and turned the key in the lock. "Let's go, Jim." When Kidd was next to him he prodded Moons with the gun barrel. "Over on the bed. Mister, if I see or hear about you on the street before train time, you'll face an attempted murder charge." He motioned Kidd past him, then stepped into the hall and locked the door.

They went down the stairs and crossed the lobby to the front door, Scallen a stride behind with the shotgun barrel almost touching Kidd's back. Passing through the doorway he said as calmly as he could, "Turn left on Stockman and keep walking. No matter what you hear, keep walking."

As they stepped out into Commercial, Scallen glanced at the ramada where Charlie Prince had been standing, but now the saloon porch was an empty shadow. Near the corner, two horses stood under a sign that said *Eat*, in red letters; and on the other side of Stockman the signs continued, lining the rutted main street to make it seem narrower. And beneath the signs, in the shadows, nothing moved. There was a whisper of wind along the ramadas. It whipped sand specks from the street and rattled them against clapboard, and the sound was hollow and lifeless. Somewhere a screen door banged, far away.

They passed the cafe, turning onto Stockman. Ahead, the deserted street narrowed with distance to a dead end at the rail station—a single-story building standing by itself, low and sprawling with most of the platform in shadow. The westbound was there, along the platform, but the engine and most of the cars were hidden by the station house. White steam lifted above the roof to be lost in the sun's glare.

They were almost to the platform when Kidd said over his shoulder, "Run like hell while you're still able."

"Where are they?"

Kidd grinned, because he knew Scallen was afraid. "How should I know?"

"Tell them to come out in the open!"

"Tell them yourself."

"Dammit, *tell* them!" Scallen clenched his jaw and jabbed the short barrel into Kidd's back. "I'm not fooling. If they don't come out, I'll kill you!"

Kidd felt the gun barrel hard against his spine and suddenly he shouted, "Charlie!"

It echoed in the street, but after there was only the silence. Kidd's eyes darted over the shadowed porches. "Dammit, Charlie—hold on!"

Scallen prodded him up the warped plank steps to the shade of the platform and suddenly he could feel them near. "Tell him again!"

"Don't shoot, Charlie!" Kidd screamed the words.

From the other side of the station they heard the trainman's call trailing off, ". . . Gila Bend. Sentinel, Yuma!"

The whistle sounded loud, wailing, as they passed into the shade of the platform, then out again to the naked glare of the open side. Scallen squinted, glancing toward the station office, but the train dispatcher was not in sight. Nor was anyone. "It's the mail car," he said to Kidd. "The second to last one." Steam hissed from the iron cylinder of the engine, clouding that end of the platform. "Hurry it up!" he snapped, pushing Kidd along.

Then, from behind, hurried footsteps sounded on the planking, and, as the hiss of steam died away—"Stand where you are!"

The locomotive's main rods strained back, rising like the legs of a grotesque grasshopper, and the wheels moved. The connecting rods stopped on an upward swing and couplings clanged down the line of cars.

"Throw the gun away, brother!"

Charlie Prince stood at the corner of the station house with a pistol in each hand. Then he moved around carefully between the two men and the train. "Throw it far away, and unhitch your belt," he said.

"Do what he says," Kidd said. "They've got you."

The others, six of them, were strung out in the dimness of the platform shed. Grim-faced, stubbles of beard, hat brims low. The man nearest Prince spat tobacco lazily.

Scallen knew fear at that moment as fear had never gripped him before; but he kept the shotgun hard against Kidd's spine. He said, just above a whisper, "Jim—I'll cut you in half!"

Kidd's body was stiff, his shoulders drawn up tightly. "Wait a minute . . ." he said. He held his palms out to Charlie Prince, though he could have been speaking to Scallen.

Suddenly Prince shouted, "Go down!"

There was a fraction of a moment of dead silence that seemed longer. Kidd hesitated. Scallen was looking at the gunman over Kidd's shoulder, seeing the two pistols. Then Kidd was gone, rolling on the planking, and the pistols were coming up, one ahead of the other. Without moving, Scallen squeezed both triggers of the scatter gun.

Charlie Prince was going down, holding his hands tight to his chest, as Scallen dropped the shotgun and swung around drawing his Colt. He fired hurriedly. *Wait for a target!* Words in his mind. He saw the men under the platform shed, three of them breaking for the station office, two going full length to the planks . . . one crouched, his pistol up. *That one! Get him quick!* Scallen aimed and squeezed the heavy revolver and the man went down. *Now get the hell out!*

Charlie Prince was face down. Kidd was crawling, crawling frantically and coming to his feet when Scallen reached him. He grabbed Kidd by the collar savagely, pushing him on and dug the pistol into his back. "Run, damn you!"

Gunfire erupted from the shed and thudded into the wooden caboose as they ran past it. The train was moving slowly. Just in front of them a bullet smashed a window of the mail car. Someone screamed, "You'll hit Jim!" There was another shot, then it was too late. Scallen and Kidd leaped up on the car platform and were in the mail car as it rumbled past the end of the station platform.

Kidd was on the floor, stretched out along a row of mail sacks. He rubbed his shoulder awkwardly with his manacled hands and watched Scallen who stood against the wall next to the open door.

Kidd studied the deputy for some minutes. Finally he said, "You know, you really earn your hundred and a half."

Scallen heard him, though the iron rhythm of the train wheels and his breathing were loud in his temples. He felt as if all his strength had been sapped, but he couldn't help smiling at Jim Kidd. He was thinking pretty much the same thing.

THE MAN WHO SHOT
LIBERTY VALANCE

BY DOROTHY M. JOHNSON
(The Man Who Shot Liberty Valance)

*The work of Dorothy M. Johnson (b. 1905) has been compared to that
of several prominent writers past and present, among them Bret Harte
and Mark Twain; but Ms. Johnson has a style and a historical vision all
her own, as is evidenced by her two outstanding collections,* Indian
Country *and* The Hanging Tree. *"The Man Who Shot Liberty Valance" (1949) is a carefully crafted and restrained tale (not so the 1962
film version with James Stewart and John Wayne) about a confrontation
between good and evil in a Montana frontier town. Two other fine
stories by Ms. Johnson have also been made into well-known films:* The
Hanging Tree *(1959; Gary Cooper's next to last Western role) and* A
Man Called Horse *(1970; starring Richard Harris).*

Bert Barricune died in 1920. Not more than a dozen persons showed
up for his funeral. Among them was an earnest young reporter who
hoped for a human-interest story; there were legends that the old man
had been something of a gunfighter in the early days. A few aging men
tiptoed in, singly or in pairs, scowling and edgy, clutching their battered hats—men who had been Bert's companions at drinking or penny
ante while the world passed them by. One woman came, wearing a
heavy veil that concealed her face. White and yellow streaks showed in
her black-dyed hair. The reporter made a mental note: Old friend from
the old District. But no story there—can't mention that.

One by one they filed past the casket, looking into the still face of
old Bert Barricune, who had been nobody. His stubbly hair was white,

and his lined face was as empty in death as his life had been. But death had added dignity.

One great spray of flowers spread behind the casket. The card read, "Senator and Mrs. Ransome Foster." There were no other flowers except, almost unnoticed, a few pale, leafless, pink and yellow blossoms scattered on the carpeted step. The reporter, squinting, finally identified them: son of a gun! Blossoms of the prickly pear. Cactus flowers. Seems suitable for the old man—flowers that grow on prairie wasteland. Well, they're free if you want to pick 'em, and Barricune's friends don't look prosperous. But how come the Senator sends a bouquet?

There was a delay, and the funeral director fidgeted a little, waiting. The reporter sat up straighter when he saw the last two mourners enter.

Senator Foster—sure, there's the crippled arm—and that must be his wife. Congress is still in session; he came all the way from Washington. Why would he bother, for an old wreck like Bert Barricune?

After the funeral was decently over, the reporter asked him. The Senator almost told the truth, but he caught himself in time. He said, "Bert Barricune was my friend for more than thirty years."

He could not give the true answer: He was my enemy; he was my conscience; he made me whatever I am.

Ransome Foster had been in the Territory for seven months when he ran into Liberty Valance. He had been afoot on the prairie for two days when he met Bert Barricune. Up to that time, Ranse Foster had been nobody in particular—a dude from the East, quietly inquisitive, moving from one shack town to another; just another tenderfoot with his own reasons for being there and no aim in life at all.

When Barricune found him on the prairie, Foster was indeed a tenderfoot. In his boots there was a warm, damp squidging where his feet had blistered, and the blisters had broken to bleed. He was bruised, sunburned, and filthy. He had been crawling, but when he saw Barricune riding toward him, he sat up. He had no horse, no saddle and, by that time, no pride.

Barricune looked down at him, not saying anything. Finally Ranse Foster asked, "Water?"

Barricune shook his head. "I don't carry none, but we can go where it is."

He stepped down from the saddle, a casual Samaritan, and with one heave pulled Foster upright.

"Git you in the saddle, can you stay there?" he inquired.

"If I can't," Foster answered through swollen lips, "shoot me."

Bert said amiably, "All right," and pulled the horse around. By twisting its ear, he held the animal quiet long enough to help the anguished stranger to the saddle. Then, on foot—and like any cowboy Bert Barricune hated walking—he led the horse five miles to the river. He let Foster lie where he fell in the cottonwood grove and brought him a hat full of water.

After that, Foster made three attempts to stand up. After the third failure, Barricune asked, grinning, "Want me to shoot you after all?"

"No," Foster answered. "There's something I want to do first."

Barricune looked at the bruises and commented, "Well, I should think so." He got on his horse and rode away. After an hour he returned with bedding and grub and asked, "Ain't you dead yet?"

The bruised and battered man opened his uninjured eye and said, "Not yet, but soon." Bert was amused. He brought a bucket of water and set up camp—a bedroll on a tarp, an armload of wood for a fire. He crouched on his heels while the tenderfoot, with cautious movements that told of pain, got his clothes off and splashed water on his body. No gunshot wounds, Barricune observed, but marks of kicks, and a couple that must have been made with a quirt.

After a while he asked, not inquisitively, but as one who has a right to know how matters stood, "Anybody looking for you?"

Foster rubbed dust from his clothes, being too full of pain to shake them.

"No," he said. "But I'm looking for somebody."

"I ain't going to help you look," Bert informed him. "Town's over that way, two miles, when you get ready to come. Cache the stuff when you leave. I'll pick it up."

Three days later they met in the town marshal's office. They glanced at each other but did not speak. This time it was Bert Barricune who was bruised, though not much. The marshal was just letting him out of the one-cell jail when Foster limped into the office. Nobody said anything until Barricune, blinking and walking not quite steadily, had left. Foster saw him stop in front of the next building to speak to a girl.

They walked away together, and it looked as if the young man were being scolded.

The marshal cleared his throat. "You wanted something, Mister?"

Foster answered, "Three men set me afoot on the prairie. Is that an offense against the law around here?"

The marshal eased himself and his stomach into a chair and frowned judiciously. "It ain't customary," he admitted. "Who was they?"

"The boss was a big man with black hair, dark eyes, and two gold teeth in front. The other two—"

"I know. Liberty Valance and a couple of his boys. Just what's your complaint, now?" Foster began to understand that no help was going to come from the marshal.

"They rob you?" the marshal asked.

"They didn't search me."

"Take your gun?"

"I didn't have one."

"Steal your horse?"

"Gave him a crack with a quirt, and he left."

"Saddle on him?"

"No. I left it out there."

The marshal shook his head. "Can't see you got any legal complaint," he said with relief. "Where was this?"

"On a road in the woods, by a creek. Two days' walk from here."

The marshal got to his feet. "You don't even know what jurisdiction it was in. They knocked you around; well, that could happen. Man gets in a fight—could happen to anybody."

Foster said dryly, "Thanks a lot."

The marshal stopped him as he reached the door. "There's a reward for Liberty Valance."

"I still haven't got a gun," Foster said. "Does he come here often?"

"Nope. Nothing he'd want in Twotrees. Hard man to find." The marshal looked Foster up and down. "He won't come after you here." It was as if he had added, *Sonny!* "Beat you up once, he won't come again for that."

And I, Foster realized, am not man enough to go after him.

"Fact is," the marshal added, "I can't think of any bait that would bring him in. Pretty quiet here. Yes sir." He put his thumbs in his galluses and looked out the window, taking credit for the quietness.

Bait, Foster thought. He went out thinking about it. For the first time in a couple of years he had an ambition—not a laudable one, but something to aim at. He was going to be the bait for Liberty Valance and, as far as he could be, the trap as well.

At the Elite Cafe he stood meekly in the doorway, hat in hand, like a man who expects and deserves to be refused anything he might ask for. Clearing his throat, he asked, "Could I work for a meal?"

The girl who was filling sugar bowls looked up and pitied him. "Why, I should think so. Mr. Anderson!" She was the girl who had walked away with Barricune, scolding him.

The proprietor came from the kitchen, and Ranse Foster repeated his question, cringing, but with a suggestion of a sneer.

"Go around back and split some wood," Anderson answered, turning back to the kitchen.

"He could just as well eat first," the waitress suggested. "I'll dish up some stew to begin with."

Ranse ate fast, as if he expected the plate to be snatched away. He knew the girl glanced at him several times, and he hated her for it. He had not counted on anyone's pitying him in his new role of sneering humility, but he knew he might as well get used to it.

When she brought his pie, she said, "If you was looking for a job . . ."

He forced himself to look at her suspiciously. "Yes?"

"You could try the Prairie Belle. I heard they needed a swamper."

Bert Barricune, riding out to the river camp for his bedroll, hardly knew the man he met there. Ranse Foster was haughty, condescending, and cringing all at once. He spoke with a faint sneer, and stood as if he expected to be kicked.

"I assumed you'd be back for your belongings," he said. "I realized that you would change your mind."

Barricune, strapping up his bedroll, looked blank. "Never changed it," he disagreed. "Doing just what I planned. I never give you my bedroll."

"Of course not, of course not," the new Ranse Foster agreed with sneering humility. "It's yours. You have every right to reclaim it."

Barricune looked at him narrowly and hoisted the bedroll to sling it up behind his saddle. "I should have left you for the buzzards," he remarked.

Foster agreed, with a smile that should have got him a fist in the teeth. "Thank you, my friend," he said with no gratitude. "Thank you for all your kindness, which I have done nothing to deserve and shall do nothing to repay."

Barricune rode off, scowling, with the memory of his good deed irritating him like lice. The new Foster followed, far behind, on foot.

Sometimes in later life Ranse Foster thought of the several men he had been through the years. He did not admire any of them very much. He was by no means ashamed of the man he finally became, except that he owed too much to other people. One man he had been when he was young, a serious student, gullible and quick-tempered. Another man had been reckless and without an aim; he went West, with two thousand dollars of his own, after a quarrel with the executor of his father's estate. That man did not last long. Liberty Valance had whipped him with a quirt and kicked him into unconsciousness, for no reason except that Liberty, meeting him and knowing him for a tenderfoot, was able to do so. That man died on the prairie. After that, there was the man who set out to be the bait that would bring Liberty Valance into Twotrees.

Ranse Foster had never hated anyone before he met Liberty Valance, but Liberty was not the last man he learned to hate. He hated the man he himself had been while he waited to meet Liberty again.

The swamper's job at the Prairie Belle was not disgraceful until Ranse Foster made it so. When he swept floors, he was so obviously contemptuous of the work and of himself for doing it that other men saw him as contemptible. He watched the customers with a curled lip as if they were beneath him. But when a poker player threw a white chip on the floor, the swamper looked at him with half-veiled hatred—and picked up the chip. They talked about him at the Prairie Belle, because he could not be ignored.

At the end of the first month, he bought a Colt .45 from a drunken cowboy who needed money worse than he needed two guns. After that, Ranse went without part of his sleep in order to walk out, seven mornings a week, to where his first camp had been and practice target shooting. And the second time he overslept from exhaustion, Joe Mosten of the Prairie Belle fired him.

"Here's your pay," Joe growled, and dropped the money on the floor.

A week passed before he got another job. He ate his meals frugally in the Elite Cafe and let himself be seen stealing scraps off plates that other diners had left. Lillian, the older of the two waitresses, yelled her disgust, but Hallie, who was young, pitied him.

"Come to the back door when it's dark," she murmured, "and I'll give you a bite. There's plenty to spare."

The second evening he went to the back door, Bert Barricune was there ahead of him. He said gently, "Hallie is my girl."

"No offense intended," Foster answered. "The young lady offered me food, and I have come to get it."

"A dog eats where it can," young Barricune drawled.

Ranse's muscles tensed and rage mounted in his throat, but he caught himself in time and shrugged. Bert said something then that scared him: "If you wanted to get talked about, it's working fine. They're talking clean over in Dunbar."

"What they do or say in Dunbar," Foster answered, "is nothing to me."

"It's where Liberty Valance hangs out," the other man said casually. "In case you care."

Ranse almost confided then, but instead said stiffly, "I do not quite appreciate your strange interest in my affairs."

Barricune pushed back his hat and scratched his head. "I don't understand it myself. But leave my girl alone."

"As charming as Miss Hallie may be," Ranse told him, "I am interested only in keeping my stomach filled."

"Then why don't you work for a living? The clerk at Dowitts' quit this afternoon."

Jake Dowitt hired him as a clerk because nobody else wanted the job.

"Read and write, do you?" Dowitt asked. "Work with figures?"

Foster drew himself up. "Sir, whatever may be said against me, I believe I may lay claim to being a scholar. That much I claim, if nothing more. I have read law."

"Maybe the job ain't good enough for you," Dowitt suggested.

Foster became humble again. "Any job is good enough for me. I will also sweep the floor."

"You will also keep up the fire in the stove," Dowitt told him. "Seven in the morning till nine at night. Got a place to live?"

"I sleep in the livery stable in return for keeping it shoveled out."

Dowitt had intended to house his clerk in a small room over the store, but he changed his mind. "Got a shed out back you can bunk in," he offered, "You'll have to clean it out first. Used to keep chickens there."

"There is one thing," Foster said. "I want two half-days off a week."

Dowitt looked over the top of his spectacles. "Now what would you do with time off? Never mind. You can have it—for less pay. I give you a discount on what you buy in the store."

The only purchase Foster made consisted of four boxes of cartridges a week.

In the store, he weighed salt pork as if it were low stuff but himself still lower, humbly measured lengths of dress goods for the women customers. He added vanity to his other unpleasantnesses and let customers discover him combing his hair admiringly before a small mirror. He let himself be seen reading a small black book, which aroused curiosity.

It was while he worked at the store that he started Twotrees' first school. Hallie was responsible for that. Handing him a plate heaped higher than other customers got at the café, she said gently, "You're a learned man, they say, Mr. Foster."

With Hallie he could no longer sneer or pretend humility, for Hallie was herself humble, as well as gentle and kind. He protected himself from her by not speaking unless he had to.

He answered, "I have had advantages, Miss Hallie, before fate brought me here."

"That book you read," she asked wistfully, "what's it about?"

"It was written by a man named Plato," Ranse told her stiffly. "It was written in Greek."

She brought him a cup of coffee, hesitated for a moment, and then asked, "You can read and write American, too, can't you?"

"English, Miss Hallie," he corrected. "English is our mother tongue. I am quite familiar with English."

She put her red hands on the cafe counter. "Mr. Foster," she whispered, "will you teach me to read?"

He was too startled to think of an answer she could not defeat.

"Bert wouldn't like it," he said. "You're a grown woman besides. It wouldn't look right for you to be learning to read now."

She shook her head. "I can't learn any younger." She sighed. "I always wanted to know how to read and write." She walked away toward the kitchen, and Ranse Foster was struck with an emotion he knew he could not afford. He was swept with pity. He called her back.

"Miss Hallie. Not you alone—people would talk about you. But if you brought Bert—"

"Bert can already read some. He don't care about it. But there's some kids in town." Her face was so lighted that Ranse looked away.

He still tried to escape. "Won't you be ashamed, learning with children?"

"Why, I'll be proud to learn any way at all," she said.

He had three little girls, two restless little boys, and Hallie in Twotrees' first school sessions—one hour each afternoon, in Dowitt's storeroom. Dowitt did not dock his pay for the time spent, but he puzzled a great deal. So did the children's parents. The children themselves were puzzled at some of the things he read aloud, but they were patient. After all, lessons lasted only an hour.

"When you are older, you will understand this," he promised, not looking at Hallie, and then he read Shakespeare's sonnet that begins:

> *No longer mourn for me when I am dead*
> *Than you shall hear the surly sullen bell . . .*

and ends:

> *Do not so much as my poor name rehearse,*
> *But let your love even with my life decay,*
> *Lest the wise world should look into your moan*
> *And mock you with me after I am gone.*

Hallie understood the warning, he knew. He read another sonnet, too:

> *When in disgrace with Fortune and men's eyes,*
> *I all alone beweep my outcast state . . .*

and carefully did not look up at her as he finished it:

> For thy sweet love remember'd such wealth brings
> That then I scorn to change my state with kings.

Her earnestness in learning was distasteful to him—the anxious way she grasped a pencil and formed letters, the little gasp with which she always began to read aloud. Twice he made her cry, but she never missed a lesson.

He wished he had a teacher for his own learning, but he could not trust anyone, and so he did his lessons alone. Bert Barricune caught him at it on one of those free afternoons when Foster, on a horse from the livery stable, had ridden miles out of town to a secluded spot.

Ranse Foster had an empty gun in his hand when Barricune stepped out from behind a sandstone column and remarked, "I've seen better."

Foster whirled, and Barricune added, "I could have been somebody else—and your gun's empty."

"When I see somebody else, it won't be," Foster promised.

"If you'd asked me," Barricune mused, "I could've helped you. But you didn't want no helping. A man shouldn't be ashamed to ask somebody that knows better than him." His gun was suddenly in his hand, and five shots cracked their echoes around the skull-white sandstone pillars. Half an inch above each of five cards that Ranse had tacked to a dead tree, at the level of a man's waist, a splintered hole appeared in the wood. "Didn't want to spoil your targets," Barricune explained.

"I'm not ashamed to ask you," Foster told him angrily, "since you know so much. I shoot straight but slow. I'm asking you now."

Barricune, reloading his gun, shook his head. "It's kind of late for that. I come out to tell you that Liberty Valance is in town. He's interested in the dude that anybody can kick around—this here tenderfoot that boasts how he can read Greek."

"Well," said Foster softly. "Well, so the time has come."

"Don't figure you're riding into town with me," Bert warned. "You're coming all by yourself."

Ranse rode into town with his gun belt buckled on. Always before, he had carried it wrapped in a slicker. In town, he allowed himself the luxury of one last vanity. He went to the barbershop, neither sneering nor cringing, and said sharply, "Cut my hair. Short."

The barber was nervous, but he worked understandably fast.

"Thought you was partial to that long wavy hair of yourn," he remarked.

"I don't know why you thought so," Foster said coldly.

Out in the street again, he realized that he did not know how to go about the job. He did not know where Liberty Valance was, and he was determined not to be caught like a rat. He intended to look for Liberty.

Joe Mosten's right-hand man was lounging at the door of the Prairie Belle. He moved over to bar the way.

"Not in there, Foster," he said gently. It was the first time in months that Ranse Foster had heard another man address him respectfully. His presence was recognized—as a menace to the fixtures of the Prairie Belle.

When I die, sometime today, he thought, they won't say I was a coward. They may say I was a damn fool, but I won't care by that time.

"Where is he?" Ranse asked.

"I couldn't tell you that," the man said apologetically. "I'm young and healthy, and where he is is none of my business. Joe'd be obliged if you stay out of the bar, that's all."

Ranse looked across toward Dowitt's store. The padlock was on the door. He glanced north, toward the marshal's office.

"That's closed, too," the saloon man told him courteously. "Marshal was called out of town an hour ago."

Ranse threw back his head and laughed. The sound echoed back from the false-fronted buildings across the street. There was nobody walking in the street; there were not even any horses tied to the hitching racks.

"Send Liberty word," he ordered in the tone of one who has a right to command. "Tell him the tenderfoot wants to see him again."

The saloon man cleared his throat. "Guess it won't be necessary. That's him coming down at the end of the street, wouldn't you say?"

Ranse looked, knowing the saloon man was watching him curiously.

"I'd say it is," he agreed. "Yes, I'd say that was Liberty Valance."

"I'll be going inside now," the other man remarked apologetically. "Well, take care of yourself." He was gone without a sound.

This is the classic situation, Ranse realized. Two enemies walking to meet each other along the dusty, waiting street of a western town. What reasons other men have had, I will never know. There are so many things I have never learned! And now there is no time left.

He was an actor who knew the end of the scene but had forgotten the lines and never knew the cue for them. One of us ought to say something, he realized. I should have planned this all out in advance. But all I ever saw was the end of it.

Liberty Valance, burly and broad-shouldered, walked stiff-legged, with his elbows bent.

When he is close enough for me to see whether he is smiling, Ranse Foster thought, somebody's got to speak.

He looked into his own mind and realized, This man is afraid, this Ransome Foster. But nobody else knows it. He walks and is afraid, but he is no coward. Let them remember that. Let Hallie remember that.

Liberty Valance gave the cue. "Looking for me?" he called between his teeth. He was grinning.

Ranse was almost grateful to him; it was as if Liberty had said, The time is now!

"I owe you something," Ranse answered. "I want to pay my debt."

Liberty's hand flashed with his own. The gun in Foster's hand exploded, and so did the whole world.

Two shots to my one, he thought—his last thought for a while.

He looked up at a strange, unsteady ceiling and a face that wavered like a reflection in water. The bed beneath him swung even after he closed his eyes. Far away someone said, "Shove some more cloth in the wound. It slows the bleeding."

He knew with certain agony where the wound was—in his right shoulder. When they touched it, he heard himself cry out.

The face that wavered above him was a new one, Bert Barricune's.

"He's dead," Barricune said.

Foster answered from far away, "I am not."

Barricune said, "I didn't mean you."

Ranse turned his head away from the pain, and the face that had shivered above him before was Hallie's, white and big-eyed. She put a hesitant hand on his, and he was annoyed to see that hers was trembling.

"Are you shaking," he asked, "because there's blood on my hands?"

"No," she answered. "It's because they might have been getting cold."

He was aware then that other people were in the room; they stirred and moved aside as the doctor entered.

"Maybe you're gonna keep that arm," the doctor told him at last. "But it's never gonna be much use to you."

The trial was held three weeks after the shooting, in the hotel room where Ranse lay in bed. The charge was disturbing the peace; he pleaded guilty and was fined ten dollars.

When the others had gone, he told Bert Barricune, "There was a reward, I heard. That would pay the doctor and the hotel."

"You ain't going to collect it," Bert informed him. "It'd make you too big for your britches." Barricune sat looking at him for a moment and then remarked, "You didn't kill Liberty."

Foster frowned. "They buried him."

"Liberty fired once. You fired once and missed. I fired once, and I don't generally miss. I ain't going to collect the reward, neither. Hallie don't hold with violence."

Foster said thoughtfully, "That was all I had to be proud of."

"You faced him," Barricune said. "You went to meet him. If you got to be proud of something, you can remember that. It's a fact you ain't got much else."

Ranse looked at him with narrowed eyes. "Bert, are you a friend of mine?"

Bert smiled without humor. "You know I ain't. I picked you up off the prairie, but I'd do that for the lowest scum that crawls. I wisht I hadn't."

"Then why—"

Bert looked at the toe of his boot. "Hallie likes you. I'm a friend of Hallie's. That's all I ever will be, long as you're around."

Ranse said, "Then I shot Liberty Valance." That was the nearest he ever dared come to saying "Thank you." And that was when Bert Barricune started being his conscience, his Nemesis, his lifelong enemy and the man who made him great.

"Would she be happy living back East?" Foster asked. "There's money waiting for me there if I go back."

Bert answered, "What do you think?" He stood up and stretched. "You got quite a problem, ain't you? You could solve it easy by just going back alone. There ain't much a man can do here with a crippled arm."

He went out and shut the door behind him.

There is always a way out, Foster thought, if a man wants to take it. Bert had been his way out when he met Liberty on the street of Twotrees. To go home was the way out of this.

I learned to live without pride, he told himself. I could learn to forget about Hallie.

When she came, between the dinner dishes and setting the tables for supper at the café, he told her.

She did not cry. Sitting in the chair beside his bed, she winced and jerked one hand in protest when he said, "As soon as I can travel, I'll be going back where I came from."

She did not argue. She said only, "I wish you good luck, Ransome. Bert and me, we'll look after you long as you stay. And remember you after you're gone."

"How will you remember me?" he demanded harshly.

As his student she had been humble, but as a woman she had her pride. "Don't ask that," she said, and got up from the chair.

"Hallie, Hallie," he pleaded, "how can I stay? How can I earn a living?"

She said indignantly, as if someone else had insulted him, "Ranse Foster, I just guess you could do anything you wanted to."

"Hallie," he said gently, "sit down."

He never really wanted to be outstanding. He had two aims in life: to make Hallie happy and to keep Bert Barricune out of trouble. He defended Bert on charges ranging from drunkenness to stealing cattle, and Bert served time twice.

Ranse Foster did not want to run for judge, but Bert remarked, "I think Hallie would kind of like it if you was His Honor." Hallie was pleased but not surprised when he was elected. Ranse was surprised but not pleased.

He was not eager to run for the legislature—that was after the Territory became a state—but there was Bert Barricune in the background, never urging, never advising, but watching with half-closed, bloodshot eyes. Bert Barricune, who never amounted to anything, but never intruded, was a living, silent reminder of three debts: a hat full of water under the cottonwoods, gunfire in a dusty street, and Hallie, quietly sewing beside a lamp in the parlor. And the Fosters had four sons.

All the things the opposition said about Ranse Foster when he ran for the state legislature were true, except one. He had been a lowly swamper in a frontier saloon; he had been a dead beat, accepting handouts at the alley entrance of a cafe; he had been despicable and despised. But the accusation that lost him the election was false. He had not killed Liberty Valance. He never served in the state legislature.

When there was talk of his running for governor, he refused. Handy Strong, who knew politics, tried to persuade him.

"That shooting, we'll get around that. 'The Honorable Ransome Foster walked down a street in broad daylight to meet an enemy of society. He shot him down in a fair fight, of necessity, the way you'd shoot a mad dog—but Liberty Valance could shoot back, and he did. Ranse Foster carries the mark of that encounter today in a crippled right arm. He is still paying the price for protecting law-abiding citizens. And he was the first teacher west of Rosy Buttes. He served without pay.' You've come a long way, Ranse, and you're going further."

"A long way," Foster agreed, "for a man who never wanted to go anywhere. I don't want to be governor."

When Handy had gone, Bert Barricune sagged in, unwashed, unshaven. He sat down stiffly. At the age of fifty, he was an old man, an unwanted relic of the frontier that was gone, a legacy to more civilized times that had no place for him. He filled his pipe deliberately. After a while he remarked. "The other side is gonna say you ain't fitten to be governor. Because your wife ain't fancy enough. They're gonna say Hallie didn't even learn to read till she was growed up."

Ranse was on his feet, white with fury. "Then I'm going to win this election it if kills me."

"I don't reckon it'll kill you," Bert drawled. "Liberty Valance couldn't."

"I could have got rid of the weight of that affair long ago," Ranse reminded him, "by telling the truth."

"You could yet," Bert answered. "Why don't you?"

Ranse said bitterly, "Because I owe you too much . . . I don't think Hallie wants to be the governor's lady. She's shy."

"Hallie don't never want nothing for herself. She wants things for you. The way I feel, I wouldn't mourn at your funeral. But what Hallie wants, I'm gonna try to see she gets."

"So am I," Ranse promised grimly.

"Then I don't mind telling you," Bert admitted, "that it was me reminded the opposition to dig up that matter of how she couldn't read."

As the Senator and his wife rode out to the airport after old Bert Barricune's barren funeral, Hallie sighed. "Bert never had much of anything. I guess he never wanted much."

He wanted you to be happy, Ranse Foster thought, and he did the best he knew how.

"I wonder where those prickly-pear blossoms came from," he mused.

Hallie glanced up at him, smiling. "From me," she said.

TOWN TAMER

BY FRANK GRUBER

(Town Tamer)

Frank Gruber (1904–65) was a popular writer of both mystery and Western fiction, as well as of film and TV scripts (he authored over 200 teleplays, in particular for such frontier series as Tales of Wells Fargo *and* Shotgun Slade). *Among his novels adapted for the screen are his first Western,* Peace Marshal, *which became the 1943 release* The Kansan, *featuring Richard Dix;* Fighting Man of the Plains, *the film which in 1949 marked the screen debut of Dale Robertson; and* Town Tamer, *the saga of a tough freelance lawman named Buchanan Smith, which Gruber first wrote as a short story in 1957, then expanded into a novel in 1958, and finally developed into a screenplay in 1965. He once went on record as calling the version which follows "my best Western short story."*

Buchanan Smith, town tamer, tied his weary horse to the hitchrail in front of Keeley's Emporium; going into the store, he found John Keeley alone, checking over a shipment of cotton print dresses. It was just as well, for Keeley preferred his first talk with the town tamer to be a private one.

"Let's save time, Mr. Keeley," Smith said, after the amenities were over, "you want this town tamed. All right, the price is five hundred, now, and at the end of a month, another five hundred."

"You can do the job in a month?"

"There'll be no second payment if I don't."

"That's good enough for me." Keeley hesitated. "The supervisors empowered me to send for you, as a last resort." Keeley drew a deep breath. "We've a town marshal, Sam Olds, but he can't handle the job. I told him we were sending for an outside man. He doesn't mind."

"As long as he doesn't interfere," Smith warned. "I've got to do it my own way. In my own time."

"That's understood. If you don't mind, I'd like to make this official. I'll swear you in as a deputy." He went down to the end of the counter, rummaged about behind it. "Got a book here somewhere."

Smith heard the footsteps out in front and was turning, when the door opened and Ethel Keeley came into the store. She was fresh and young, he saw in his first glance, like some of the girls he had seen in other trail towns—girls who dropped their eyes when they saw him and sometimes even crossed the street to keep from passing near him.

Keeley saw his daughter and exclaimed in relief, "Here you are, Ethel. I seem to have mislaid the Bible."

"It's in the drawer, second from the bottom," Ethel Keeley said. She walked by Smith, giving him a cool, appraising glance, her lips parted in a half smile.

Keeley found the Bible before his daughter reached him, then brought it forward, wiping dust from it. He extended it to Smith. "Raise your right hand. Now, do you swear that you will perform your duties, true and faithfully, for which you have been engaged? So help you—" There was the slightest pause before he added the word "God."

"I do," said Buchanan Smith.

Keeley fished a nickeled star out of his vest pocket, handed it to Smith. "You're now the deputy marshal of Broken Lance. I—I'll have your advance pay for you within the hour."

Marvin Potter came into the store from the rear. He was in his mid-twenties, a serious young man who was working at Keeley's to earn enough money to stock a little ranch on which he had made a down payment, and to which he hoped to take Ethel Keeley as his bride.

Ethel saw him coming and, turning her back, faced Smith. "I guess you're going to be with us awhile, Mr.—?"

Keeley frowned. "Buchanan Smith. My daughter, Ethel."

Smith nodded. "Ma'am," he said. Then, pinning the star on his shirt front, he left the store.

Ethel turned to her father. "I didn't know the town could afford two marshals."

"Can't afford not to have 'em," growled Keeley, "the way things have been going lately."

"Buck Smith," said Marvin Potter, "the gunfighter. That's who he is."

"Gunfighter?" asked Ethel Keeley, sharply.

"He's a hired killer," Potter went on, with smoldering resentment. "Makes his living, going from town to town—killing."

Keeley said, peevishly. "You pile up those flour sacks, Marvin!"

"Yes, Mr. Keeley. I've cleaned up everything in the storeroom." The clerk's eyes were on Ethel, who was trying her best not to meet his glance.

"I've got some marketing to do," she said, addressing her father. Then, wickedly: "Perhaps you'll ask the new marshal to supper?"

Marvin Potter's eyes showed anguish and Keeley felt a little sorry for the man. Yet he was not sure that he wanted Potter for a son-in-law. He had a tendency to bring out the touch of waspishness in his daughter's character.

Sam Olds was forty. He had grown too fat. What had been muscle a few years ago was now flabbiness. The job of marshal of a town as tough as Broken Lance was too much for him. He had not protested, therefore, when he had been told by Mayor Keeley that the Board of Supervisors had decided to give him a temporary deputy.

Buck Smith's name and repute were known to him and as he looked at the town tamer now, he knew that there were violent days ahead and wondered if he himself would be alive at the end.

He said, in reply to Smith's question, "The saloonkeepers want an everything-goes town, the other businessmen don't."

"How many saloons are there?"

"Six. The Lone Star, the Bull's Head—"

Smith made a deprecating gesture of dismissal. "I'll get acquainted with them." His pale blue eyes searched the face of the fat marshal and Olds felt a little shiver go through him. "What's the real trouble in Broken Lance?"

Olds hesitated. "It's a trail town. The Texas men are troublemakers, every mother's son of them. They're still fighting the war. We're the Yankees and they think it's fun to hurrah a Yankee town."

"Texas men come and go. You can handle them yourself. Who's behind the trouble here?"

"I don't think I know what you mean."

"There's always one man. But let it ride. It's better I find things out for myself."

Smith went out of the marshal's office and rode his horse to the livery stable. Gutterman, the liveryman, noted his star. "The town tamer, eh?"

"It's around, is it?"

"Before you came," replied Gutterman. "Sam Olds is too fat, too soft. Everybody knows that."

"Who's the man behind the trouble?"

"Eh?"

Smith hadn't expected an answer to his question and was not disappointed. Olds had also evaded the question. He nodded and, leaving instructions for the care of his horse, left the stable and strolled into the street. It consisted of two short blocks of business buildings, with some square houses on a cross street and some a short distance away from the town itself.

There were four saloons in the first hotel, two in the second. The big saloon had a sign over it: *Long Jack's Kansas House.* There was a defiance in the name, since the patronage of the saloons was largely Texans, who hated all things Northern.

Smith went into the saloon and found it well patronized for midafternoon. Fargo and poker games were going on and there were a half-dozen booted and spurred Texans at the long bar.

There were three bartenders. One of them came up and polished the mahogany in front of Smith.

"Beer," said Smith.

The man drew a short glass, so that the suds did not spill over the rim. A swarthy man, with long mustaches drooping over the ends of his mouth, came and stood beside Smith as he lowered the empty glass.

"Hello, Smith," he said.

Smith had never seen the man, but it was to be expected that his name and his occupation would be known in this place by now. He nodded.

"Name's Breed," the swarthy one went on, "Joe Breed."

The name was known in the Kansas towns. Joe Breed had once challenged Wild Bill Hickok and lived to tell about it.

"You work for Long Jack?" Smith asked.

A man some inches over six feet and not much fleshier than a fence rail came out of an office at the far end of the bar. A thin stogie was clamped between his lips. Breed jerked his thumb in the direction of the lean man.

"Ask him."

Long Jack let his eyes run along the bar, held them briefly on Breed. Then continued on to Smith. He nodded almost imperceptibly, then worked his way along behind the bar.

"Howdy, Marshal," he said, with a sardonic twist to his lips. "I'm Jack Long, commonly known as Long Jack." He obviously had no intention of offering his hand, and Buchanan Smith thought it just as well. Any amenities between a town tamer and Long Jack would be meaningless.

This is the man, Smith thought.

At the poker table, a thick, angry voice suddenly rose. A chair was sent crashing. Smith turned swiftly to see a Texan reach for his gun. He never got it clear of leather. A short gun appeared in the hand of the house man and uttered a spiteful crack. The cowboy reeled back, swayed for a moment, then slid to the floor.

The voice of the house man said, ringingly, "He went for his gun. It was self-defense."

Smith walked to the poker table. He held out his hand. "Give me that."

The house man's eyes bulged. "Smith," he said, thickly. "Buck Smith. They didn't tell me—" Then he caught himself and his eyes flickered to Joe Breed and Long Jack, who were coming up. Sight of them gave Hudkins, the gambler, courage.

"Now, wait a minute, Marshal," he said. "This Texan accused me—"

"—of cheating! And he was quite right." Smith walked around the table and again held out his hand. "Give me the gun—or use it!"

Hudkins' eyes went desperately to the face of Long Jack, who was only a short distance away. He caught no signal there.

With his left foot, Smith kicked the gun away. At the same time he made a half pivot and his fist crashed against Hudkins' jaw. Hudkins went to the floor, then scrambled up to a sitting position. But that was as far as he rose for the moment.

Smith said, "Don't be in Broken Lance by sundown." He turned to meet the mocking light in Long Jack's eyes.

"I always heard you were tough," Long Jack said, "but you saw it yourself. Hudkins had to shoot in self-defense."

"Sure," said Smith, "with a sleeve gun."

"Any law against a sleeve gun?" asked Joe Breed.

"Yes," Smith replied, grimly. "I just made it."

He walked out of the Kansas saloon.

The news spread swiftly about the town. On his way home from his office, Ortinger, the banker, stopped in at Keeley's Emporium. "It's a half hour to sundown," he said to the merchant-mayor of Broken Lance.

Keeley looked through the window, to where the town tamer was leaning against the hitchrail, carelessly noting everyone who went in or out of Long Jack's place.

"I think he'll leave," Keeley said.

"I hope so," the banker replied soberly. "I went along with this town tamer idea, but I've had my doubts about it. The cure," he added, "might be worse than the disease."

Marshal Olds sat on his reinforced armchair on the porch of the jail, whittling. His mind was preoccupied, but not so much that he did not throw an occasional glance up the street. A loaded shotgun and a repeating Winchester stood just inside the door, where he could reach them in a quick step or two. If he had time to make the steps.

Up the street, Buchanan Smith watched Long Jack's and wondered idly if this was the town, the time. One day it would happen, he knew that. He had tamed numerous towns, his luck had held, but one day it would run out. Perhaps here, in Broken Lance.

It didn't worry him. He had made his peace with himself, a long time ago.

The young man in Keeley's store, who was having trouble with Keeley's daughter, the future was for him and his kind. Men like Smith were necessary, because there were men like Long Jack and Joe Breed, but their time was today. Tomorrow, they would scarcely remain a memory.

The sun had sunk below the buildings on the western side of the street. Through a chink between two buildings, Smith saw that the great reddish orb was already touching the horizon. Another ten minutes and it would be gone.

Ten minutes. Perhaps that was Smith's time.

The batwing doors of Long Jack's saloon burst open and a man carrying a valise rushed out and clambered aboard one of the horses at the hitchrail.

Smith straightened and moved out into the street. When Hudkins came along, he said, clearly: "Don't come back!"

Hudkins made no reply, but there was no fear on his face. Only malice. And a trace of triumph? He knew something that Smith did not know. It didn't matter. Smith did not expect Long Jack to yield. He would bide his time, perhaps, but his kind did not surrender.

Ethel Keeley came out of Fisher's Market, with a basket. She saw Hudkins riding by and came to the edge of the wooden sidewalk. Smith saw her and wanted to turn away, but knew that he could not do that. He crossed to her and stood in the dust of the street.

"I am sorry I could not accept your invitation."

"Why?" she asked. "Didn't you expect to live until supper?"

He shook his head. "Men in my profession are not asked to people's homes. We make no attachments."

"It's easier that way, is it? You come into town, kill a few men who need killing and then you go off. You're like the hangman. You do your work for pay."

The words were rough. They had never actually been said to Smith before, but he had seen them in people's eyes. He had known women to step aside so their skirts would not brush against him.

He touched the brim of his flat-crowned Stetson, nodded and turning, crossed the street to the marshal's office.

Olds had finished with his whittling and stood in the doorway.

Smith said, "How are you fixed for guns?"

Olds sent a brief look over his shoulder, into the office. "I've got a Greener and a Winchester."

Smith nodded. "Put the Greener in the livery stable, the Winchester in Carmody's shop, if he doesn't mind. My own Winchester I'll drop at the barber shop. I may need a heavy gun in a hurry."

"One at each end of the street and one in the middle," said Olds.

He hesitated. "Hudkins leaving doesn't mean much. He's only a short card man with a sleeve gun."

"I know. Breed's the man."

Olds started to say, "And Long Jack," but changed his mind.

Marvin Potter had seen Ethel Keeley and Buchanan Smith through the window of the Emporium. It was only a few minutes before closing time and he finally finished putting things away and locking up the rear. At precisely six o'clock he got his coat and hat and putting them on, left the store, omitting his customary "goodnight" to his employer.

Keeley came forward and stood worriedly by the window. He watched Marvin Potter cross the street and enter Long Jack's. His clerk's drinking, he knew, consisted of a glass or two of beer on a Saturday evening. This was Thursday.

Marvin did not order a glass of beer at Long Jack's. He pointed to a whiskey bottle and poured out a stiff jigger. He tossed it off and it did nothing for him. He poured out a second glass and then the bartender caught Joe Breed's eye and made an almost imperceptible signal.

Marvin was tasting his third whiskey when Joe Breed sauntered up.

"Your future pa-in-law know you're drinkin' moose milk?" Breed asked, wickedly. Marvin finished drinking his whiskey and started to pour another glassful. He paid no attention to Joe Breed and the gunfighter prodded him. "Or ain't you gonna be his loving son-in-law?"

Marvin hit him then. It was intended to be a heavy, back-handed sidesweep, but Breed, half-expecting the blow, rolled with it and it was no more than the flicking of a hand across his face.

He stepped back. "Why doggone me if the ribbon clerk ain't got spunk!"

Marvin lowered his head and lunged at Breed. Long Jack came out of his office just as Breed met Potter's charge with a smashing uppercut that lifted the attacking Potter a full two inches off the floor and smashed him back against the bar.

"Your business may be marryin' the boss' daughter," Breed observed, "but mine's fighting."

He stepped in, then, and gave a short demonstration of his business. It wasn't a pretty thing to watch. He could have knocked Potter into insensibility in seconds, but he knew how to place his blows so they did the most damage, yet kept Potter on his feet. At the end, which was not long in coming, he caught the bleeding, battered young clerk by the scuff of his trousers and the back of his coat collar, ran him to the batwing doors, and gave him a violent heave.

Potter landed face down on the wooden sidewalk outside of Long Jack's. Buchanan Smith, coming up, gave the man only a cursory look. He went into Long Jack's, where Joe Breed was licking a knuckle.

"Damn those people who can't hold their liquor," Breed growled.

Ethel Keeley had baked a dried apple pie for supper and Keeley was finishing off a generous slab of it, when he said, "It's time we talked about it."

"Talked about what, Dad?"

"You and Marvin. You've been acting badly toward him. He doesn't deserve it. I think you know that Marvin hasn't been my idea of the kind of man you'd marry one day, but he's a good man. Steady."

"Marvin," said Ethel, not letting her eyes meet her father's, "will make a fine farmer. But I don't think I'd be happy on a farm, milking cows, churning butter, cooking for farm hands, and raising children."

"That may be my fault," Keeley said, heavily. He wiped his mouth with the heavy linen napkin. "Marvin had a fight with Joe Breed."

Ethel's reaction was instantaneous. "Is he hurt?"

"Not seriously, but—he may be a little hard to recognize for a few days." He looked dourly at his daughter. "He got drunk at Long Jack's."

Friday was a quiet day in Broken Lance. A trail herd reached the grazing area south of the town, but the hands were not paid off and only two or three of them drifted into Broken Lance. They had a drink or two and caused no trouble.

Buchanan Smith spent most of the day sitting in front of the marshal's office, watching the traffic flow back and forth up the dusty street. A considerable number of farmers were in town, he noted, and he decided that it would not be long before the businessmen of the town ceased to cater to the cattle trade. The herds would go to other towns. The future of Broken Lance would be farming.

It had happened to other trail towns. Unbroken prairie one day, a roaring, hell-raising boom town the next; and then, after a while, a quiet community of modest business establishments surrounded by prosperous farmsteads.

Late in the day, Marshal Olds came from upstreet and stopped on the porch near Buchanan Smith. He stoked his pipe, puffed a few moments, then said in a casual tone of voice: "Tom Rodabaugh's in town."

"I saw him ride in."

Olds nodded. "Didn't know if you knew him. He's a little man and don't look like much, until he's got a gun in his hand—then he's big."

"I ran him out of Black River," said Smith.

Ethel Keeley had gone into the market ten minutes before and Smith saw her come out now, with her filled basket, and saw, too, that she was careful not to look in the direction of the jail, even when she started diagonally across the street to Keeley's Emporium.

A heaviness settled over Smith. Somewhere along the road, he had taken the wrong fork. Had he taken the right road, he might now be living in a town like Broken Lance, with someone like Ethel Keeley as his wife.

He got heavily to his feet and, stepping down to the sidewalk, walked slowly up the street. As he passed the Emporium his eyes went to the interior. Ethel and young Potter were standing together, the young man's face ugly from bruises. There was a slump to his shoulders. Smith saw him make a gesture of helplessness and despair.

He continued on, but heard the door of the Emporium slam and then Ethel's voice: "Mr. Smith!"

He took another step, stopped and turned. "Miss Keeley," he said, evenly.

She came toward him, determined, smiling. "I thought you might be interested to know that there's a dance tomorrow night at the Masonic Hall."

"I may stop in," he said, "in the course of my duties as a marshal."

"That wasn't exactly what I had in mind."

"I have never learned to dance." Smith looked past her, toward her father's store. She was aware of his glance and a spot of color appeared in her cheeks.

"There's nothing between Marvin Potter and me," she said, tartly. "Because he works in my father's store, he may have presumed—" She broke off, biting her lower lip, looked wildly at him an instant, then whirled and went off swiftly.

Smith looked after her a moment, then wearily resumed his walk. He reached the end of the street, crossed and started back.

He reached Long Jack's and entered.

Long Jack, Joe Breed and Tom Rodabaugh were in a small clump at the far end of the bar. Buchanan Smith stopped at the near end.

He ordered a beer, paid for it and drank it, not too slowly, not too fast. Breed and Rodabaugh remained at the other end of the bar; they were aware of him, but since they did not come toward him, Smith knew that their plans had not yet been fully formed.

The farmers came early to Broken Lance on Saturday. The men stood in groups on the sidewalk, discussing the weather, their crops, the things farmers talk about. The women shopped in the stores, gossiped with their friends. The children roamed the street, went into stores and played games here and there.

Buchanan Smith sat much of the day before the marshal's office. It was a warm day, getting hot and sticky in mid-afternoon. Smith felt a tightness in his chest and shrugged it off as the heat; he had got past nervousness about the time he had tamed his first town. What was the name of it? Belgrove? Garden City? Yes, Garden City; an odd name for the hellspot along the Union Pacific.

In the late afternoon some of the farmers left Broken Lance. There were chores to do at home. There was a lull along the street for a while, but then the farmers who had worked all day and performed their evening chores early began coming to town.

A woman appeared, dressed in a flowery muslin dress, ready for the dance at the Masonic Hall, the last building on the west side of the street. A man carrying a drum soon came out and walked toward the hall.

Smith went to the Elite Barber Shop, got his ticket and saw from the number that he had a good half-hour to wait. He left the shop and heard a violin tuning up across the street at the Masonic Hall. Several buckboards and a farm wagon or two stood outside.

Tom Rodabaugh stood in front of the Kansas saloon. Smith remained on the east side of the street, but he knew that Rodabaugh's eyes were following him. He strolled to the south end of the street, stopped in at Carmody's and saw the Winchester Marshal Olds had left there.

Olds was standing outside his office, as Smith came back up the street. He was puffing at his pipe, a frown on his fat face. Smith stopped on the sidewalk and leaned against the porch railing.

After a moment, he said: "Is it usually as quiet as this on Saturday?"

Olds took the pipe from his mouth. "It's only the shank of the evening." He gestured with his pipe up the street. "Bunch of cowboys just went into Long Jack's."

Smith wrote off Olds as a possible ally. The man had grown too flabby mentally, as well as physically. He resumed his walk down the street, stopped in at the two-chair barber shop and saw from the number that he would not have to wait more than ten minutes to get his shave.

He picked up a copy of the *Broken Lance Point* and sat down on a chair. After awhile, his eyes flickered across the top of the newspaper, toward his own Winchester, which stood against the wall, just inside the window.

He met the head barber's eye. The barber quickly averted his look, and said to his customer, "A little hair tonic, Mr. Fultz?"

The farmer debated the matter a moment, then decided in favor of the hair tonic, Smith folded up the newspaper, but held it in his lap. His right elbow touched the butt of the .45 in his holster.

The tightness in his chest was more pronounced.

It was perhaps a minute later that the gun was fired inside the Kansas saloon. It was a spiteful crack, sharp and loud, despite the distance it had to travel to reach Smith's ears.

Smith got quickly to his feet, stepped around the head barber and reached for the Winchester. As he turned away, he caught the barber's frightened look, saw his opened mouth.

Outside, he started quickly across the wooden sidewalk, stepped out into the dust of the street, then stopped abruptly.

An instinct, finely developed through the years of his hazardous career, told him it was a trap. Instinct—and the fact that no men came spilling out of Long Jack's. About half of the crowd usually disperses promptly from a scene of violence, especially shooting violence.

The batwing doors of the Kansas Saloon remained closed.

Inside Long Jack's, Tom Rodabaugh and Joe Breed stood to one side of the batwing doors, guns in their hands. Long Jack was on the other side of the door.

"Is he coming?" asked Long Jack.

Joe Breed put his head close to the door and, standing on his toes, peered over the top of the door.

"He's stopped!"

"Damn the man," swore Long Jack. "He's suspicious." He looked over his shoulder, about his saloon. All games had come to a halt, men nervously watching the scene by the door.

At the bar, Marvin Potter, who had left his work early, stood with his hand tightly gripping a glass of whiskey.

Out on the street, Smith stood uncertainly, the Winchester in both hands, ready for a quick shot. Out of the corner of his eye he saw people coming out of the Masonic Hall.

In the Kansas saloon, Joe Breed said to Tom Rodabaugh, "He's got the rifle. How much of an edge do you need?"

Tom Rodabaugh swore roundly. "You're so damn' brave, *you* go out and take him. I've seen Buck Smith in action, you haven't."

"What the hell," said Breed. "He's got an empty gun in his hand." He drew a deep breath, stepped out, so that he faced the batwing doors. "You comin'?"

Rodabaugh hesitated, then moved forward.

Smith saw the batwing doors swing open as he started across the street. He stopped again. Joe Breed and Tom Rodabaugh appeared.

"All right, town tamer," snarled Breed across the distance. His gun shipped up, roared and bucked in his hand.

Smith pulled the trigger of the Winchester, a fraction of a second before Breed's bullet hit him. In that horrified instant, he knew the truth. The Winchester had been emptied. He recalled the scared look on the barber's face. The barber had known—had been afraid to tell him.

Breed's bullet tore through his left side like a triphammer. It spun Smith half around, so that Rodabaugh's bullet missed him by a fraction of an inch. Smith threw the Winchester aside with his left hand, while his right went for his revolver, which *was* loaded.

He let himself sag forward, even as his hand touched the Frontier Model, brought it out. He was on his knees when his first bullet killed

Breed. He was flat on his stomach when he fired the second time, at Tom Rodabaugh.

A man came violently through the doors of Long Jack's, smashed out by someone on the inside. A second figure followed the first. A gun exploded, a fist smacked against flesh and then the man with the gun was down on his back—and young Marvin Potter straddled Long Jack.

"Empty a man's gun, so you can murder him!" cried Marvin Potter.

Buchanan Smith climbed to his feet, holstered his Frontier Model and walked across the street. He reached Joe Breed's body as Ethel Keeley came running up from the direction of the Masonic Hall. Her eyes went first to Marvin Potter, he noted.

"You're hurt!" she cried.

Potter brushed the back of his hand, across the trickle of blood on his forehead where Long Jack's bullet had creased him.

Smith did not hear Potter's reply. He was busy with Long Jack. Hauling the man to his feet, he slammed him against the wall of the Kansas saloon.

"I'm going to count up to twenty—now," Smith was saying to the saloonkeeper.

Long Jack looked at Smith for one shuddering moment. When Smith started counting, he whirled and rushed for the horses at the hitchrail. He was scrambling onto one of them when fat Marshal Olds rolled up, tore him from the saddle and took him by the coat collar.

"Oh, no, you don't," Marshal Olds said, "you're coming down to the nice cell I been savin' for you for a long time. And then you stand trial —for the attempted murder." He started propelling the former "boss" of Broken Lance down the street.

When Smith entered Keeley's Emporium, the storekeeper was counting up the day's receipts. Keeley nodded approvingly.

"Doc Karnes patch you up, all right?" He drew a deep breath. "Want the rest of your pay now, Mr. Smith?"

"Breed and Rodabaugh are dead," Smith said, "and Long Jack's in jail. I don't think you need me around here any more. However," he paused a moment, "if you should have any more trouble, I think young Potter could handle it very well."

"Yes," said Keeley slowly, "the boy kind of surprised me. All of us, I guess."

"Including your daughter."

"Especially Ethel," said Keeley, smiling.

"The five hundred," said Smith, "give it to them—for a wedding present."

A tiny frown creased Keeley's forehead. "I'll do that, Mr. Smith."

Buchanan Smith, town tamer, smiled, nodded and turning, walked out of the store. At the livery stable he paid his bill, got his horse and rode out of Broken Lance.

Somewhere there was another town to be tamed. And somewhere, perhaps in the next town, Buchanan Smith would meet—his destiny.

JEREMY RODOCK
BY JACK SCHAEFER
(Tribute to a Bad Man)

Jack Schaefer (b. 1907) is another writer of high-quality Western fiction who has had several films made from his work. The classic, of course, is Shane *(1953), based on his short novel of the same title.* Monte Walsh, *the novel most critics and aficionados consider his best (and that many feel is one of the best of all Western novels), was filmed in 1970 with Lee Marvin and Jack Palance in the lead roles. And two of his strongest short stories, "Sergeant Houck" and "Jeremy Rodock," were brought to the screen, respectively, as* Trooper Hook *(1957), starring Joel McCrea and Barbara Stanwyck, and* Tribute to a Bad Man *(1956), with James Cagney in the role of Jeremy Rodock, a tough old horse rancher who "was a hanging man when it came to horse thieves."*

Jeremy Rodock was a hanging man when it came to horse thieves.

He hanged them quick and efficient, and told what law there was about it afterwards. He was a big man in many ways and not just in shadow-making size. People knew him. He had a big ranch—a horse ranch—about the biggest in the Territory, and he loved horses, and no one, not even a one of his own hands—and they were careful picked—could match him at breaking and gentling his big geldings for any kind of road work. Tall they were, those horses, and rawboned, out of Western mares by some hackney stallions he'd had brought from the East, and after you'd been working with cowponies they'd set you back on your heels when you first saw them. But they were stout in harness with a fast, swinging trot that could take the miles and a heavy coach better than anything else on hooves. He was proud of those horses, and he had a right to be. I know. I was one of his hands for a time. I was with him once when he hanged a pair of rustlers. And I was with him the one time he didn't.

That was a long ways back. I was young then with a stretch in my legs, about topping twenty, and Jeremy Rodock was already an old man. Maybe not so old, maybe just about into his fifties, but he seemed old to me—old the way a pine gets when it's through growing, standing tall and straight and spreading strong, but with the graying grimness around the edges that shows it's settling to the long last stand against the winds and the storms. I remember I was surprised to find he could still outwork any of his men and be up before them in the morning. He was tough fiber clear through, and he took me on because I had a feeling for horses and they'd handle for me without much fuss, and that was what he wanted. "You'll earn your pay," he said, "and not act your age more than you can help, and if your sap breaks out in sass, I'll slap you against a gatepost and larrup the hide off your back." And he would, and I knew it. And he taught me plenty about horses and men, and I worked for him the way I've never worked for another man.

That was the kind of work I liked. We always paired for it, and Rodock was letting me side him. The same men, working as a team, always handled the same horses from the time they were brought in off the range until they were ready and delivered. They were plenty wild at first, four- and five-year-olds with free-roaming strong in their legs, not having had any experience with men and ropes from the time they were foaled except for the few days they were halter-broken and bangtailed as coming two-year-olds. They had their growth and life was running in them, and it was a pleasure working with them.

Rodock's system was quick and thorough; you could tell a Rodock horse by the way he'd stand when you wanted him to stand and give all he had when you wanted him to move, and respond to the reins like he knew what you wanted almost before you were certain yourself. We didn't do much with saddle stock except as needed for our personal use. Rodock horses were stage horses. That's what they were bred and broke for. They were all right for riding, maybe better than all right if you could stick their paces, because they sure could cover ground, but they were best for stage work.

We'd rope a horse out of the corral and take him into a square stall and tie a hind leg up to his belly so he couldn't even try to kick without falling flat, and then start to get acquainted. We'd talk to him till he was used to voices, and slap him and push him around till he knew we weren't going to hurt him. Then we'd throw old harness on him and yank it off and throw it on again, and keep at this till he'd stand without flicking an inch of hide no matter how hard the harness hit. We'd take him out and let the leg down and lead him around with the old harness flapping till that wouldn't mean any more to him than a breeze blowing. We'd fit him with reins and one man would walk in front with the lead-rope and the other behind holding the reins and ease him into knowing what they meant. And all the time we'd speak sharp when he acted up and speak soft and give him a piece of a carrot or a fistful of corn when he behaved right.

Hitching was a different proposition. No horse that'll work for you because he wants to, and not just because he's beat into it, takes kindly to hitching. He's bound to throw his weight about the first time or two and seem to forget a lot he's learned. We'd take our horse and match him with a well-broke trainer, and harness the two of them with good leather to a stout wagon. We'd have half-hobbles on his front feet fastened to the spliced ends of a rope that ran up through a ring on the underside of his girth and through another ring on the wagon tongue and up to the driving seat. Then the two of us would get on the seat and I'd hold the rope and Rodock'd take the reins. The moment we'd start to move, the trainer heaving into the traces, things would begin to happen. The new horse would be mighty surprised. He'd likely start rearing or plunging. I'd pull on the rope and his front legs would come out from under him and down he'd go on his nose. After trying that a few times, he'd learn he wasn't getting anywhere and begin to steady and remember some of the things he'd learned before. He'd find he had to step along when the wagon moved, and after a while he'd find that stepping was smoothest and easiest if he did his share of the pulling. Whenever he'd misbehave or wouldn't stop when he should, I'd yank on the rope and his nose would hit the soft dirt. It was surprising how quick he'd learn to put his weight into the harness and pay attention to the boss riding behind him. Sometimes, in a matter of three weeks, we'd have one ready to take his place in a four-horse pull of the old coach we had for practice runs. That would be a good horse.

Well, we were readying twenty-some teams for a new stage line when this happened. Maybe it wouldn't have happened, not the way it did, if one of the horses hadn't sprung a tendon and we needed a replacement. I don't blame myself for it, and I don't think Rodock did either, even though the leg went bad when I pulled the horse down on his nose. He was something of a hollow-head anyway, and wasn't learning as he should and had kept on trying to smash loose every time the wagon moved.

As I say, this horse pulled a tendon, not bad, but enough to mean a limp, and Rodock wouldn't send a limping horse along even to a man he might otherwise be willing to trim on a close deal. Shoo him out on the range, he told me, and let time and rest and our good grass put him in shape for another try next year. "And saddle my bay," he said, "and take any horse you'd care to sit, son. We'll ramble out to the lower basin and bring in another and maybe a spare in case something else happens."

That was why we were riding out a little before noon on a hot day, leaving the others busy about the buildings, just the two of us loafing along toward the first of the series of small natural valleys on Rodock's range where he kept the geldings and young studs. We were almost there, riding the ridge, when he stopped and swung in the saddle toward me. "Let's make a day of it, son. Let's mosey on to the next basin and have a look-see at the mares there and this year's crop of foals. I like to see the little critters run."

That's what I mean. If we hadn't been out already, he never would have taken time to go there. We'd checked the mares a few weeks before and tallied the foals and seen that everything was all right. If that horse hadn't gone lame, it might have been weeks, maybe months, before any of us would have gone up that way again.

We moseyed on, not pushing our horses because we'd be using them hard on the way back, cutting out a couple of geldings and hustling them home. We came over the last rise and looked down into that second small valley, and there wasn't a single thing in sight. Where there ought to have been better than forty mares and their foals, there wasn't a moving object, only the grass shading to deeper green down the slope to the trees along the stream and fading out again up the other side of the valley.

Jeremy Rodock sat still in his saddle. "I didn't think anyone would have the nerve," he said, quiet and slow. He puts his horse into a trot around the edge of the valley, leaning over and looking at the ground, and I followed. He stopped at the head of the valley where it narrowed and the stream came through, and he dismounted and went over the ground carefully. He came back to his horse and leaned his chest against the saddle, looking over it and up at me.

"Here's where they were driven out," he said, still quiet and slow. "At least three men. Their horses were shod. Not more than a few days ago. A couple of weeks and there wouldn't have been any trail left to follow." He looked over his saddle and studied me. "You've been with me long enough, son," he said, "for me to know what you can do with horses. But I don't know what you can do with that gun you're carrying. I wish I'd brought one of the older men. You better head back and give the word. I'm following this trail."

"Mister Rodock," I said, "I wish you wouldn't make so many remarks about my age. One thing a man can't help is his age. But anywhere you and that bay can go, me and this roan can follow. And as for this gun I'm carrying, I can hit anything with it you can and maybe a few things you'd miss."

He looked at me over his saddle and his eyebrows twitched a little upwards.

"Careful, son," he said. "That comes close to being sass." His jawline tightened, and he had that old-pine look, gray and grim and enduring. "You'll have hard riding," he said, and swung into his saddle and put his horse into a steady trot along the trail, and that was all he said for the next four-five hours.

Hard riding it was. Trotting gets to a man even if he's used to being on a horse. It's a jolting pace, and after a time your muscles grow plain tired of easing the jolts and the calluses on your rump warm up and remind you they're there. But trotting is the way to make time if you really intend to travel. Some people think the best way is to keep to a steady lope. That works on the back of your neck after a while and takes too much out of the horse after the first couple of hours. Others like to run the horse, then give him a breather, then run him again, and keep that up. You take it all out of him the first day doing that. Trotting is the best way. A good horse can trot along steady, his shoulders and legs relaxed and his hooves slapping down almost by their own weight, do it hour after hour and cover his fifty-to-sixty miles with no more than a nice even sweat and be ready to do the same the next day and the next after that, and a lot longer than any man riding him can hope to take it.

Rodock was trotting, and his long-legged bay was swinging out the miles, and far as I could tell the old man was made of iron and didn't even know he was taking a beating. I knew I was, and that roan I'd picked because he looked like a cowpony I'd had once, was working with his shorter legs to hold the pace, and I was shifting my weight from one side to the other about every fifteen minutes so I'd burn only half of my rump at a time.

It was dark night when Rodock stopped by water and swung down and hobbled his horse and unsaddled, and I did the same.

"Might miss the trail in the dark," he said. "Anyways, they're moving slow on account of the colts. I figure we've gained at least a day on them already. Maybe more. Better get some sleep. We'll be traveling with the first light." He settled down with his saddle for a pillow and I did the same, and after a few minutes his voice drifted out of the darkness. "You came along right well, son. Do the same tomorrow and I'll shut up about your age."

Next thing I knew he was shaking me awake and the advance glow of the sun was climbing the sky, and he was squatting beside me with a hatful of berries from the bushes near the water. I ate my share and we saddled and started on, and after I shook the stiffness I felt fresh and almost chipper. The trail was snaking in wide curves southwest, following the low places, but rising, as the whole country was, gradually up through the foothills toward the first tier of mountains.

About regular breakfast time, when the sun was a couple of hours over the horizon behind us, Rodock waved to me to come alongside close.

"None of this makes sense," he said, without slacking pace. "A queer kind of rustling run-off. Mares and foals. I've tangled with a lot of thievery in my time, but all of it was with stock could be moved fast and disposed of quick. Can't do that with mares and sucking colts. How do you figure it, son?"

I studied that awhile. "Mister Rodock," I said, "there's only one advantage I see. Colts that young haven't felt a branding iron yet. Get away with them and you can slap on any brand you want."

"You're ageing fast, son," he said. "That's a right good thought. But these foals couldn't be weaned for three months yet. Say two months if you were the kind could be mean and not worry about getting them started right. What good would they be, even with your brand on them, still nursing mares that have got my J-tailed-R brand?"

"I'd be mighty embarrassed," I said, "every time anybody had a look at a one of them. Guess I'd have to keep them out of sight till they could be weaned."

"For two-three months, son?" he said. "You'd ride herd on them two-three months to keep them from heading back to their home range? Or coop them some place where you'd have to feed them? And be worrying all the time that maybe Jeremy Rodock would jump you with a hanging rope in his hand?"

"No," I said, "I wouldn't. I don't know what I'd do. Guess I just don't have a thieving mind."

"But somebody's doing it," he said. "Damned if I know what."

And we moved along at that steady fast trot, and my roan dropped back where he liked to stay, about twenty feet behind where he could set his own rhythm without being bothered trying to match the strides of the longer-legged bay. We moved along, and I began to feel empty clear down into my shanks and I began to hunch forward to ease the calluses on my rump. The only break all morning was a short stop for brief watering. We moved along and into the afternoon, and I could tell the roan felt exactly as I did. He and I were concentrating on just one thing, putting all we had into following twenty feet after an old iron ramrod of a man on one of the long-legged, tireless horses of his own shrewd breeding.

The trail was still stale, several days at least, and we were not watching sharp ahead, so we came on them suddenly. Rodock, being ahead and going up a rise, saw them first and was swinging to the ground and grabbing his horse's nose when I came beside him and saw the herd, bunched, well ahead and into a small canyon that cut off to the right. I swung down and caught the roan's nose in time to stop the nicker starting, and we hurried to lead both horses back down the rise and a good ways more and over to a clump of trees. We tied them there and went ahead again on foot, crawling the last stretch up the rise and dropping on our bellies to peer over the top. They were there all right, the whole herd, the mares grazing quietly, some of the foals lying down, the others skittering around the way they do, daring each other to flip their heels.

We studied that scene a long time, checking every square yard of it as far as we could see. There was not a man or a saddled horse in sight. Rodock plucked a blade of grass and stuck it in his mouth and chewed on it.

"All right, son," he said. "Seems we'll have to smoke them out. They must be holed up somewhere handy waiting to see if anyone's following. You scout around the left side of that canyon and I'll take the right. Watch for tracks and keep an eye cocked behind you. We'll meet way up there beyond the herd where the trees and bushes give good cover. If you're jumped, get off a shot and I'll be on my way over ahumping."

"Mister Rodock," I said, "you do the same and so will I."

We separated, slipping off our different ways and moving slow behind any cover that showed. I went along the left rim of the canyon, crouching by rocks and checking the ground carefully each time before moving on and peering down into the canyon along the way. I came on a snake and circled it and flushed a rabbit out of some bushes, and those were the only living things or signs of them I saw except for the horses below there in the canyon. Well up beyond them, where the rock wall slanted out into a passable slope, I worked my way down and to where we were to meet. I waited, and after a while Rodock appeared, walking toward me without even trying to stay under cover.

"See anything, son?" he said.

"No," I said.

"It's crazier than ever," he said. "I found their tracks where they left. Three shod horses moving straight out. Now what made them chuck and run like that? Tracks at least a day old too."

"Somebody scared them," I said.

"It would take a lot," he said, "to scare men with nerve enough to make off with a bunch of my horses. Who'd be roaming around up here anyway? If it was anyone living within a hundred miles, they'd know my brand and be taking the horses in." He stood there straight, hands on his hips, and stared down the canyon at the herd. "What's holding them?" he said.

"Holding who?" I said.

"Those horses," he said. "Those mares. Why haven't they headed for home? Why aren't they working along as they graze?"

He was right. They weren't acting natural. They were bunched too close and hardly moving, and when any of them did move there was something wrong. We stared at them, and suddenly Rodock began to run toward them and I had trouble staying close behind him. They heard us and turned to face us and they had trouble turning, and Rodock stopped and stared at them and there was a funny moaning sound in his throat.

"My God!" he said. "Look at their front feet!"

I looked, and I could see right away what he meant. They had been roped and thrown and their front hooves rasped almost to the quick, so that they could barely put their weight on them. Each step hurt, and they couldn't have traveled at all off the canyon grass out on the rocky ground beyond. It hurt me seeing them hurt each time they tried to move, and if it did that to me I could imagine what it did to Jeremy Rodock.

They knew him, and some of them nickered at him, and the old mare that was their leader, and was standing with head drooping, raised her head and started forward and dropped her head again and limped to us with it hanging almost to the ground. There was a heavy iron bolt tied to her forelock and hanging down between her eyes. You know how a horse moves its head as it walks. This bolt would have bobbed against her forehead with each step she took, and already it had broken through the skin and worn a big sore that was beginning to fester.

Rodock stood still and stared at her and that moaning sound clung in his throat. I had to do something. I pulled out my pocketknife and cut through the tied hairs and tossed the bolt far as I could. I kicked up a piece of sod and reached down and took a handful of clean dirt and rubbed it over the sore on her forehead and then wiped it and the oozing stuff away with my neckerchief, and she stood for me and only shivered as I rubbed. I looked at Rodock and he was someone I had never seen before. He was a gaunt figure of a man, with eyes pulled back deep in their sockets and burning, and the bones of his face showing plain under the flesh.

"Mister Rodock," I said, "are we riding out on that three-horse trail?"

I don't think he even heard me.

"Not a thing," he said. "Not a single solitary goddamned thing I can do. They're traveling light and fast now. Too much of a start and too far up in the rocks for trailing. They've probably separated and could be heading clean out of the Territory. They're devilish smart and they've done it, and there's not a goddamned thing I can do."

"We've got the mares," I said. "And the foals."

He noticed me, a flick of his eyes at me. "We've got them way up here and they can't be moved. Not till those hooves grow out." He turned toward me and threw words at me, and I wasn't anyone he knew, just someone to be a target for his bitterness. "They're devils! Three devils! Nothing worth the name of man would treat horses like that. See the devilishness of it? They run my horses way up here and cripple them. They don't have to stay around. The horses can't get away. They know the chances are we won't miss the mares for weeks, and by then the trail will be overgrown and we won't know which way they went and waste time combing the whole damn country in every direction, and maybe never get up in here. Even if someone follows them soon, like we did, they're gone and can't be caught. One of them can slip back every week or two to see what's doing, and if he's nabbed, what can tie him to the run-off? He's just a fiddlefoot riding through. By weaning-time, if nothing has happened, they can hurry in and take the colts and get off clean with a lot of unbranded horseflesh. And there's not a thing we can do."

"We can watch the mares," I said, "till they're able to travel some, then push them home by easy stages. And meantime be mighty rough on anyone comes noseying around."

"We've got the mares," he said. "They're as well off here as anywhere now. What I want is those devils. All three of them. Together and roped and in my hands." He put out his hands, the fingers clawed, and shook them at me. "I've got to get them! Do you see that? I've got to!" He dropped his hands limp at his sides, and his voice dropped too, dry and quiet with a coldness in it. "There's one thing we can do. We can leave everything as it is and go home and keep our mouths shut and wait and be here when they come for the colts." He took hold of me by the shoulders and his fingers hurt my muscles. "You see what they did to my horses. Can you keep your mouth shut?"

He didn't wait for me to answer. He let go of my shoulders and turned and went straight through the herd of crippled mares without looking at them and on down the canyon and out and over the rise where we first sighted them and on to the clump of trees where we had tied our horses.

I followed him and he was mounted and already starting off when I reached the roan and I mounted and set out after him. He was in no hurry now and let the bay walk part of the time, and the roan and I were glad of that. He never turned to look at me or seemed to notice whether I followed or not. A rabbit jumped out of the brush and I knocked it over on the second shot and picked it up and laid it on the saddle in front of me, and he paid no attention to me, not even to the shots, just steadying the bay when it started at the sharp sounds and holding it firm on the back trail.

He stopped by a stream while there was still light and dismounted, and I did the same. After we had hobbled and unsaddled the horses, he sat on the ground with his back to a rock and stared into space. I couldn't think of anything to say, so I gathered some wood and made a fire. I took my knife and gutted the rabbit and cut off the head. I found some fairly good clay and moistened it and rolled the rabbit in a ball of it and dropped this in the fire. When I thought it would be about done, I poked it out of the hot ashes and let it cool a bit. Then I pried off the baked clay and the skin came with it and the meat showed juicy and smelled fine. It was still a little raw, but anything would have tasted good then. I passed Rodock some pieces and he took them and ate the meat off the bones mechanically like his mind was far away some place. I still couldn't think of anything to say, so I stretched out with my head on my saddle, and then it was morning and I was chilled and stiff and staring up at clear sky, and he was coming toward me leading both horses and his already saddled.

It was getting toward noon, and we were edging onto our home range when we met two of the regular hands out looking for us. They came galloping with a lot of questions and Rodock put up a palm to stop them.

"Nothing's wrong," he said. "I took a sudden mind to circle around and look over some of the stock that's strayed a bit and show the boy here parts of my range he hadn't seen before. Went farther'n I intended to and we're some tuckered. You two cut over to the lower basin and take in a pair of four-year-olds. Hightail it straight and don't dawdle. We've got that stage order to meet."

They were maybe a mite puzzled as they rode off, but it was plain they hadn't hit the second basin and seen the mares were missing.

Rodock and I started on, and I thought of something to say and urged the roan close.

"Mister Rodock," I said, "I don't like that word 'boy.' "

"That's too damn bad," he said, and went steadily on and I followed, and he paid no more attention to me all the rest of the way to the ranch buildings.

Things were different after that around the place. He didn't work with the horses himself any more. Most of the time he stayed in his sturdy frame house where he had a Mexican to cook for him and fight the summer dust, and I don't know what he did in there. Once in a while he'd be on the porch, and he'd sit there hours staring off where the foothills started their climb toward the mountains. With him shut away like that, I was paired with Hugh Claggett. This Claggett was a good enough man, I guess. Rodock thought some of him. They had knocked around together years back, and when he had showed up needing a job sometime before I was around the place, Rodock gave him one, and he was a sort of acting foreman when Rodock was away for any reason. He knew horses, maybe as much as Rodock himself in terms of the things you could put down as fact in a book. But he didn't have the real feel, the deep inside feel, of them that means you can sense what's going on inside a horse's head; walk up to a rolled-eye maverick that's pawing the sky at the end of a rope the way Rodock could, and talk the nonsense out of him and have him standing there quivering to quiet under your hand in a matter of minutes. Claggett was a precise, practical sort of a man, and working with him was just that, working, and I took no real pleasure in it.

When Rodock did come down by the stables and working corral, he was different. He didn't come often, and it would have been better if he hadn't come at all. First thing I noticed was his walk. There was no bounce to it. Always before, no matter how tired he was, he walked rolling on the soles of his feet from heels to toes and coming off the toes each step with a little bouncy spring. Now he was walking flat-footed, plodding, like he was carrying more weight than just his body. And he was hard and driving in a new way, a nasty and irritable way. He'd always been one to find fault, but that had been because he was better at his business than any of us and he wanted to set us straight. He'd shrivel us down to size with a good clean tongue-whipping, then pitch in himself and show us how to do whatever it was and we'd be the better for it. Now he was plain cussed all through. He'd snap at us about anything and everything. Nothing we did was right. He'd not do a lick of work himself, just stand by and find fault, and his voice was brittle and nasty, and he'd get personal in his remarks. And he was mighty touchy about how we treated the horses. We did the way he had taught us and the way I knew was right by how the horses handled, still he would blow red and mad and tear into us with bitter words, saying we were slapping on leather too hard or fitting bridles too snug, little things, but they added to a nagging tally as the days passed and made our work tiring and troublesome. There was a lot of grumbling going on in the bunkhouse in the evenings.

Time and again I wanted to tell the others about the mares so maybe they would understand. But I'd remember his hands stretching toward me and shaking and then biting into my shoulders and I'd keep what had happened blocked inside me. I knew what was festering in him. I'd wake at night thinking about those mares, thinking about them way up there in the hills pegged to a small space of thinning grass by hooves that hurt when weight came on them and sent stabs of pain up their legs when they hit anything hard. A good horse is a fine-looking animal. But it isn't the appearance that gets into you and makes something in you reach out and respond to him. It's the way he moves, the sense of movement in him even when he's standing still, the clean-stepping speed and competence of him that's born in him and is what he is and is his reason for being. Take that away and he's a pitiful thing. And somewhere there were three men who had done that to those mares. I'd jump awake at night and think about them and maybe have some notion of what it cost Jeremy Rodock to stay set there at his ranch and leave his mares alone with their misery far off up in the hills.

When the stage horses were ready to be shod for the last real road tests, he nearly drove our blacksmith crazy cursing every time a hoof was trimmed or one of them flinched under the hammer. We finished them off with hard runs in squads hitched to the old coach and delivered them, and then there was nothing much to do. Not another order was waiting. Several times agents had been to see Rodock and had gone into the house and come out again and departed, looking downright peeved. I don't know whether he simply refused any more orders or acted so mean that they wouldn't do business with him. Anyway, it was bad all around. There was too much loafing time. Except for a small crew making hay close in, no one was sent out on the range at all. The men were dissatisfied and they had reason to be, and they took to quarreling with each other. Some of them quit in disgust and others after arguing words with Rodock, and finally the last bunch demanded their time together and left, and Claggett and I were the only ones still there. That's not counting the Mexican, but he was housebroke and not worth counting. Claggett and I could handle the chores for the few horses kept regularly around the place and still have time to waste. We played euchre, but I never could beat him and then got tired of trying. And Rodock sat on his porch and stared into the distance. I didn't think he even noticed me when I figured that his bay would be getting soft and started saddling him and taking him out for exercise the same as I did the roan. One day I rode him right past the porch. Rodock fooled me on that, though. I was almost past, pretending not to see him, when his voice flicked at me. "Easy on those reins, boy. They're just extra trimming. That horse knows what you want by the feel of your legs around him. I don't want him spoiled." He was right too. I found you could put that bay through a figure eight or drop him between two close-set posts just by thinking it down through your legs.

The slow days went by, and I couldn't stand it any longer. I went to the house.

"Mister Rodock," I said, "it's near two months now. Isn't it time we made a move?"

"Don't be so damn young," he said. "I'll move when I know it's right."

I stood on one foot and then on the other and I couldn't think of anything to say except what I'd said before about my age, so I went back to the bunkhouse and made Claggett teach me all the games of solitaire he knew.

Then one morning I was oiling harness to keep it limber when I looked up and Rodock was in the stable doorway.

"Saddle my bay," he said, "and Hugh's sorrel. I reckon that roan'll do for you again. Pick out a good packhorse and bring them all around to the storehouse soon as you can."

I jumped to do what he said, and when I had the horses there he and Claggett had packs filled. We loaded the extra horse, and the last thing Rodock did was hand out Henrys and we tucked these in our saddle scabbards and started out. He led the way, and from the direction he took it was plain we were not heading straight into the hills, but were going to swing around and come in from the south.

I led the packhorse and we rode in a compact bunch, not pushing for speed. It was in the afternoon that we ran into the other riders, out from the settlement and heading our way, Ben Kern, who was federal marshal for that part of the Territory, and three of the men he usually swore in as deputies when he had a need for any. We stopped and they stopped, looking us over.

"You've saved me some miles," Kern said. "I was heading for your place."

Rodock raised his eyebrows and looked at him and was silent. I kept my mouth shut. Claggett, who probably knew as much about the mares as I did by now, did the same. This was Rodock's game.

"Not saying much, are you?" Kern said. He saw the Henrys. "Got your warpaint on too. I thought something would be doing from what I've been hearing about things at your place. What's on your mind this time?"

"My mind's my own," Rodock said. "But it could be we're off on a little camping trip."

"And again it couldn't," Kern said. "Only camping you ever do is on the tail of a horse thief. That's the trouble. Twice now you've ridden in to tell me where to find them swinging. Evidence was clear enough, so there wasn't much I could do. But you're too damn free with your rope. How we going to get decent law around here with you oldtimers crossing things up? This time, if it is a this time, you're doing it right and turn them over to me. We'll just ride along to see that you do it."

Rodock turned to me. He had that grim and enduring look and the lines by his mouth were taut. "Break out those packs, boy. We're camping right here." I saw what he was figuring and I dismounted and began unfastening the packs. I had them on the ground and was fussing with the knots when Kern spoke.

"You're a stubborn old bastard," he said. "You'd stay right here and outwait us."

"I would," Rodock said.

"All right," Kern said. "We'll fade. But I've warned you. If it's rustlers you're after, bring them to me."

Rodock didn't say a thing and I heaved the packs on the horse again, and by time I had them fastened tight, Kern and his men were a distance away and throwing dust. We started on, and by dark we had gone a good piece. By dark the next day we had made a big half-circle and were well into the hills. About noon of the next, we were close enough to the canyon where we had found the mares, say two miles if you could have hopped it straight. Claggett and I waited while Rodock scouted around. He came back and led us up a twisting rocky draw to a small park hemmed in part way by a fifteen-foot rock shelf and the rest of the way by a close stand of pine. It was about a half-acre in size, and you'd never know it was there unless you came along the draw and stumbled into it. We picketed the horses there and headed for the canyon on foot, moving slow and cautious as we came close. When we peered over the rim, the herd was there all right, the foals beginning to get some growth and the mares stepping a lot easier than before. They were used to the place now and not interested in leaving. They had taken to ranging pretty far up the canyon, but we managed to sight the whole count after a few minutes watching.

We searched along the rim for the right spot and found it, a crack in the rim wide enough for a man to ease into comfortably and be off the skyline for anyone looking from below, yet able to see the whole stretch where the herd was. To make it even better, we hauled a few rocks to the edge of the opening and piled brush with them, leaving a careful spy-hole. We brought a flat-topped rock for a seat behind the hole. The idea was that one of us could sit there watching while the other two holed in a natural hiding-place some fifty feet back under an over-hanging ledge with a good screen of brush. The signal, if anything happened, was to be a pebble chucked back toward the hiding-place.

I thought we'd take turns watching, but Rodock settled on that flat-top stone and froze there. Claggett and I kept each other company under the ledge, if you could call it keeping company when one person spent most of the time with his mouth shut whittling endless shavings off chunks of old wood or taking naps. That man Claggett had no nerves. He could keep his knife going for an hour at a time without missing a stroke or stretch out and drop off into a nap like we were just lazing around at the ranch. He didn't seem to have much personal interest in what might develop. He was just doing a job and tagging along with an oldtime partner. As I said before, he didn't have a real feel for horses. I guess to be fair to him I ought to remember that he hadn't seen those mares with their hooves rasped to the quick and flinching and shuddering with every step they took. Me, I was strung like a too-tight fiddle. I'd have cracked sure if I hadn't had the sense to bring a deck in my pocket for solitaire. I nearly wore out those cards and even took to cheating to win, and it seemed to me we were cooped there for weeks when it was only five days. And all the time, every day, Rodock sat on that stone as if he was a piece of it, getting older and grayer and grimmer.

Nights we spent back with the horses. We'd be moving before dawn each morning, eating a heavy breakfast cooked over a small quick fire, then slipping out to our places with the first streaks of light carrying a cold snack in our pockets. We'd return after dark for another quick meal and roll right afterwards into our blankets. You'd think we hardly knew each other the way we behaved, only speaking when that was necessary. Claggett was never much of a talker, and Rodock was tied so tight in himself now he didn't have a word to spare. I kept quiet because I didn't want him smacking my age at me again. If he could chew his lips and wear out the hours waiting, I could too, and I did.

We were well into the fifth day and I was about convinced nothing would ever happen again, any time ever anywhere in the whole wide world, when a pebble came snicking through the brush and Rodock came hard after it, ducking low and hurrying.

"They're here," he said. "All three." And I noticed the fierce little specks of light beginning to burn in his eyes. "They're stringing rope to trees for a corral. Probably planning to brand here, then run." He looked at me and I could see him assessing me and dismissing me, and he turned to Claggett. "Hugh," he started to say, "I want you to—"

I guess it was the way he had looked at me and the things he had said about my age. Anyway, I was mad. I didn't know what he was going to say, but I knew he had passed me by. I grabbed him by the arm.

"Mister Rodock," I said, "I'm the one rode with you after those mares."

He stared at me and shook his head a little as if to clear it.

"All right, boy," he said. "You do this and, by God, you do it right. Hurry back and get your horse and swing around and come riding into the canyon. Far as I can tell at the distance, these men are strangers, so there's not much chance they'd know you worked for me. You're just a drifter riding through. Keep them talking so Hugh and I can get down behind them. If they start something, keep them occupied long as you can." He grabbed me by the shoulders the way he had when we found the mares. "Any shooting you do, shoot to miss. I want them alive." He let go of me. "Now scat."

I scatted. I never went so fast over rough country on my own feet in my life. When I reached the roan, I had to hang onto his neck to get some breath and my strength back. I slapped my saddle on and took him at a good clip out of the draw and in a sharp circle for the canyon mouth, a good clip, but not too much to put him in a lather. I was heading into the canyon, pulling him to an easy trot, when it hit me, what a damn fool thing I was doing. There were three of them in there, three mighty smart men with a lot of nerve, and they had put a lot of time and waiting into this job and wouldn't likely be wanting to take chances on its going wrong. I was scared, so scared I could hardly sit the roan, and I came near swinging him around and putting my heels to him. Maybe I would have. Maybe I would have run out on those mares. But then I saw that one of the men had spotted me and there was nothing much to do but keep going toward them.

The one that had spotted me was out a ways from the others as a lookout. He had a rifle and he swung it to cover me as I came near and I stopped the roan. He was a hardcase specimen if ever I saw one and I didn't like the way he looked at me.

"Hold it now, sonny," he said. "Throw down your guns."

I was glad he said that, said "sonny," I mean, because it sort of stiffened me and I wasn't quite so scared, being taken up some with being mad. I tried to act surprised and hold my voice easy.

"Lookahere," I said, "that's an unfriendly way to talk to a stranger riding through. I wouldn't think of using these guns unless somebody pushed me into it, but I'd feel kind of naked without them. Let's just leave them alone, and if you're not the boss, suppose you let me talk to him that is."

I figured he wouldn't shoot because they'd want to know was I alone and what was I doing around there, and I was right. He jerked his head toward the other two.

"Move along, sonny," he said. "But slow. And keep your hands high in sight. I'll blast you out of that saddle if you wiggle a finger."

I walked the roan close to the other two and he followed behind me and circled around me to stand with them. They had been starting a fire and had stopped to stare at me coming. One was a short, stocky man, almost bald, with a fringe of grizzled beard down his cheeks and around his chin. The other was about medium height and slender, with clean chiseled features and a pair of the hardest, shrewdest, bluest eyes I ever saw. It was plain he was the boss by the way he took over. He set those eyes on me and I started shivering inside again.

"I've no time to waste on you," he said. "Make it quick. What's your story?"

"Story?" I said. "Why, simple enough. I'm footloose and roaming for some months and I get up this way with my pockets about played out. I'm riding by and I see something happening in here and I drop in to ask a few questions."

"Questions?" he said, pushing his head forward at me. "What kind of questions?"

"Why," I said, "I'm wondering maybe you can tell me, if I push on through these hills do I come to a town or some place where maybe I can get a job?"

The three of them stood there staring at me, chewing on this, and I sat my saddle staring back, when the bearded man suddenly spoke.

"I ain't sure," he said, looking at the roan. "But maybe that's a Rodock horse."

I saw them start to move and I dove sideways off the roan, planning to streak for the brush, and a bullet from the rifle went whipping over the saddle where I'd been, and I hadn't more than bounced the first time when a voice like a chill wind struck the three of them still. "Hold it, and don't move!"

I scrambled up and saw them stiff and frozen, slowly swiveling their necks to look behind them at Rodock and Hugh Claggett and the wicked ready muzzles of their two Henrys.

"Reach," Rodock said, and they reached. "All right, boy," he said. "Strip them down."

I cleaned them thoroughly and got, in addition to the rifle and the usual revolvers, two knives from the bearded man and a small but deadly derringer from an inside pocket of the slender man's jacket.

"Got everything?" Rodock said. "Then hobble them good."

I did this just as thoroughly, tying their ankles with about a two-foot stretch between so they could walk short-stepped, but not run, and tying their wrists together behind their backs with a loop up and around their necks and down again so that if they tried yanking or pulling they'd be rough on their own Adam's apples.

They didn't like any of this. The slender man didn't say a word, just clamped his mouth and talked hate with his eyes, but the other two started cursing.

"Shut up," Rodock said, "or we'll ram gags down your throats." They shut up, and Rodock motioned to me to set them in a row on the ground leaning against a fallen tree and he hunkered down himself facing them with his Henry across his lap. "Hugh," he said, without looking away from them, "take down those ropes they've been running and bring their horses and any of their stuff you find over here. Ought to be some interesting branding irons about." He took off his hat and set it on the ground beside him. "Hop your horse, boy," he said; "get over to our hide-out and bring everything back here."

When I returned leading our other horses, the three of them were still right in a row leaning against the log and Rodock was still squatted on the ground looking at them. Maybe words had been passing. I wouldn't know. Anyway, they were all quiet then. The hardcase was staring at his own feet. The bearded man's eyes were roaming around and he had a sick look on his face. The slender man was staring right back at Rodock and his mouth was only a thin line in his face. Claggett was standing to one side fussing with a rope. I saw he was fixing a hangman's knot on it and had two others already finished and coiled at his feet. When I saw them I had a funny empty feeling under my belt and I didn't know why. I had seen a hanging before and never felt like that. I guess I had some kind of a queer notion that just hanging those three wouldn't finish the whole thing right. It wouldn't stop me waking at night and thinking about those mares and their crippled hooves.

My coming seemed to break the silence that had a grip on the whole place. The slender man drew back his lips and spit words at Rodock.

"Quit playing games," he said. "Get this over with. We know your reputation."

"Do you?" Rodock said. He stood up and waggled each foot in turn to get the kinks out of his legs. He turned and saw what Claggett was doing and a strange little mirthless chuckle sounded in his throat. "You're wasting your time, Hugh," he said. "We won't be using those. I'm taking these three in."

Claggett's jaw dropped and his mouth showed open. I guess he was seeing an old familiar pattern broken and he didn't know how to take it. I wasn't and I had caught something in Rodock's tone. I couldn't have said what it was, but it was sending tingles through my hair roots.

"Don't argue with me, Hugh," Rodock said. "My mind's set. You take some of the food and start hazing the herd toward home. They can do it now if you take them by easy stages. The boy and I'll take these three in."

I helped Claggett get ready and watched him go up the canyon to bunch the herd and get it moving. I turned to Rodock and he was staring down the back trail.

"Think you could handle four horses on lead ropes, boy?" he said. "The packhorse and their three?"

"Expect I could, strung out," I said. "But why not split them? You take two and I take two."

"I'll be doing something else," he said, and that same little cold chuckle sounded in his throat. "How far do you make it, boy, to the settlement and Kern's office?"

"Straight to it," I said, "I make it close to fifty mile."

"About right," he said. "Kind of a long hike for those used to having horses under them. Hop over and take the hobbles off their feet."

I hopped, but not very fast. I was feeling some disappointed. I was feeling that he was letting me and those mares down. A fifty-mile hike for those three would worry them plenty, and they'd be worrying, too, about what would come at the end of it. Still it was a disappointment to think about.

"While you're there," Rodock said, "pull their boots off too."

I swung to look at him. He was a big man, as I said before, but I'd run across others that stood taller and filled a doorway more, but right then he was the biggest man I ever saw anywhere any time in my whole life.

I didn't bother to take off the hobbles. I left them tied so they'd hold the boots together in pairs and I could hang them flapping over the back of the packhorse. I pulled the boots off, not trying to be gentle, just yanking, and I had a little trouble with the hardcase. He tried to kick me, so I heaved on the rope between his ankles and he came sliding out from the log flat on his back and roughing his bound hands under him, and after that he didn't try anything more. But what I remember best about the three of them then is the yellow of the socks the slender man wore. Those on the others were the usual dark gray, but his were bright yellow. I've thought about them lots of times and never been able to figure why and where he ever got them.

Rodock was rummaging in their stuff that Claggett had collected. He tossed a couple of branding irons toward me. "Bring these along," he said. "Maybe Kern will be interested in them." He picked up a whip, an old but serviceable one with a ten-foot lash, and tested it with a sharp crack. "Get up," he said to the three, and they got up. "I'll be right behind you with this. You'll stay bunched and step right along. Start walking."

They started, and he tucked his Henry in his saddle scabbard and swung up on the bay.

By time I had the other horses pegged in a line with the packhorse as an anchor at the end and was ready to follow, they were heading out of the canyon and I hurried to catch up. I had to get out of the way, too, because Claggett had the herd gathered and was beginning to push the mares along with the foals skittering around through the bushes. Anyone standing on the canyon edge looking down would have seen a queer sight, maybe the damndest procession that ever paraded through that lonesome country. Those three were out in front, walking and putting their feet down careful even in the grass to avoid pebbles and bits of deadwood, with Rodock big and straight on his bay behind them, then me with my string of three saddled but riderless horses and the packhorse, and behind us all the mares and the skittering foals with Claggett weaving on his sorrel to keep the stragglers on the move.

Once out of the canyon we had to separate. Rodock and I and our charges turned southeast to head for the settlement. Claggett had to swing the herd toward the northeast to head for the home range. He had his trouble with the mares because they wanted to follow me and my string. But he and his sorrel knew their business and by hard work made the break and held it. I guess he was a bit huffy about the whole thing because I waved when the distance was getting long between us, and he saw me wave and didn't even raise an arm. I don't know as I blame him for that.

This was mid-afternoon and by camping time we had gone maybe ten miles and had shaken down to a steady grind. My horses had bothered the roan some by holding back on the rope and had bothered themselves a few times by spreadeagling and trying to go in different directions, but by now the idea had soaked in and they were plugging along single-file and holding their places. The three men out in front had learned to keep moving or feel the whip. The slender man stepped along without paying attention to the other two and never looked back at Rodock and never said a word. The bearded man had found that shouting and cursing simply wore out his throat and had no effect on the grim figure pacing behind them. The hardcase had tried a break, ducking quick to one side and running fast as he could, but Rodock had jumped the bay and headed him the same as you do a steer, and being awkward with his hands tied he had taken a nasty tumble. Not a one of them was going to try that again. Their feet were too tender for hard running, anyway, especially out there in the open where the grass was bunchy with bare spaces aplenty, and there were stretches with a kind of coarse gravel underfoot. When Rodock called a halt by water, they were ready to flop on the ground immediately and hitch around and dabble their feet in the stream, and I noticed that the bottoms of their socks were about gone and the soles of their feet were red where they showed in splotches through the dirt ground in. I enjoyed those ten miles, not with a feeling of fun, but with a sort of slow, steady satisfaction.

I prepared food and Rodock and I ate, and then we fed them, one at a time. Rodock sat watch with his Henry on his lap while I untied them and let them eat and wash up a bit and tied them again. We pegged each of them to a tree for the night, sitting on the ground with his back to the trunk and a rope around so he wouldn't topple when he slept. I was asleep almost as soon as I stretched out, and I slept good, and I think Rodock did too.

The next day was more of the same except that we were at it a lot longer, morning and afternoon, and our pace slowed considerably as the day wore on. They were hard to get started again after a noon stop and the last hours before we stopped, they were beginning to limp badly. They weren't thinking any more of how to make a break. They were concentrating on finding the easiest spots on which to set each step. I figured we covered twenty miles, and I got satisfaction out of every one of them. But the best were in the morning because along late in the afternoon I began to feel tired, not tired in my muscles but tired and somehow kind of shrinking inside. When we stopped, I saw that their socks were just shredded yarn around their ankles and their feet were swelling and angry red and blistery through the dirt. With them sullen and silent and Rodock gray and grim and never wasting a word, I began to feel lonesome, and I couldn't go to sleep right away and found myself checking and rechecking in my mind how far we had come and how many miles we still had to go.

The day after that we started late because there was rain during the night and we waited till the morning mists cleared. The dampness in the ground must have felt better to their feet for a while because they went along fairly good the first of the morning after we got under way. They were really hard to get started, though, after the noon stop. During the afternoon they went slower and slower, and Rodock had to get mean with the whip around the heels of the hardcase and the bearded man. Not the slender one. That one kept his head high and marched along and you could tell he was fighting not to wince with every step. After a while, watching him, I began to get the feel of him. He was determined not to give us the satisfaction of seeing this get to him in any serious way. I found myself watching him too much, too closely, so I dropped behind a little more, tagging along in the rear with my string, and before Rodock called the halt by another stream, I began to see the occasional small red splotches in the footprints on dusty stretches that showed the blisters on their feet were breaking. The best I could figure we had come maybe another ten miles during the day, the last few mighty slow. That made about forty all together, and when I went over it in my mind I had to call it twelve more to go because we had curved off the most direct route some to avoid passing near a couple of line cabins of the only other ranch in that general neighborhood north of the settlement.

There weren't many words in any of us as we went through the eating routine. I didn't know men's faces were capable of such intense hatred as showed plain on the hardcase and the bearded man. They gobbled their food and glared at Rodock from their night-posts against trees, and for all I know glared without stopping all night because they had the same look the next morning. It was the slender man who suddenly took to talking. The hatred he'd had at the start seemed to have burned away. What was left was a kind of hard pride that kept his eyes alive. He looked up from his food at Rodock.

"It was a good try," he said.

"It was," Rodock said. "But not good enough. Your mistake was hurting my horses."

"I had to," the man said. "That was part of it. I saw some of your horses on a stage line once. I had to have a few."

"If you wanted some of my horses," Rodock said, "why didn't you come and buy them?"

"I was broke," the man said.

"You were greedy," Rodock said. "You had to take all in that basin. If you'd cut out a few and kept on going, you might have made it."

"Maybe," the man said. "Neither of us will ever know now. You planning to keep this up all the way in?"

"I am," Rodock said.

"Then turn us over?" the man said.

"Yes," Rodock said.

"You're the one that's greedy," the man said.

He shut up and finished his food and crawled to his tree and refused to look at Rodock again. I fixed his rope and then I had trouble getting to sleep. I lay a long time before I dozed and what sleep I got wasn't much good.

In the morning Rodock was grayer and grimmer than ever before. Maybe he hadn't slept much either. He stood off by himself and let me do everything alone. I couldn't make the hardcase and the bearded man get on their feet, and I found my temper mighty short and was working up a real mad when the slender man, who was up and ready, stepped over and kicked them, kicked them with his own swollen feet that had the remains of his yellow socks flapping around the ankles.

"Get up!" he said. "Damn you, get up! We're going through with this right!"

They seemed a lot more afraid of him than of me. They staggered up and they stepped along with him as Rodock came close with the whip in his hand and we got our pathetic parade started again. We couldn't have been moving much more than a mile an hour, and even that pace slowed, dropping to about a crawl when we hit rough stretches, and more and more red began to show in the footprints. And still that slender man marched along, slow but dogged, the muscles in his neck taut as he tried to stay straight without wincing.

Rodock was mean and nasty, crowding close behind them, using the whip to raise the dust around the lagging two. I didn't like the look of him. The skin of his face was stretched too tight and his eyes were too deep-sunk. I tried riding near him and making a few remarks to calm him, but he snapped at me like I might be a horse thief myself, so I dropped behind and stayed there.

He didn't stop at noontime, but kept them creeping along, maybe because he was afraid he'd never get them started again. It was only a short while after that the bearded man fell down, just crumpled and went over sideways and lay still. It wasn't exactly a faint or anything quite like that. I think he had cracked inside, had run out his score and quit trying, even trying to stay conscious. He was breathing all right, but it was plain he wouldn't do any more walking for a spell.

Rodock sat on his horse and looked down at him. "All right, boy," he said. "Hoist him on one of your string and tie him so he'll stay put." I heaved him on the first of the horses behind me and slipped a rope around the horse's barrel to hold him. Rodock sat on his bay and looked at the other two men, not quite sure what to do, and the slender one stared back at him, contempt sharp on his face, and Rodock shook out the whip. "Get moving, you two!" he said, and we started creeping along again.

It was about another hour and maybe another mile when the hardcase began screaming. He threw himself on the ground and rolled and thrashed and kept screaming, then stretched out taut and suddenly went limp all over, wide awake and conscious, but staring up as if he couldn't focus on anything around him.

Rodock had to stop again, chewing his lower lip and frowning. "All right, boy," he said. "Hoist that one too." I did, the same as the other one, and when I looked around, damned if that slender man wasn't walking on quite a distance ahead with Rodock right behind him.

I didn't want to watch, but I couldn't help watching that man stagger on. I think he had almost forgotten us. He was intent on the terrible task of putting one foot forward after the other and easing his weight onto it. Rodock, bunched on his bay and staring at him, was the one who cracked first. The sun was still up the sky, but he shouted a halt and when the man kept going he had to jump down and run ahead and grab him. It was a grim business making camp. The other two had straightened out some, but they had no more spirit in them than a pair of limp rabbits. I had to lift them down, and it wasn't until they had some food in them that they began to perk up at all. They seemed grateful when I hiked a ways and brought water in a folding canvas bucket from one of the packs and let them take turns soaking their swollen bloody feet in it. Then I took a saddle blanket and ripped it in pieces and wrapped some of them around their feet. I think I did that so I wouldn't find myself always sneaking looks at their feet. I did the same for the slender man, and all the time I was doing it he looked at me with that contempt on his face and I didn't give a damn. I did this even though I thought Rodock might not like it, but he didn't say a word. I noticed he wouldn't look at me and I found I didn't want to look at him either. I tried to keep my mind busy figuring how far we had come and made it six miles with six more still to go, and I was wishing those six would fade away and the whole thing would be over. The sleep I got that night wasn't worth anything to me.

In the morning I didn't want any breakfast and I wasn't going to prepare any unless Rodock kicked me into it. He was up ahead of me, standing quiet and chewing his lower lip and looking very old and very tired, and he didn't say a word to me. I saddled the horses the way I had been every morning because that was the easiest way to tote the saddles along and tied them in the usual string. The slender man was awake, watching me, and by time I finished the other two were too. They were thoroughly beaten. They couldn't have walked a quarter of a mile with the devil himself herding them. I thought to hell with Rodock and led the horses up close and hoisted the two, with them quick to help, into their saddles. They couldn't put their feet in the stirrups, but they could sit the saddles and let their feet dangle. I went over to the slender man and started to take hold of him, and he glared at me and shook himself free of my hands and twisted around and strained till he was up on his feet. I stood there gaping at him and he hobbled away, heading straight for the settlement. I couldn't move. I was sort of frozen inside watching him. He made about fifty yards and his legs buckled under him. The pain in his feet must have been stabbing up with every step and he simply couldn't stand any longer. And then while I stared at him he started crawling on his hands and knees.

"God damn it, boy!" Rodock's voice behind me made me jump. "Grab that man! Haul him back here!"

I ran and grabbed him and after the first grab, he didn't fight and I hauled him back. "Hoist him on his horse," Rodock said, and I did that. And then Rodock started cursing. He cursed that man and he cursed me and then he worked back over us both again. He wasn't a cursing man and he didn't know many words and he didn't have much imagination at it, but what he did know he used over and over again and after a while he ran down and stopped and chewed his lower lip. He turned and stalked to the packhorse and took the pairs of tied boots and came along the line tossing each pair over the withers of the right horse. He went back to the packs and pulled out the weapons I'd found on the three and checked to see that the guns were empty and shook the last of the flour out of its bag and put the weapons in it with the rifle barrel sticking out the top. He tied the bag to the pommel of the slender man's saddle.

"All right, boy," he said. "Take off those lead ropes and untie their hands."

When I had done this and they were rubbing their wrists, he stepped close to the slender man's horse and spoke up at the man.

"Back to the last creek we passed yesterday," he said, "and left along it a few miles you come to Shirttail Fussel's shack. From what I hear for a price he'll hide out anything and keep his mouth shut. A man with sense would fix his feet there and then keep traveling and stay away from this range the rest of his days."

The slender man didn't say a word. He pulled his horse around and started in the direction of the creek and the other two tagged him, and what I remember is that look of hard pride still in his eyes, plain and sharp against the pinched and strained bleakness of his face.

We watched them go and I turned to Rodock. He was old, older even than I thought he was when I first saw him, and tired with heavy circles under his eyes. At that moment I didn't like him at all, not because he had let them go, but because of what he had put me through, and it was my turn to curse him. I did it right. I did a better job than he had done before and he never even wagged a muscle. "Shut up," he said finally. "I need a drink." He went to his bay and mounted and headed for the settlement. I watched him, hunched forward and old in the saddle, and I was ashamed. I took the lead rope of the packhorse and climbed on the roan and followed him. I was glad when he put the bay into a fast trot because I was fed up with sitting on a walking horse.

He bobbed along ahead of me, a tired old man who seemed too small for that big bay, and then a strange thing began to happen. He began to sit straighter in the saddle and stretch up and look younger by the minute, and when we reached the road and headed into the settlement he was Jeremy Rodock riding straight and true on a Rodock horse and riding it like it was the part of him that in a way it really was. He hit a good clip the last stretch and my roan and the packhorse were seesawing on the lead rope trying to keep up when we reached the buildings and pulled in by a tie-rail. I swung down right after him and stepped up beside him and we went toward the saloon. We passed the front window of Kern's office and he was inside and came popping out.

"Hey, you two," he said. "Anything to report?"

We stopped and faced him and he looked at us kind of funny. I guess we did look queer, dirty and unshaved and worn in spots.

"Not a thing," Rodock said. "I told you we could be taking a camp trip and that's all I'll say. Except that I'm not missing any stock and haven't stretched any rope."

We went into the saloon and to the bar and downed a stiff one apiece.

"Mister Rodock," I said, "when you think about it, that man beat us."

"Damned if he didn't," Rodock said. He didn't seem to be bothered by it and I know I wasn't. "Listen to me, son," he said. "I expect I haven't been too easy to get along with for quite a few weeks lately. I want you to know I've noticed how you and that roan have stuck to my heels over some mighty rough trail. Now we've got to get home and get a horse ranch moving again. We'll be needing some hands. Come along with me, son, and we'll look around. I'd like your opinion on them before hiring any."

That was Jeremy Rodock. They don't grow men like that around here any more.